BLACK ROCK

DAVID ODLE

Black Rose Writing | Texas

The author grants the final approval for this literary material.

First printing

This is a work of fiction. Names, characters, businesses, places, events, and incidents are either the products of the author's imagination or used in a fictitious manner. Any resemblance to actual persons, living or dead, or actual events is purely coincidental.

ISBN: 978-1-68433-932-7
PUBLISHED BY BLACK ROSE WRITING
www.blackrosewriting.com

Printed in the United States of America
Suggested Retail Price (SRP) $19.95

Black Rock is printed in Baskerville

*As a planet-friendly publisher, Black Rose Writing does its best to eliminate unnecessary waste to reduce paper usage and energy costs, while never compromising the reading experience. As a result, the final word count vs. page count may not meet common expectations.

For Tammy,

It was that tablet and box of pencils

20-years ago that brought it all

back.

I love you

BLACK ROCK

The Beginning

Lewis squirmed in his seat and barreled toward death.

"Kim, I'm telling you right now," he glanced at his wife, "if we don't see something soon, I'll have to go right here on the side of the road." He hated being so blunt, but she wasn't grasping the sense of urgency.

Kim rolled her eyes. "This is so dumb."

He shrugged. "We need gas too. Who knows how long it'll be before we see another station."

She turned to Caleb and Lori in the back seat. "Get your shoes on. Daddy has to stop. Any of you have to pee?"

"I do!" Caleb said and grinned. Lewis shot him a playful glance in the rearview mirror. Caleb was a toddler, of course he had to pee.

Lori's face unglued from her cell phone, and she mumbled, "I don't have to." Lewis swore since she turned fifteen, she never went to the bathroom.

Kim checked Caleb's shoes. "You can go in with Daddy since he can't wait for a rest area." Lewis sensed the jab in her voice but ignored it. "There should be a gas station or something coming up soon."

"You need to be ready, little man. I won't be able to wait on ya. I have to go now."

"There." Kim pointed to a blue sign perched along the interstate. A faded gas symbol stenciled above the word BLACK ROCK. She said, "Only two miles. Doesn't look promising though."

"Nope, it doesn't." There wasn't shit out here. Just trees, trees, and more trees. Maybe no one had discovered this part of Indiana yet. Except for the people of Black Rock, apparently, wherever the hell *that* was. "But I don't know how far it is to the next one."

Kim scrolled on her phone. "There's not much along here until we get close to a town called Boswell. About 20 miles. We have enough gas to get there?"

Lewis thought about it. Another twenty miles down the highway. *Shit.* "Let's just stop here and see."

Kim's lips pressed to a thin line, but she didn't say anything.

He flipped on his turn signal, even though there were no other cars in sight, and drifted off the interstate.

"It's like we're heading to the Twilight Zone," Kim said.

So far, he hadn't seen the first sign of civilization other than this potholed road. As they neared the stop sign, he spotted a placard nailed to a battered fencepost sporting the word *Gas*. A hand-drawn arrow pointed to the right with the words, BLACK ROCK stenciled in black paint. He didn't like that at all. It reminded him of those movies where teenagers wandered into the territory of mutant cannibals.

"Great," Kim said, "I guess we have to hunt for it."

"Damn." Why did shit always have to be complicated?

"Maybe we should just keep going to that Boswell exit," she said.

Lewis considered this. Actually, he'd prefer that. But how far would it be? He was in agony *now*. He pictured himself suddenly unable to hold it. Kim and the kids would see him piss his pants.

"I'll just jump out here," he said and pointed to a bushy spot next to the road.

"God." Kim shook her head. "Just drive and see if the gas station's down there." She flicked her hand.

He debated, then hit the gas and headed down a black top road lined with trees stretching their skeletal branches over the top. He wiggled in his seat. Time to stop. Right now.

He slowed as a building inched into view. A break in the trees revealed just enough to see a porch overhang jutting out from an old structure where two gas pumps stood like lost soldiers. *We're not getting gas here*, he thought, but he could still take a leak.

"There it is." Lewis smashed the accelerator.

"Thank god." Kim turned to the back. "Caleb, you got your shoes on?"

"Yep," he said.

Big sister Lori diverted her attention from her phone long enough to confirm. "He's got 'em on."

Lewis thought, *I don't like this.* Perhaps at some point in its past, the place had been a gas station, but now it resembled a graveyard. Tall weeds crowded the outside, climbing past windows with sparse shards of glass dangling in the rotting frames. A decrepit mobile home, collapsing on one end, squatted at the edge of the trees. This place wasn't old, it was goddamn ancient. Lewis decided right then that he'd just piss behind the Suburban in the weed-infested parking lot. He and Caleb could just step back there, let it fly, and get right back on the road. The place gave him the creeps. A nagging feeling that life here ended long ago.

Nope, we ain't hangin' out here.

He brought the Suburban to a hurried stop, shoved the shifter to Park, and said to Kim, "We're stepping behind the car real quick. No damn way I'm gonna go stomping around here." He smiled and Kim shook her head in that exasperated way she sometimes did. She didn't like it here either.

Caleb climbed over the seat and flopped into his lap. Lewis smiled. "Let's go, little man."

He opened the door and chilly air wafted inside. Spring was still young. He left the car running and climbed out with Caleb wedged in the crook of his arm. He shut the door behind him and let his son down gently. Crickets chirped across the deserted parking lot from the tree line. What a dismal place.

Gravel crunched under his shoes like brittle bones.

Lewis would never know which one he reacted to first—seeing the dog or Caleb's panicked shout. As they rounded the back of the Suburban, the first dog appeared; large and filthy with its head hunkered low. It bared its teeth and Lewis froze. His chest fluttered as if his blood suddenly changed to cold water.

"Lewis!" Kim's shout ripped through the air. "Get back in here! Wild dogs!"

Lewis swallowed a hard lump in his throat and gripped Caleb's hand. She said *wild dogs*, though he saw only one. He stole quick glances about, but saw nothing. He settled his terrified gaze on the one in front of him.

Black and scrawny. Probably hadn't seen a decent meal in months. Its fur rose in a spiked clump.

Caleb squealed and tugged at Lewis's tightening grip.

Lewis's hands tingled and his heart quivered. His first thought was *if we turn to run, it'll attack us*. He pictured the car door – a good five yards back. If he sprinted, he might make it.

The dog crept closer. "Easy," Lewis said. He yanked Caleb into his arms. *Back up slowly… no sudden moves*, but his feet screamed to run. Now. "Easy. Good dog." *Oh dear god.*

Caleb squirmed and whimpered.

Lewis flipped his attention behind him and spotted a second dog circling around the front of the Suburban, growling in the same hateful way as the first. This one was twice the size as the first one. Saliva drooled from its mouth and splattered in wet smacks.

Lewis darted his head back and forth between the two. Kim's voice echoed in some distant, unrecognizable part of the universe. His balls shriveled to hard rocks. He thought, *if Lori rolled down her window, I could shove Caleb in.* Then he'd deal with the dogs. So clear, so right.

He opened his mouth to yell at Lori, keeping one eye on the Labrador.

It charged.

Lewis whirled and pinned Caleb between his body and the back window of the Suburban. At first, it felt like someone kicked him squarely in the ass, but then hot pain shot through his legs and the dog yanked. The back of the Suburban offered nothing to grip onto.

He screamed as something ripped.

The bigger dog bit him in the left thigh, latching its teeth firmly into the meat of his leg. The animal's strength terrified him and the dreadful idea that Caleb may slip away and die in this weed-infested parking lot slammed into his brain with loathsome clarity.

Caleb.

He wedged his hands under Caleb's arms and hoisted his bawling son onto the Suburban's roof. Just as Caleb's little feet disappeared over the top edge of the vehicle, the large dog yanked on Lewis's leg again. A chunk of his muscle tore away in a wet sucking sound. He fell to his knees. *Get up!* But nothing worked.

A swarm of shadows engulfed him. Lewis tried to bring his arms up to protect his face, but they no longer worked. Powerful jaws clamped onto his neck. Hot breath flooded his ear and the stench of something rotten enveloped him. The dog wrenched, twisting Lewis in a violent twirl until his face collided with gravel.

Blood filled his vision. On the ground. On his clothes. Was that *his* blood?

Oh lord god, they're eating me... they're...

A white flash lanced his eyes and stars floated like small ghosts. Everything fell away, even the fear.

And then he was gone.

. . . . .

Officer Jack Snider held the woman's bloody hand, hoping to offer some measure of comfort. "You're safe now, ma'am. You and your kids, you're all safe." He winced as the words came out, thinking about the dead husband.

The radio squawked and Jack thumbed the mic. "Yeah."

"Jack?" Patti's voice.

"Yeah, it's me. What's up?"

"Sheriff with you?"

"Yeah," he said. "But we're kinda busy here." His eyes landed on one of the dead dogs. It took three bullets from his Smith and Wesson to bring it down. The woman on the ground wailed. Thank God the kids were still in the vehicle. They didn't need to see all this. An ambulance backed up toward the blood smeared Suburban. Jesus, what a mess.

"I can't raise him," Patti said, "And we've got another situation."

"Now what?"

"Ronnie Castle called again. Said Sherri has been kidnapped. That a man took her."

"What do you mean a man took her?"

"That's what he's saying. That a man named Michael took her."

What the Christ is going on out there? The whole world's gone fucking nuts.

A paramedic leapt from the ambulance and scrambled to the woman. Jack let go of her hand and glanced at the paramedic. "You got her and the kids?" he asked.

"We got 'em," the paramedic said.

Jack hustled to his car and climbed inside. He keyed his mic again and said, "I'm in my car and heading to Black Rock now, Patti."

Watch out for those dogs, those men who do evil,
those mutilators of the flesh.
–Philippians 3:2

For the wages of sin are death.
–Romans 3:23

Part 1
Black Rock

Everyone has a story to tell.

Some see ghosts, some see UFOs; hell, some even say that the good Lord Himself spoke right to them. How do you respond to shit like that? I guess you just nod, say wow, and move on, like giving a street bum a quarter so he'll leave you alone. But the story you're about to hear transcends all bullshit, and honestly, I still blame myself for not acting sooner.

It started when that *thing* named Benjamin Clark came to Black Rock. I still don't know exactly what it was. I'll get more into that later, but I should mention, *it* has haunted us twice since I've been here, only the first time it bore a different name. More on that later also.

Aside from the story I'm about to tell you, Black Rock ain't a lot different than any other small town. Just a blip off the main path sprinkled with all the small-town ingredients; an old courthouse that sits on a quiet little main street. A school, a few churches, and couple of bars. There's a group of nosy old women who play Bingo on Friday nights down at the Lions Club. I swear they spend most of their time gossiping on about how Mike Markel's teenage daughter is pregnant or harping on about the affair the Methodist minister is havin' with that trashy girl that plays the piano for church. I personally don't think she's trashy, but you know how old women like to carry on.

Like I said, typical small-town living. Calm. Predictable. At least it had been for the past 15 years.

You'll soon learn what I mean by that.

What happened 15-years ago? That's a lot to unpack, but to give you an idea; a guy was killed by dogs out at the old gas station. A teenage girl was kidnapped and never found. Archie Winthrop, the guy who mows cemeteries, went nuts.

And then everything stopped. At least for a long time, it did.

That is until a couple of months ago when Black Rock became a shit-show again, to put it lightly. Granted, some people had no clue anything was goin' on at all. But those who did, and lived through it; they sure as hell knew. People like me, Pastor Loggins and his daughter, Abigail, and Ronnie - people like us, we knew. There was evil in this little town. Real evil.

And guess what? I'm fixin' to tell you all about it.

Walk with me, if you don't mind. We'll stroll up the main street here and as we do, I'll tell the story.

You'll start to notice things about this town – things you might miss at first glance; until you look deeper. Like how the trees seem to lean inward and stretch their branches over you. Or how the older buildings, long deserted, stand hauntingly empty with their dark windows facing the night. God knows what lurks behind them. It's the type of town that makes a person want to hurry up and get through it.

Oh look! See that guy stumbling out the front door of Ada's bar? That's Jesse England. He's drunk, like always. Jesse's a dumb-ass and everyone knows it; you can tell by looking at him. Not because of his stringy hair or his Harley Davidson attire, even though the dipshit has never owned a Harley in his life, but because idiots like Jesse live in every town.

Look at him.

He stops at the edge of the sidewalk, the streetlamp casts a gloomy glow so that only his silhouette is visible to us, and stuffs his hands into his jeans pocket. He spits belligerently into the gutter. Just then, the front door to Ada's bar bursts open and a big man named Bill Hoskins glares outside until his eyes find Jesse. Bill's nostrils flare and he yells, "I see your ass in here again, I'll kick your damn head in! You understand me, you son of a bitch?"

Don't worry, you're witnessing a regular event. Jesse could give a shit less. He's always been fine with pissing people off. Jesse's only shining moment was years ago when he married a pretty girl named Britney Darnell, but he screwed that up like we all knew he would.

Jesse lights a cigarette and saunters away. Alone. As he walks, he murmurs. He talks to himself a lot nowadays. Let's move closer, keeping out of sight, and see if we can hear what he's saying. This is important because Jesse's been a little off since meeting Benjamin Clark, like so many things in Black Rock are.

"No one owns me," Jesse says and smokes his cigarette. He sways, but never stumbles. He's got the drunk-walk down to an art. There's hardly anyone out on the streets tonight, so the scrape of his shoes echoes off sleeping buildings. "And I don't own no one." He slaps his hand down on his thigh with a dull splat and laughs hysterically, then yells, "You got the eyes, boy! You got the soul!"

He stops and gazes toward the sky. "Where are you?" he says, barely loud enough to hear. He stands that way for several minutes. His breaths are raspy, like something wet inside him; like there might be something wrong with him.

He'll go home now and pass out. In the scheme of things, Jesse doesn't matter much, but he played a small part in what happened to Pastor Loggins three-months ago, so I pointed him out.

.　.　.　.　.

It's muggy tonight. It gets that way when summer arrives. At least there's no thunderstorms rolling in! Looks like we're pretty safe. The stars are shining; splattering the sky. Twinkling reflections.

Most things around here are closed this time of night. Just up ahead there's the public library. An old building – built around 1855. They've done a great job preserving it. I love the inside of that place. It's quaint and has that comforting aroma of old books. There's been rumors that the city council plans to build a new, bigger library, but nothing ever comes of it. Without that old library, this just wouldn't be Black Rock.

We'll keep walking straight down Perry Street, but if we turned left onto Twin Bridges Road, and went out by the old cemetery, we'd end up out by Donna Johnson's old place. A lot of folks say that's where all the bad stuff started.

So buckle up, my friend; here we go. If there was a beginning to all the madness, it started the morning Donna died.

Chapter 1

Donna strained to sit up as pain flared in her side. Her hand fell asleep, like she'd laid on it wrong, and she couldn't wake it up. In all her 82 years, she'd never felt pain like that in her side, not like this.

"Can't wake my hand up," she told her cat, Charlie. She flicked her wrist like shooing off a bee; then waited for that uncomfortable tingle to settle in as blood rushed back to the limb. But nothing changed. Charlie remained curled up at the foot of the bed and watched her with indifference.

Winter mornings were sometimes fraught with odd ailments. Cooped up in the house all the time. She hated winters and had always fancied a move south, maybe to Florida or Texas, someplace warm, and leave this buggery old house and butt-cold Indiana for the birds.

Ha. Like she'd *ever* move.

The chorus of familiar barks echoed outside her window and she plucked her glasses off the nightstand. "I'm comin', I'm comin'," she said.

Maybe if she got busy feeding the animals, her hand would wake up. She needed to quit thinking about it. Just move on and let things go away on their own. That's what her mother always said.

Donna heaved her 164 pounds off the bed and stood for a moment, making sure she wouldn't get dizzy. She'd nearly fallen down the stairs a few months back after getting dizzy from standing up too fast. Getting old was horrible, and for Donna, there was no one to call if she fell and busted a hip or broke an arm.

She didn't have one of those fancy air phones that everyone seemed to have their face stuck in nowadays. And if she kept it her way, she never would.

She pushed her feet into thick slippers, picked her house-coat off the bed, and slipped it on while briskly rubbing her arms to calm the goose-bumps. It was like living in an icebox here. The hardwood floors didn't help a damn thing. But those slippers were wonderful. She'd picked them up the last time she was at the Wal-Mart in Lafayette.

Outside, the goats bleated, the chickens crowed, and the dogs barked, all begging for food. If there was one thing in this world that Donna loved, had always loved, it was this time of day; the time of day when she was closest to the animals.

"Oh, I'm comin'!" she yelled while hobbling down the stairs. "My goodness!" Before going outside, she waddled over to the woodstove and opened the little metal door and peered inside. The two chunks of wood she'd put in last night were nothing but embers now. No wonder it was so damn cold in here. She grabbed a handful of timber she kept stacked in a metal bucket next to the stove and tossed it in. That should be burning well by the time she got back in.

She went to the sink while flexing her left hand and filled the percolator, placing two spoonfuls of coffee in the basket, and set it on the burner. Nothing like coming in from outside and having a hot cup of coffee while sitting on the couch, snuggled in her afghan and watching Good Morning America.

That pain in her side swelled again, this time like a bubble, and it floated from her side to the middle of her chest. She knew damned good and well it was gas. Gas pains could be the worst kind of pain there was. She wondered if maybe she shouldn't go out to the outhouse and try going to the bathroom. But the thought of sitting out there in that cold little building on that frozen wooden seat was as appealing as eating broken glass. She'd wait until she warmed up a little; maybe after she got back from feeding the animals. Besides, after a good cup of coffee, going to the bathroom was easier anyway.

With her flannel coat on and a sock-hat pulled on her head, Donna stepped outside. *Not too bad out here.* No wind, which made all the difference. She moved carefully down the wooden steps to the ground, her feet crunching in old snow. This was where she had to be careful. Hit a patch of ice and you'll be on your ass quicker than shit through a goose.

Donna didn't notice the man standing at the end of her driveway, his dark clothes silhouetting him against the snowy backdrop. If she had, she probably would have turned back to the house immediately. She didn't like strangers.

"Petey!" she yelled. "Where are you boy?"

A black Labrador came barreling around the corner with his tongue hanging out. Donna knew it was his way of saying *good morning, good morning, I'm so glad to see you!*

She'd loved Petey from the day he'd wandered up to her front porch. At first, he'd been scared to come within twenty feet of her. Her heart ached imagining horrors the poor dog had gone through. Diligently, she'd sat out bowls of food, moving them closer to her each day, until finally, Petey was eating right in front of her. Eventually she was able to touch him and he warmed up to her. That was last Fall and now he was like a big puppy again.

As Donna reached down to give Petey his morning hug, something caught his attention. He glared at the driveway. His ears perked up and for a just a second, the hair on his back furled. A growl rumbled deep in his throat.

"Hey now," Donna said, "You quit that." And Petey did. "Where's everyone else, Petey? Where are your brothers and sisters?"

One by one, each of the other nine dogs emerged, falling in behind Petey as he led the pack toward the barn. Donna smiled as she watched them. Her adopted kids, she liked to think of them. A mixture of breeds, some big, some *really* big, nearly all had been stray dogs at some point and by the good graces of Donna's heart, had found a home. The cacophony of barks, yelps, and whines surrounded her and she held out her hands as they sniffed and nudged forward. They were hungry. Heck, they were always hungry.

"I'm gettin' it, just give me a second," she said.

She kept their food in the old barn about fifty feet behind the house. She filled it every autumn with bags of dog food, grain, and hay. Enough to last all winter.

Three large steel bowls sat empty and lined up against the outside of the barn. Donna struggled to drag out one of the forty-pound bags. With her hand numb, it was hard to keep hold of the bag. She tore the top off and then dumped the food evenly between the three bowls. The dogs plunged in, heads smashed against each other, eating as if they'd never been fed before.

She glanced at the goats, who gawked back at her. "You're next, fellas", she said. Donna stepped back inside the barn, tossed the empty dogfood bag into the wheel-barrow, and grabbed a smaller bag of grain. Much easier. Just as she locked the barn-door behind her, a jolt of pain shot through her left shoulder and she winced. She didn't feel well at all. She gasped. What the Christ was going on? Her entire left arm felt numb and that bubble of pain in her chest heated up, like hot lead.

A deep fear washed over her. *Oh my God.*

She shook her head. *Just calm down and this will pass.* She had to get inside and set down, that was all. A good cup of coffee and getting warm by the stove would help. But panic crept closer, rising like a black cloud. Something was wrong, terribly wrong. It dawned on her. *Help. I need help. Back to the house. The phone…*

She turned feebly, a small moan escaping her mouth, and that's when she saw him. A man, standing in the driveway, staring directly at her. *Help me, please.*

Had she been able to draw a breath, she would have screamed.

It wouldn't have mattered.

Blackness engulfed her and she fell forward. Donna Johnson was dead before she hit the ground.

Petey raised his head and looked at her. Still chewing his last mouthful of food, he ambled over and started to whine. He stuck his nose in Donna's hair, sniffing, and then licked her exposed ear. Donna's sock-hat had fallen off and lay next to her head, her grimaced face buried in the snow. Petey's tail dropped and his head lowered as he made one last circle around Donna's body, the woman who'd loved him. Finally, he lay down next to her and gave a quick bark.

The other dogs watched and a few joined him lying next to Donna. The two goats, as if realizing they weren't getting fed, started to bleat again. Up in the bedroom window, Charlie the cat watched the scene as if he didn't give a shit.

The man in the driveway walked to the front door.

Chapter 2

Two things weighed on Pastor Thomas Loggins's mind the day he met Benjamin Clark for breakfast; that he'd be late for his daughter's school Spring program and that she would grossly overreact to said tardiness. Nothing was easy since Abby turned fifteen. *Girls turn into mean creatures when they become teenagers.* That's what his friends told him. Thomas had always laughed it off thinking that his dear, sweet little Abigail, the girl who drew him wonderful crayon pictures and kissed him every night, would never change.

Thomas had been wrong. Abby had changed. She'd morphed into a complete stranger, and she was mean sometimes. Thomas leaned heavily on his wife for help, but the gulf between him and his daughter grew wider and wider.

Deep down, Thomas recognized his own contribution to the problem. He battled his own demons. Free passes didn't exist for pastors. The perception of perfection carried its burdens. He preached that *he* himself had faults, that *he* sinned constantly, that *he* was nothing more than a man who relied on God's mercy daily. But let one of his sins slip out and people would turn on him like starving wolves. Maybe unfair, maybe hypocritical, but it came with the job, and Thomas would never look at it any other way.

But arriving late to Abby's program prompted trepidation he'd prefer to avoid.

Benjamin Clark called two days ago and asked if Thomas could meet for breakfast on Friday. Thomas tried to recall who Benjamin Clark was, then determined that it didn't matter and considered his schedule, going off memory (never a good thing) and said, "yeah, that shouldn't be a problem". Not five minutes later, when he told his wife about the scheduled breakfast, he realized he'd screwed up. *Abby's program starts at 9 AM*, she'd said.

Great.

Surely Benjamin would understand. If worse came to worst and Thomas had to tell him, *I'm sorry, but my daughter has a program*, Benjamin would surely understand. Men of God are busy, busy, busy. So many people to save, so little time to do it. Thomas spent more time on his cell phone than he did in his Bible these days. He hadn't asked Jesus what he thought about *that* yet.

He should've just cancelled the breakfast and rescheduled. Easy peasy. But the pastor worried about perception. He had the fastest growing church in Taylor County. *Who would have thought?* The man who moved here from Texas, the man with the *past* (with the tattoos to prove it). What if he suddenly had to start missing appointments because he was too busy for the congregation? He was too new here. If Benjamin needed help finding Jesus, then Thomas would be there for him.

. . . . .

Thomas arrived earlier than their scheduled meet time. He wanted to have a cup of coffee and ponder his own thoughts before Benjamin arrived. The young waitress set the steaming mug on the table and asked, "You want anything besides coffee, pastor?" *What a sweet voice.*

Most folks in the restaurant knew him. "No thanks," he said and smiled, not making eye contact with anyone. "I'll just wait."

"Okay." She walked to another table carrying the coffee pot and Thomas resumed his spiritual self-reflection.

He frequented this place three or four times a week. It was the perfect place for meetings just like the one he was about to have with Benjamin. It offered the right combination of X's and Y's. People needed that. Just yesterday he'd sat in this exact same booth with Myrtle Blankenship. They spoke for an hour about her suspicions that her husband didn't love her anymore and she wanted to know how to get him into church. Seldom did anyone actually listen to Thomas or apply any of the advice he gave.

Too often that meant taking accountability for their own actions, which wasn't everyone's cup of tea. People love to complain, but doing something, taking action, was a different game entirely. But it was his job to listen, to be there when needed. To lead people to Jesus one soul at a time.

He stared directly into his cup of coffee, watching the creamer swirl in the brown liquid, spiraling like a galaxy. *If your eyes cause you to sin, cut them out.* Why? A question he'd asked himself for the past twenty-four years. Since that day in college. The day he prayed to forget. Just then, the front door opened with a ding.

Benjamin stepped inside, glanced around, and then smiled. Thomas waved, painted on his own smile, and stood up. What a sweet looking man. Older. Not like senile old, but much older than Thomas.

Benjamin moved through the small restaurant with an uncanny grace, taking slow steps to avoid running into anything, almost drifting through. A shy smile painted the man's face. He wore a black suit. A typical candidate to request a meeting with a middle-aged pastor. In Thomas's experience, the criteria for wanting to change the direction of one's life consisted of three main ingredients: kids, marriage, and regret. All things, that in most cases, required time to fully mature, like a fine wine, only then to be uncorked and consumed. Only time revealed the basic fact that we, as people, need God in our lives to provide fulfillment and harmony. Or said a different way, you need time to screw things up.

Benjamin reached the table and Thomas said, "Good morning, Benjamin." He stuck his hand out to shake.

Benjamin took it, shook it vigorously, and grinned back – and that's when Thomas noticed something odd about this man. The grin. A simple gesticulation that didn't settle quite right, something out of place and not in a good way.

"Mornin' sir," Benjamin said. "I really appreciate you meeting with me."

"Don't thank me, this is what I do."

"You can call me Ben." That strange grin revealed teeth too large. What appeared at first to be a typical, older guy deteriorated and melted into something... different. But different wasn't the word he wanted;

different didn't quite fit. A word danced on the end of Thomas's tongue. *Stop focusing on this man's physical imperfections.*

"Ben it is," Thomas said. "Please, have a seat."

"Sounds great," Ben plopped down.

"Ever eat here?" Thomas asked and chuckled as he settled into his chair.

"Nope. But I'm starving. Any suggestions?"

"I always get the bacon, egg, and potato taco. The potato makes all the difference. They use some magical spice in there. Best breakfast in Black Rock."

"Guess I'll get a few of those." Ben scooted the plastic menu off to the side and rested his forearms on the table. *My dad used to do that,* Thomas thought. Of course, his father also used to lounge around the house drunk, wearing nothing but underwear when the rest of the family huddled under blankets in front of the TV.

"I'm guessing you're new to town? Where were you before this?" Thomas asked. Always the small talk first.

"I'm from Indiana." One corner of Ben's mouth curled into a smile.

Thomas nodded, not sure if Ben answered his question.

Ben continued, "I moved here to Black Rock, oh…" he glanced up at the ceiling. "Probably a week or so ago."

"What brought you here?" Thomas could guess the answer, because it was always one of two things; either a job in Lafayette or relatives. People didn't simply choose to settle in Black Rock. Unless, of course, a church needed a pastor and you happened to be a pastor out of work.

"A job," Ben said. "Seemed too good to pass up."

"What do you do?"

Ben thought and said, "I build houses. Work dried up quite a bit down by Vincennes, but around Lafayette, it's still pretty strong, considering the economy and all. I don't like living in big towns, especially after all that Coronavirus crap happened, so I moved out here."

"Ah, that's understandable. We have to follow the opportunities, right?" *Why do I feel like he's lying to me?*

"Yeah, I like it. But it's a little way from home."

"You still got family down in Vincennes?"

Again, Ben hesitated. Then said, "Sort of."

Thomas wasn't sure what *sort of* meant, but did it matter? Strangely, he couldn't relax, as if bad news lurked around the corner. Thomas nodded and sipped his coffee.

The waitress wandered back over, flipped out her pad and pen, and asked for their order. Throughout the interaction, Thomas noticed that Ben never once looked at her. Making eye contact was common courtesy, after all. Not to mention, a pretty girl typically garnered a quick glance. To Thomas, the whole thing felt a bit rude and more than a bit odd.

Thomas checked his watch. 7:47 AM. He'd have to leave by 8:40 at the latest to make it to Abby's program. Normally, people took their time opening up, but once they did, the crap spilled from their mouths like sewage from a clogged pipe.

Ben seemed to be taking his time, asking all kinds of questions about Thomas's preaching career; how long he'd been doing it, where all he'd been, what was his favorite part, and other boring nonsense. Thomas was relieved when the waitress arrived with their order, hopeful that it would move the conversation along.

Thomas checked his watch again. 8:22 AM.

"You short on time?" Ben asked. "I don't wanna hold you up."

"Sort of," Thomas smiled. "My daughter's got a school program this morning. She's in the choir."

"Ah," Ben's smile stretched across his face and suddenly the word that had eluded Thomas earlier jumped into his mind… sinister. Ben seemed *sinister*. Like staring at a corpse. A chill crept across the back of his neck as Ben spoke. "You wouldn't wanna be late. She'll hate you for that."

"She seems to hate me all the time now anyway," Thomas said and for some reason, wished he hadn't said it.

"You gotta go now?"

"I do, actually. We'll have breakfast again next week if you want. I don't usually have other commitments like this. Truth be known, I forgot about the program when I agreed to our breakfast."

"That'd be great," Ben said. "Sorry, I sort of diddle-daddled around this morning about talking."

"Oh, no," Thomas shook his head, "It can take a while to get into things. At least we got a lot of small talk out of the way. I'd like to get together next week, if you can." It occurred to him that he'd just lied to Benjamin. Thomas didn't want to see this man again. Ever.

"Let's do that," Ben sipped his coffee. "I really do have some things I need to run past you."

Thomas was on auto-pilot now, regurgitating the same stuff he said to everyone. "I think the first step in any walk with God is accountability, and we all need help with that." He pictured the drive to the house and how many minutes it would take to get there.

Ben nodded and smiled, but not in a friendly way. It was more of a smirk. "Yeah." Ben stared at him, a glint of accusation painted on his darkening face. "I think you're right. Accountability is important. It seems these days nobody wants to be held accountable for what they've done."

A sudden, and horrifying thought burst open in Thomas's mind; *does he KNOW about me?*

He tried to push the thought away. "Let me pick up the check, Benjamin."

"It's Ben, pastor. And no, I'm paying for breakfast. I insist. After all, I'm the one who droned on and on all morning while you've got important business to attend to."

Thomas started to protest, but Ben raised a hand to silence him.

"Ok, Ben. Thank you for breakfast."

As soon as the words came out of his mouth, Thomas felt a sense of relief. He was almost done with this strange man.

Almost done.

Chapter 3

The program went amazingly well. Thomas arrived on time and he thanked God for small blessings. Abby sang, but stood in the back with a mopey frown on her face, making no attempt to hide her discontent, which always prompted Thomas to think, *then why do you do it?*

Linda recorded the entire event on her iPad.

"God, she's so beautiful up there," Linda said while aiming the awkward looking iPad at the stage.

"She doesn't look happy about it," Thomas said. Why couldn't she be like the other girls up there whose gleeful expressions reflected their joy? Nope, not Abby, she hated the world. No one else was like that; at least, not that Thomas could tell.

She really was beautiful, though, and no longer in a little girl sort of way. A young woman, that's what she was. This wasn't the first time he'd noticed, of course, but sometimes reality slugged you in the gut.

A few weeks back, reality struck home like lightning on gasoline when Abby had divulged a secret about one of her friends in the Ninth grade. Carol-Lee had gotten caught passing a note that detailed her plans to give her boyfriend a blowjob. After the initial shock of hearing the word *blowjob* flow from Abby's mouth, Thomas prayed that he wouldn't over-react and say something stupid. He wasn't ready for that. Not that he lived life in a bubble; he'd known things like this were coming. His relationship with Abby was already rocky. Certainly not prepared for talk of *blowjobs*. Thomas had sat like a lump on a frog's butt, listening to Linda and Abby discuss it. Things were changing so fast.

After the program, on the drive home, they stopped for some hot chocolate.

"I think you sang the best," Linda said, "I couldn't understand the others nearly as well." She clasped her hands together in a strained gesture, as if regretting what she'd just said. Thomas read her mind; *oh my god, I'm over-doing it.* "I've heard you sing and you're wonderful."

Abby rolled her eyes and sipped her drink.

Thomas felt disconnected. He wished he could join in the conversation like he used to. Not anymore.

Blowjob.

His little Abby. The childhood fancier of Snow White. The young beautician who painted her mother's nails.

Now a frightening creature he barely recognized.

He glanced at Abby. Thomas knew how these things worked. He counseled people all the time who struggled with their teenage children. They come back, eventually. As long as relationships are based in the fundamental foundation of Christ, it all works out.

Which all sounded great until your daughter turned fifteen and started talking about blowjobs.

"…before we go?" Linda's voice slapped him and he blinked. He hadn't heard a word she said.

"What?"

"Do you want to grab anything else before we go?" *Where'd you go?* her look asked.

"You're in the Twilight Zone, dad." Abby shook her head.

"I guess." Thomas sipped from his cup and played it off. "I don't need anything."

"Whatever," Abby said, rolling her eyes. *Whatever? Why would she say that?*

She's not trying to be mean, he reminded himself. She's just saying what comes to mind – that filter that prevents the mouth from spewing crap hasn't quite matured yet. "Maybe I need some meds." He meant it as a joke, but no one laughed.

Abby shrugged.

He almost said, *Is my angel too cool to joke with her old man?* But he held his tongue. He hadn't called her angel in over a year and it'd probably just sound stupid.

She took a sip and said something that shocked him. "I love you, even though I don't act like it sometimes."

Linda's head snapped to Abby and she said, "Would you quit. Your dad knows you love him."

He wanted to tell Linda to hush. He loved his wife, God knew he did, but not everything required her intervention.

The drive home settled into the usual silence. *Even though I don't act like it sometimes.* The ghost of a smile touched his face in the silence of the car.

. . . . .

Thomas met with Benjamin the following Monday. Thomas would have preferred to wait until the following Friday, but Benjamin insisted. Thomas concluded that not liking someone very much was no reason to deny them the path to righteousness.

They met at the same restaurant. Same waitress. Same table.

Just before Benjamin arrived, Thomas sipped his coffee and mouthed silently, "Thank you for your power, God, and your refuge." He thought of Proverbs, of lessons of wisdom. That's when Benjamin Clark stepped through the door, dressed in the same black suit he'd worn the last time. *Didn't Ben say he was in construction?* Some people felt the need to overdress when talking to a pastor.

Benjamin's face bore the same familiar oddness; but Thomas couldn't put a finger on why. Maybe the jaw too large or the eyes too narrow.

Thomas stood and held out his hand. "Hey, Ben." He truly did not like this man and using the familiar name felt wrong.

That same smile, the one that made Thomas cringe, spread across Ben's face. Thomas glanced away thinking, *it's all in my head*, and said, "Please, sit down."

"Thanks pastor." Ben scooted out a chair and eased himself down, then rested his hands in his lap. "I appreciate you meeting me today."

"No problem. Sorry about last Friday," Thomas said and Ben shook his head and smiled.

"I completely understand." Ben held Thomas's gaze. "If we don't show our kids they're important to us, they'll grow up thinking no one cares about them."

"We do the best we can," Thomas said.

"Everyone's too busy now days."

Thomas thought about it and added for conversation's sake, "I think people are under a lot of pressure. It's hard."

"Yes," Ben nodded and shifted his gaze upward, as if watching a ghost dance on the ceiling. "People are selfish."

"You think People have changed?"

"I believe there was a time when people genuinely cared about others more than they do now. Things used to be better."

What a strange statement. It was hard to concentrate on anything but Ben's cold, piercing stare; like trying to think about mathematical equations in a room full of wasps. "I'll bet every generation says that." Thomas said. *Maybe not the way you said it.*

"No," Ben's solemn face straightened. "They don't, pastor."

Thomas painted a fake smile, confused as hell, and decided to change the subject, maybe get down to Ben's business. He said, "I love talking history, but let's talk about you."

Ben waved a hand and said, "Yes, let's get down to business." The waitress brought a cup of coffee over and sat it down next to Ben. He picked it up and sipped. "It's really more your business than mine."

Thomas crinkled his eyebrows. His unease burrowed deeper. "Oh, in what way?"

"That waitress remind you of anyone?" Ben's gravelly voice sank low.

Thomas's fingers tingled and his vision grayed, like someone about to faint, and sweat tickled his palms. "What are you talking about?" Thomas's words stammered. His breath hitched. He fought a maddening urge to jump to his feet and charge out of there; to run and never stop.

"I asked you, does she remind you of anyone from your past?" Ben glared at Thomas.

"I'm sorry Ben, I don't know what you mean."

Ben's words stabbed deeper. "Did you think you'd get away with it?"

A chill crept up Thomas's spine, spreading like a spider unfurling its spiny legs inside him. His lip quivered.

"Your payment is due, pastor."

. . . . .

Thomas trembled. Old guilt swept through him and a moan seeped from his throat in a steady hum.

Ben said, "Hey, I get it." His head bobbed like someone trying to relate. "You were young and drunk. So was she. Could'a happened to anyone, right?"

A cold tear slipped down Thomas's cheek. He shivered as if his heart were pumping ice-water.

Ben glanced around the room, then said, "She's a pretty little thing, your girl."

Thomas said, "What?"

"Abby. She's pretty. Like her mom."

"What the hell do you know about my family?" Thomas trailed off at the end, realizing that several patrons were looking their way.

"I know plenty," Ben nodded and that sinister smile spread across his face. "I'm afraid you've got a tough choice to make, pastor."

Thomas's mouth straightened to a thin line. His ears grew hot.

"You see, here's the deal," Ben leaned closer. "Maybe no one caught you, but you've got to pay. The balance is due. I'm gonna give you a simple choice. You. Or your daughter. You choose which."

Thomas's chest tightened, then loosened, then tightened again. He felt like an observer, as if this were all happening on a movie screen. He stammered, "What?"

The voice of his long dead father whispered in his ear, *you can't let him get away with saying that kind of stuff, boy*.

Ben shook his head and sipped his coffee, then said, "You committed a dreadful sin against humanity, pastor. Now the balance is due. Someone has got to pay. It's either going to be you, or Abby. That simple. Your choice."

Thomas shot to his feet. His chair crashed to the floor behind him. Conversations ceased and every eye darted to him. Thomas's eyes locked on Ben.

"I don't know what you think you're doing here," Thomas growled. He felt stupid. Weak. Like he should be punching this old man's lights out. The little coward inside him sprang to life. Thomas, who'd never been in a fight his entire life, didn't know how to do it. His eyes watered.

Help me, God. I need you to help, my Lord Jesus.

"Sit down," Ben hissed and stared up at him. "You're making a scene."

Thomas's breath hitched. "You leave my daughter alone."

Ben said, "Well, that's up to you. But sit down, pastor, or I'm gonna tell everyone in this place your little secret."

Thomas's nostrils flared with each harsh breath; his heart galloped in his chest. *Who is this man? How does he know? Why now?*

"Look," Ben glanced around the place then back at Thomas, "You can either sit down here and talk to me, or I swear, I'll tell everyone here you're a rapist."

Thomas glared at him. "Nobody will believe you."

Ben shook his head, as if annoyed, and said, "August 17th, wasn't it? Twenty-four years ago?"

Thomas's mouth fell open.

"Emily." Ben flipped a finger at him. "That was her name, wasn't it? She was wearing that sweet blue dress that she bought from Dillards the day before? Oh, they'll believe me. That they will."

Holy God, who is this man? Some sick-o cop, maybe. A tormented relative. But none of those things felt right.

Ben smiled and said, "You even left flowers for her – secretly, of course. How sweet of you. You must have really felt like shit. As if flowers could make up for raping her."

Thomas reached behind him, his heart ka-thudding like a jackhammer. Sweat broke out in his arm pits and one droplet trickled coldly down his side. His fingers tingled as they found the edge of his fallen chair. He eased it upright then scooted it back up to the table. *I shouldn't be sitting down right now*, he thought madly, *I should be...*

What?

Think. "Are you a cop?" Thomas asked and thought, *oh, you coward.*

He pictured Abby before she'd left for school. What had she worn this morning? For the life of him, he couldn't remember and it suddenly seemed so utterly pathetic that he couldn't.

Ben chuckled and said, "Oh, good heavens, no."

Thomas clamped down until his teeth ached. Had someone seen him all those years ago? A camera? Even Emily had never known (at least, he never thought she did... he'd never seen her again. Ever). Even the flowers he left for her must have been a mystery to her. Why was this happening now?

"I'm here to grant absolution," Ben touched Thomas's arm and the fingertips stung like jagged ice. Thomas jerked his arm off the table, but Ben didn't seem to notice. "It's you or her, you understand me? And don't even think of going to the cops. Don't make *any* trouble. I'll tell your secret and you'll go to jail and I'll still take Abby."

Words tumbled out of Ben's mouth like bloody vomit. Thomas tried to appear strong, but he felt defeat creeping into his posture. "I get it. This is a hard decision. I'm happy to give you some time to think about it. You simply tell me what you want by the end of this week. I'll even make it easy for you. If you don't respond, I'll assume you're willing to let your little girl pay the balance. That way, you don't have to *make* the decision." Ben's face morphed into sunken skin clinging to dead bones, the teeth grew long and sharp, and for a moment, a moment seared into Thomas's mind forever, Ben stank of rot.

Thomas slunk back and tears stung his eyes. His courage, if he'd ever had any, scampered away like a scared rabbit. He bent his head down and stared at his lap, praying silently that Ben would just leave.

Whatever Ben was.

A hand touched his shoulder and Thomas cried out, whirled around, and nearly fell out of his chair. For one horrifying second, he had no idea where he was. Emily hovered next to him. Then the waitress's face swam into focus.

"Are you okay?" she asked, her eyes wide and scared.

He nodded in little jerks, then he tried to speak, "I... I..."

Holy Christ, he couldn't talk. He glanced at Ben and gasped.

Ben wasn't there.

"Where'd the man go that was with me?" he asked, speaking through breathless hitches.

"He left about ten minutes ago," the waitress said. She leaned over and gently rubbed his back.

Ten minutes!

"You've just been sitting here. Crying," the waitress said. "Are you okay, pastor?"

Thomas noticed everyone staring at him; some concerned, some with something less trusting. He couldn't deal with their dubious eyes, and wiped his arm across his forehead. Sweat drenched the hair on his wrist.

He needed to get out of here and get to the police station. Now.

"Uhm," his voice shook, "How much do I owe you?"

"You don't owe nothin'," she said, "He paid for you both."

Good 'ole Benjamin.

Thomas pulled on his coat and willed his rubbery legs toward the door. The bright sunshine lanced his eyes and he put his hand up to shadow it. He checked in both directions to see if Benjamin might be out there waiting for him somewhere and saw no sign of him. Thank God for that. He planned to march straight to the police station and tell the Sheriff.

Thomas swiped a hand across his forehead again.

She remind you of anyone?

Emily.

I'll tell them your secret.

How could this possibly be happening? He had to do something. Tell someone. No. He'd pick up Abby first. Get her safe. He didn't plan to let her out of his sight.

He stumbled to his car and climbed inside, gasping.

Did you think you'd get away with it?

Your balance is due.

What if people find out? What if Linda finds out?

Don't get sidetracked. We're dealing with a crazy man.

Man? Really? That face *changed.* Those teeth.

First, get Abby safe.

Chapter 4

Nosy people.

Abby hated this pathetic town. *Town* used sparingly. Nothing but a bunch of nosy people, all trying to get the upper hand in a strange game with no prize. Another day in stupid Black Rock.

"Tell me, Abigail," the principal gazed at her, his folded hands tucked neatly beneath his chin, as if he was *on her side* (and yes, he's actually said that). She despised him. Just another man trying to have sympathy on poor little her, the preacher's girl who *won't apply herself*. "Why aren't you doing your work?"

She didn't answer him. She stared at her feet instead, concentrating on the grass stains etched on the end of her Vans sneakers in dark-green swirls.

As the principal released an exasperated breath, an absurd urge to apologize swept over her and she forced it back, clenching her fist to maintain composure. *I can't let them win. No way.*

"Don't you realize what will happen if you start failing classes?" the principal, Mr. Pearson, shuffled through papers, frustrated. Good. Everyone in the school called him "dogface" Pearson because of his shaggy beard and curly hair.

He continued. "You won't graduate. You're two years away, Abigail..."

"Abby," she corrected him. She hated Abigail. Sounded like a nun or something.

"Okay. Abby." He cleared his throat. "You're two years from graduating. If you lose anymore credits, you'll wind up in summer school, and possibly not graduate."

"Maybe I *don't want to* graduate." Take *that* you piece of shit. Maybe she meant it, maybe she didn't, but blurting the words sparked dark satisfaction, like dropping the f-bomb when alone in a room.

"Don't talk like that. You're too smart. Your mom and dad would be very upset if they knew your situation and it'd kill them to hear that kind of talk from you."

Oh, you patronizing weasel! *He's so worried about my parents. Everyone's worried about my parents.* Apparently, everyone just assumed *she* was fine. Why wouldn't she be fine? Her dad is a preacher. Dogface could go to hell for making that assumption. *And tonight, I'll go home and put on my fake face for my mom and dad to make them think I'm well and good. Blah, blah, blah.*

Mr. Pearson sat silent, the mood growing awkward, until he finally said, "Look, Abby, you're a very smart young woman. It seems like the past year has been tough for you." Her eyes shot up at him, met his gaze, and saw nothing but truth there. For a weird second, she liked him. *Ask me why. Please ask me why this year's been tough and then let me tell you.*

Then he ruined it like everyone seems to ruin everything with stupid lectures. "But you can't keep making excuses for failure. I can't imagine you'd want that, you're *not* a failure. You need to keep pressing forward, to be the best you can be. Isn't that…"

Her anger boiled, her face grew hot and sweat broke out on her palms. "You don't know *anything* about what I want." She didn't scream, but listening to her own voice, it sounded strange, as if spoken by someone else. Someone hidden in the room. Someone dangerous.

He blinked, stunned. "I wasn't trying…"

"You and everyone else in this stupid town think I'm perfect. You all think that."

"Abigail, I wasn't…"

"Abby! It's Abby, you jackass! *ABBY!*" She shot to her feet.

He leaned back in his chair, flattened his hands on his desk, and swallowed hard. She had him confused, unsure of what to do, against the ropes. She remembered her dad watching boxing matches years ago, leaning forward in his chair, excited, and saying, *he's hurt. That right hand hurt him bad.*

"Sit down, young lady," he hissed. "Don't make this worse than what it is."

"Go to hell you moron!" She immediately regretted those final words.

His eyes widened, then quickly sharpened with anger.

She'd crossed the line. She knew it right then. Why did people push her when she felt her worst? She swore sometimes people *wanted* to see her cry. She pictured her dad's disappointed face, his expression both shocked and saddened. *Why Abby?* Her answer would stun everyone. I don't know.

I don't know! The thought drove her crazy.

The silence between her and Principal Pearson hung in the air like a dagger deciding on which body to impale.

A strand of hair slipped loose from her ponytail and dangled in front of her eye and Abby fought the urge to push it back. To hell with it, let it hang there!

"I'm calling your mother," he said, his hand moving toward the phone. "I won't have blatant disrespect in my school, young lady. You need to remember who you're talking to."

She stood there, like an idiot. She hated the thought of him calling her mom. *Please don't,* she wanted to say, *God, last Friday we all went for hot chocolate and they think the world is perfect because I sang in the stupid choir.* She suddenly felt alone. An image flashed in her mind. A baby bird fallen from its nest, shattered and abandoned with ants crawling on it.

He dialed the number and then dipped the receiver below his mouth so he could speak to her. "Please wait outside, Miss Loggins. This conversation is over."

And just like that, all the power she had, if she'd ever had any to start with, deflated like a balloon. She wanted to scream at him, but only had the guts to give a disgusted growl and whirled away, slamming the door behind her. She hated being fifteen. She had no rights whatsoever. She couldn't even drive a stinkin' car.

She plopped down in a hard, wooden chair that lined the front glass of the office and folded her hands over her chest. The secretary, Mrs.

Gleeson, gave her a nervous glance, then looked back at her computer screen.

Did Mrs. Gleeson hear what I yelled at Mr. Pearson?

That lady wanted nothing to do with Abby and her problems. That was good, because Abby didn't want to share her problems.

Abby waited for what seemed like hours, but was really only fifteen minutes. Mrs. Gleeson never looked at her again. Mr. Pearson's door eased open and he stepped out and looked right at her.

"Your father is on his way," he said. Abby's heart sank. He'd have to leave the church to come here. *Shit.* "Why don't you go and get your things from your locker. I'm suspending you for the remainder of this week."

She looked away from him and back down at the floor.

"Listen," he said, his voice turning soft. "I didn't want this, Abby." At least he got the name right, finally. "But I can't help you unless you let me. No one can."

And then his door clicked shut. She glanced up, wishing he was still there. How weird was that? Her mind did strange stuff like that sometimes. She hated admitting it. She wondered if it was a sign of something worse. Like, that maybe she had mental issues or something. She hoped it wasn't, but how would she know?

She pushed that dangling piece of hair behind her ear.

Misunderstood and unseen.

She shuffled out the door in silence and checked her phone as the door closed softly behind her. Her soon-to-be boyfriend, Michael, had still not texted her today and she needed to hear from him.

She tapped his name and typed; got suspended. Call me!

Her thumb hovered over the send icon. She didn't want to sound pathetic. Since they hadn't officially met in person, it meant technically they were still only talking, not dating, so she couldn't be too needy. Not yet.

She deleted the words and stuffed the phone back into her pocket. *Play it cool, Abby.*

The hallway reminded her of something in one of those horror movies. Lockers lined the hall, the still ghosts of uniformed soldiers, and she slowly made her way past them. As she dragged her feet across the floor, the rubber on her shoes made little squeaks with each monotonous step.

I hate my life.

. . . . .

"You okay, Abby?"

She glanced up, lost for a second. It was Scott Kee, the boy who'd been following her around lately. If she told him to paint himself blue and walk through the halls naked, he'd do it. And even though she knew he'd give anything to kiss her, she also knew he'd never give up trying, making him hers as long as she needed him. How mean did that sound?

"No, not really," she said. "I just got suspended."

"Suspended!" His mouth fell open and revealed his shiny metal braces. He was skinny, pale white, and sported a nightmarish hairstyle, one that reminded her of people in those old eighties movies where it hung long in the back and short in the front. He stopped walking and said, "Dogface suspended you for failing History? He can't do that."

"It wasn't that." She chuckled. "I told him to go to hell."

Scott gawked at her. He'd never have the balls to say such a thing to the principal (or anyone else, for that matter). Some boys were like that. Weak. She wondered what Michael would have said. He would have stood up to ole' Dogface for sure.

"He'll definitely have it in for me now." She shot him a look that said *walk with me* and his feet immediately acted, catching up with her.

He shook his head. "How long?"

"The rest of the week."

"Ah," he sighed, "that's not too bad."

"Not bad," Abby smiled, feeling wrong, but not wanting Scott to know that. "That's four days!"

"At least it's not for the rest of the year. They kicked Robbie Smith out for the whole year!"

"Robbie got caught with weed."

"Yeah, but still."

They strolled along, approaching her locker, and she said, "My dad's gonna kill me for this."

"He'll get over it," Scott said. Easy for him to say.

"What are you doing out here anyway?" Abby asked. He should be in class, not walking down the empty halls with her.

"I saw you leave for the office, waited about ten minutes and asked if I could go to the restroom. Then I just waited, wanted to make sure you were okay."

"That's cool." She had to admit, he was sweet sometimes.

"Everyone acts stupid in Ms. Carter's class anyway. I hate being in there."

She knew why Scott didn't like it. He got picked on. He weighed like 90 pounds and she doubted he'd ever been in a fight in his life.

"You think she'll come back and teach next year?"

"Probably not," he snorted, "I sure as hell wouldn't. How much more boring can you get?"

"Yeah, I wouldn't either." Why are we talking about Ms. Carter? Who cared about her besides Scott?

They stopped at Abby's locker and she popped the metal door open.

"What's your mom and dad gonna do?"

"I don't know." She wasn't lying about that. "Probably ground me for life. I'm pretty sure I'll lose my phone." Her phone existed as a bargaining chip – they always threatened to take it if she misbehaved. What's funny is that they'd never actually taken it, not in the three years since they'd bought it for her.

The idea of losing it horrified her. It was her lifeline to the world.

"I'll shoot you a text tonight, see if you still have it," he said.

"Okay. Wait until like six or so, hopefully our family shit-show will be over by that time."

"You want me to walk down by your place tonight, see if you're around?"

Abby thought about this. Scott lived close and she'd seen him walk by her house several times, staring at it. It was cute, but also kind of creepy.

"No, that's okay," she said. "Just shoot me a text. If I have my phone, I'll let you know what's happening." She'd probably slap a post on Snapchat, but didn't say anything.

She slammed the locker door shut and twirled around, pressing her palms together, and said, "Well, guess I won't need any of that stuff."

Scott shrugged and said, "Lucky you with a week off."

"I'll let you know how lucky I am."

"You can sit and jam all day."

She smiled, feeling wrong and hollow, and strolled back toward the office. Scott followed. Her dad might be here already which sparked dread, heavy and thick. The thought of seeing him made her sick. God, she wished she hadn't been so stupid!

"I'm stopping at the bathroom for a minute." She looked at Scott and he gawked back. She touched his arm and said, "Wait here." She did not want to walk back to that office alone.

He glanced first at her hand on his skin, then smiled as goofy as she'd ever seen him, and said, "No problem. I'll be here."

She had the restroom all to herself and she checked her phone.

Nothing.

Why wasn't Michael texting her? Was he dead? Was he bored with her already? Maybe he was seeing someone else? *Get ahold of yourself, Abby...*

Chapter 5

Two events shot Sheriff Jack Snider's *shit ain't right* radar into overdrive.

Daisy Howard, the nursing home caretaker, called the station around 9 PM, frazzled as hell. Jack had known her since childhood and he knew for damn sure it took a lot to rattle her. The Taylor County Nursing Home towered like a brick monument atop a hill overlooking Black Rock. As the live-in caretaker, Daisy stayed out there every night, even the weekends since her husband died eight years ago, and had never once called in a panic, not even when one of the residents died in their sleep or fell down the stairs.

Except for tonight.

The dispatcher had called Jack at home and told him what happened.

"Jesus Christ," Jack mumbled, then said, "I'll head out there now." He pulled on a pair of jeans, squirmed into a t-shirt and slipped on his brown sheriff's shirt as he stormed out the door.

He arrived at the County Home fifteen minutes later. Daisy sat across from him at a small table, her wrinkled hand trembled as she fiddled with an empty cup. They'd avoided the topic long enough. Time to get into it.

Jack sipped his coffee; his hand wrapped around the cup. "Tell me what happened."

She shook her head and her gaze reflected a confused woman, scared and questioning a world she'd assumed could no longer surprise her. She forced a painful smile. "It was just so weird, Jack. He ain't spoke a lick in the fifteen years he's been here. I bathed him, fed him, clothed him; hell, Betty Wigg usually combed his hair and shaved him; she used to be a hairdresser, ya know, and likes doing that stuff."

Jack nodded. He knew.

"Then tonight Archie talks all kinds of nonsense and then dives out a window. Why would he do that?" She spoke while staring at her hands, as if she expected them to answer.

"What did he say?"

She shook her head. "Crazy stuff. I don't know. Stuff like *take me* and *I'm sorry*. He yelled *he's back* several times. Just crazy stuff."

"Archie's always had problems, Daisy, you know that." Jack took another drink of coffee. The *he's back* comment bothered him.

She nodded. "Yeah, ever since that girl accused him of raping her, he's never been the same."

"Well, she never made an official accusation." Jack glanced at the sink. He'd read the report. That case had been a long time ago; well before Jack became a cop. "That poor girl left and no one ever saw her again."

She nodded and said, "We all heard the stories of what happened, but no one ever proved anything."

Jack ignored the *proved anything* comment and said, "And Archie sure as hell ain't been right since I found him out by the cemetery. What's that been... fifteen-years ago or so?" Jack tapped a thumb on the table and recalled that night; Archie wandering down the road, stumbling around like a clumsy drunk.

"At least fifteen." She glared at him. "But even after you found him, he ain't never acted like he'd jump out a window."

What do people who jump out windows act like?

Just then, an old memory slithered into his mind - a boy named Ronnie Castle; a kid who'd grown up in Black Rock. He'd never forget Ronnie, not in a million years, because...

Jack shook the thought away. An old man jumped out a window – a crazy old man to boot. That's all. No one in Black Rock talked about those days anymore. No one dared. Black Rock hid its scars well.

Jack pursed his lips. Dread grew inside him. "I don't know," he lied. "Maybe he just lost it."

She raised an eyebrow.

He tapped the table and said, "This kind of stuff happens all the time. Suicides and whatnot." He wasn't lying about that.

"You really believe that?" Daisy spoke like a school teacher who knew she was being bullshitted, but not having the evidence to prove it. "This is all starting to scare me, Jack. Don't put your blinders on and ignore how bizarre this is."

Put on my blinders? He sipped his coffee which was no longer hot. He decided he'd drive to Black Rock and visit with Pastor Thomas Loggins. The pastor filed a complaint earlier in the afternoon about a strange man who threatened his daughter. It suddenly seemed relevant. "I can't wait for this day to end," he said. "Whole goddamned day's been weird."

She huffed a humorless chuckle. "Weirder than this?"

"Well," he cocked his head and smiled, "Maybe not, but still strange. Do you know Pastor Loggins?"

"Not well, but I know who he is. That preacher in Black Rock?"

"Yep, that's him. The pastor's got a daughter in high school, can't recall how old, but someone apparently threatened her today."

Shock washed over Daisy's face. "Threatened the preacher's daughter?"

"Yep. Fairly serious, I believe. Pastor Loggins filed the complaint this morning. Said some new member of his church, Benjamin Clark, met him for breakfast and threatened her." Jack didn't want to share too much since he didn't exactly have all the facts, and technically it was an official case, but gleaning Daisy's insight, especially with what just happened to Archie, seemed relevant.

"Clark?" Her eyes caught his.

He nodded and glanced away. He knew what she was thinking.

"Same last name as that creep who was here all those years ago? You don't find that odd?"

He nodded and said, "Of course I do. But Clark's a common name and technically, nothin's happened yet." But did he *really* believe that?

"I told ya, Jack," she shook a finger at him. "Don't put your blinders on. I think ya might be kiddin' yourself that there ain't a connection here."

Jack clenched his jaw and let the silence hover between them.

Daisy cast her gaze down at the table. "What did that pastor say?"

He shrugged and wondered if his feeling that Daisy had taken control of the conversation meant anything. Maybe it was what he needed. "Well, I ain't talked to him myself yet, but read Wayne's report. We're keepin' an eye on the pastor's house and all."

Daisy nodded.

Jack rested his hand on the table and looked at her. "Look, I'm sorry for dumpin' this on ya in the midst of this thing with Archie and you're right, I need to keep my eyes open. I can still *hope* it's a coincidence."

Daisy smiled weakly. "Let's hope it is, for both our sakes."

He rocked back in his chair. In the other room, he heard the residents milling about, muffled voices seeped through the door.

"Well," Daisy pushed some dangling strands of gray hair out of her eyes. "I guess I oughtta get these folks moving toward bed. Everyone here's in a ruckus tonight, as you can imagine."

"I'll bet," he said. "Need me to help with anything?"

"Nah, those boys in the ambulance helped me clean up a lot of the broken glass and stuff."

Jack hoisted himself up. "You let me know if you hear of anything."

"Oh, I will," she said, "Believe me, you'll be the first to know." An edge touched her voice; a nervousness that hadn't been there before he'd told her about the pastor. Surprisingly, she stepped up and hugged him. "Thanks for coming out, Jack. I mean it, thank you. Archie jumping out that window just scared the bejesus out of me."

"That would scare anyone." He gently placed his hands on her back. His palms pressed against her shoulder blades, so frail, like the bones of a bird.

She backed away and wiped the front of his shirt as if she'd left a bunch of cookie crumbs on it, and smiled. "You stay safe," she said. "I'll call you if anything happens. We'll be alright here."

She picked up their cups and walked quickly over to the sink. He hadn't noticed before how much she leaned over, starting to get that old woman look. *We're all getting old.*

"Take care, Daisy." He adjusted his cap and stepped toward the door.

"You too."

"One more thing," he cleared his throat. "If you need anything, I want you to call me, okay? Call me at home."

She stiffened, rested her hands on the edge of the sink, and stared out the window in front of her, into the darkness draping Black Rock and everyone in it. "Thanks, Jack."

"Just wanted you to know you can call *me* directly." He paused and debated on telling her he hoped she didn't take that the wrong way, but thought better of it.

He turned and made his way out the door.

.   .   .   .   .

As Jack drove home, he pictured Archie Winthrop sitting in the passenger seat next to him, the old man's maddened eyes wide and terrified.

Why'd you jump, Archie?

He imagined Archie's mouth dropping open to say, *you know why, Jack. Because that thing is back.*

Goose bumps pebbled Jack's arms and the hairs stirred under the sleeve of his jacket. Despite mounting evidence that serious shit lurked about, his rational mind sought to shrug it off. A stranger threatens a pastor's family – nothing to panic about. A random suicide at an old folks' home – nothing to panic about. Two unrelated events. Two weird things in one day, so what?

Clark. That's what.

The same last name. He couldn't explain that one away.

Amy, help me out here, babe.

He considered fishing out her photo he kept tucked into his wallet. Easier to remember her and to focus when he saw her picture and she smiled back at him. Maybe if it wasn't so dark. Tough to see anything by the dash lights, especially the details of a photograph. Good way to wreck.

He spoke aloud to her as he often did when he visited the cemetery. "What the hell's goin' on around here, babe?" He cracked his window and lit a cigarette. "I can tell ya right now, I ain't likin' it."

What's going on? she asked from the passenger seat.

Jack smiled and said, "now *you're* a goddamn sight better than Archie Winthrop sitting over there." A single tear tracked coldly down his weathered cheek. The gravel road rumbled the car and rocks pecked the frame in little *tinks*.

"It's way more than nothin', I'm afraid. Hell, even Daisy knows it." He blew a lung full of smoke out the window. He glanced sideways at Amy.

Stop, Jack, she yelled. *Stop now!*

His eyes shot back to the road.

He gripped the steering wheel and slammed the brakes. The car kilted sideways, then shuddered to a stop. There was something in the road; a dark lump shrouded by a swelling dust plume. Amy faded away like switching off a television screen. Good bye, love.

Sonofabitch.

An animal? Had to be.

Thank God no one was behind him or they'd have smashed right into his ass-end. Thick dust circled the windows and drifted into the headlights like an eerie fog.

"Jesus Christ." He wiped his eyes. Is it a dog? Someone must've hit the fucking thing and left it lying there. He flipped his flashing lights on anyway. The blue and red reflected the dust and cast a desolate, eerie mood.

He plucked the mic off the radio and pressed the talk button. "Patti?"

"Yeah, Sheriff?" Her voice broke through loud and clear.

"There's a dead dog out by Black Rock layin' in the middle of Twin Bridges Road. I'm gettin' out to move it." He slotted the mic back into its holder. As if this day wasn't already creepy enough.

Patti's crackly voice came back, "copy that, sheriff."

He tapped his weapon holster, felt the comforting metal of the pistol grip, and opened the door. Expect nothing; be ready for anything.

The cool night air bit his skin. Thankfully, most of the dust had settled. He stepped around the front of the car and the headlights casted his shadow long and skinny ahead of him. As he crept closer, the nape of his neck began to sweat. That's not a dog; it's a goddamned goat! A dark patch of blood soaked the gravel and puddled under the fur, still wet and reflecting the light. Jack guessed the thing had stumbled out of the trees, bleeding, and picked this spot to fall down and die.

He knelt next to it and examined an enormous gash in its belly where guts bulged; the slimy insides protruded like a bubble. His hand tightened on his gun as fear settled on him like a heavy blanket. A car didn't do this.

What the hell? He glanced up at the shadowed trees and listened. Only the steady idle of the car's engine drifted through the darkness.

What would do this? Coyotes? For damn sure, whatever it was, it was still out here.

He gripped the goat's hind legs and dragged the body behind his cruiser and stopped next to the trunk lid. It might be a stupid idea to bring it back to the station, but he wanted Wayne Tillwood, his deputy, to take look at it. He debated heaving it into the weeds. Animals got killed in these woods all the time. He thought it might be one of Ray Stingle's goats and Ray only lived a half mile or so from here.

Something gnawed at him. He needed verification nothing weird lurked about. Maybe some kids with a sick sense of humor were up to no good. Maybe an unusual Coyote attack. Or maybe it was nothing.

Or maybe it was everything.

Because it looked like a dog attack and Jack had seen horrific dog attacks before.

He popped the trunk and spread a tarp across the trunk floor. He bent over and gripped the front legs in one hand and both back legs in the other, then heaved the dead animal up. Rigor hadn't settled in yet, so the head dangled like a water balloon. He grimaced and twisted his head away. Disgusting. He slammed the trunk shut with a plan to call Wayne on his way in.

That's when he heard it.

A short growl followed by the single snap of a twig, somewhere in the trees where the red and blue lights splashed against twisted branches. He froze and watched for any sign of movement. His heart pulsed into his neck. Sweat broke out on his palms and he considered a sprint for the car door. Instead, he drew his weapon and waited.

"What's out there?"

Nothing greeted him but the car's engine and the silence of the woods.

He stepped to the door of his cruiser while keeping his eyes trained on the wood-line and popped open his door. *Why am I acting like a scared little shit?* He scooted into the driver's seat, suddenly seized by a childhood terror that he'd be grabbed before he could slam the door shut.

For the second time in a single night, events occurred that thrust him back fifteen-years. To a family attacked by wild dogs out by the abandoned gas station. To a young girl kidnapped and never heard from again.

To Ronnie Castle.

Chapter 6

Thomas settled into his leather recliner and sipped a cup of hot tea. He felt hollow and exposed. He imagined being stripped naked and forced to parade across the alter of his church. Even the thought of taking his own life had crossed his mind. Would there be forgiveness for that? God forgave him decades ago during those fits of self-loathing. Thomas believed that God's forgiveness transcended even the depths of Hell. But suicide?

So, why now? Thomas had lived with his secret for nearly twenty-four years. Not even the slightest whisper or insinuation from anyone. Suddenly, this hellish stranger, in a single statement, destroyed the flimsy illusion he'd built so strongly atop a foundation of glass.

Fear gripped him like barbed-wire, piercing his flesh, tightening despite his every effort to stop it. He hadn't told Linda about Benjamin yet. Thomas knew he had to. She needed to know about the threat to their family. He knew this was true, but it presented two problems. First, was figuring out how to tell her without sparking unnecessary panic.

And what of his secret? Thomas didn't want to tell Linda about his past, but now he risked her learning of it from Benjamin. Thomas sensed it would be better if she heard the truth from his own mouth. He just wished it didn't have to be now. A hopeful fragment inside him clung to the possibility that Benjamin didn't *know* anything about what had happened with Emily. That he was using old rumors as a bluff designed to frighten the preacher. But to what end? What did this man want? Benjamin hadn't asked for money. He asked for - what had he said? Absolution? Maybe he was just some pedophile sicko? Whatever the man's motives, this was a real problem. Or was it? Did Benjamin really know? Of course not. No one could possibly know because no one had been there!

And yet, part of Thomas believed that Benjamin knew exactly what had happened twenty-four years ago. Thomas's cup trembled as he drank. A long-buried self-hatred, dormant for twenty-four years, stirred awake in his guts and he winced at its slimy feel.

I need to focus. Thomas pictured himself speaking to Linda with his jaw set and a solid determination painting his face like General Patton marching into battle. But his mind's rehearsals never matched the way things actually went in the real world. His tough demeanor always crumbled as his fear burst forth in a torrent of shameful tears. He'd do it, though. Thomas swore before God that he'd tell her right now. He'd come clean and then they'd both pray for the strength to stay strong for both of them. No panicking.

You willing to lose it all and tell your dear, sweet Linda you're a rapist?

A quiet moan seeped up from the deepest part of him and his eyes squeezed shut.

But I'm not a rapist! I made a mistake twenty-four years ago. A mistake! Emily and I both did!

Stop!

This was bigger than him. Bigger than any of them. He'd pray for the strength to force open that door and accept the consequences when Linda peered inside.

God help me.

He decided the best way was to work his way up to it slowly. First, they'd talk about Abby's suspension since that caught them both by surprise.

When Thomas had spoken to the principal earlier that day, Principal Pearson had sounded authoritarian when he'd said, "Abby's never flown off the handle like that and I'm quite concerned, hence I showed restraint." It was like the guy wanted gratitude. Like he wanted Thomas to thank him for suspending Abby.

On a normal day, Thomas may have reacted more assertively in the face of such a preposterous suggestion. But his mind had been a whirlwind blown off-course by Benjamin Clark.

"I'm sure you're aware, she's been struggling with her classes for some time now, Mr. Loggins."

Should I be here listening to this or should I haul Abby out to my car and speed away as fast as possible?

"I didn't know her grades were so bad," Thomas heard himself say as he'd gripped the smooth wood of the arm chair. Had he cared about grades right then? Benjamin's words ringing in his ears. Principal Pearson had rambled on about Abby failing two classes. What the hell did her grades matter when her very life was in danger?

"Frankly." Principal Pearson had leaned forward in his chair and cleared his throat, "I'm more concerned about her attitude."

Benjamin's face wouldn't fade and Thomas had felt his anxiety swelling. A dull thud, radiating out from the center of his skull. "Her, ah, her attitude?"

Pearson had shot him an incredulous look. "She told me to go to hell, Mr. Loggins. She yelled it from the very chair you're sitting in right now."

Though it happened hours earlier, Thomas recalled his own confusion; his utter lack of comprehension. He'd blinked. He wanted to say something to appease Principal Pearson, but what? His brain wouldn't focus and he kept hearing Benjamin's ultimatum … *you or her?* Logic told Thomas that Benjamin was bluffing. That the choice was a distraction. Benjamin was just trying to get under his skin. But in his gut, Thomas knew differently. No matter *what* he chose, the end result would be the same. Thomas had considered telling Pearson about the whole thing. The more people knew and could look out for Abby, the better, *right?* So why not say it? Because he'd have to explain the whole thing and that was impossible.

She remind you of anyone?

Emily.

I'll tell them your secret.

"Mr Loggins, I feel like I don't have your full attention here. Do you have more important matters to attend to?"

"I'm sorry." Thomas forced a smile that felt painful, as if by doing it, his lips might split and bleed. "We're just shocked." No lying about that.

"I've suspended her from school this week." Principal Pearson had been ready for the conversation to end and Thomas kept silent, like a child knowing that once the scolding finished, he'd be free to run away. "You can take Abby home now. Please speak with her, pastor. She's a good kid."

Thomas faked the smile again. A school suspension couldn't have come at a better time.

"I will," Thomas assured the principal. As Thomas stood up, he found himself wishing Abby were standing right there next to him. "Where is Abby now?"

"She's picking up her things from her locker. You can wait in the lobby for her."

Abby had shown up a few minutes later, and they'd walked to the car together, in total silence.

. . . . .

Linda trudged into the room carrying her own cup of tea and eased down onto the loveseat opposite Thomas. His new-found strength drifted away into the stuffy air. Thomas could suddenly hear the ticking of the clock on his desk, the one he'd received as a gift from his previous congregation with the words WITH GOD, ALL THINGS ARE POSSIBLE stamped into a brass plate.

I'll tell her your secret.

"I just don't understand it," Linda blurted. "She's never done anything like this."

"She's a teenager." Thomas shrugged and felt fake. "Sometimes they just get wrapped around the axle on the smallest stuff."

"Abby?" She shot him a look. "Abby doesn't get wrapped around the axle. It's Abby, Thomas, not someone else's kid. Being a teenager doesn't excuse her. She swore at the principal!" Thomas sensed a dangerous anger roiling just below the surface. A coiled snake about to strike. Was she angry with *him*?

"We need to be curious, find out what she's thinking," he said. "That's all I'm saying. I mean, we're in uncharted territory here."

Tell her about Benjamin.

Linda stared at him, as if this were somehow his fault. Finally, her eyes softened and she said, "I just don't feel like you're taking this seriously enough."

Thomas leaned forward and placed his forearms on his thighs. "I guess it just shows that you never know what someone's thinking." Dear God, if that wasn't a hypocritical statement, nothing was.

Linda rolled her eyes and he felt lame. What in the world did she expect of him? Unfamiliar anger sparked inside him and an absurd urge to stand up and walk out flared up.

Tell her!

He cleared his throat, summoning courage. "There *is* something else I need to tell you." He heard the words roll out of his mouth; unsure of what might spill out next.

"What?" Linda sipped her tea and the gesture made her look uncharacteristically old.

Her eyes set and her hard expression dissolved into something more incredulous. "This will sound weird," he said. "But you have to promise me you won't mention anything to Abby unless we both agree to do it."

A nervous smile touched her lips.

He swallowed hard. "Promise me," he said.

She sat there. She could be so difficult sometimes.

"Look, this is difficult for me." He clasped his hands together. "Please, promise me."

"Okay." She placed her cup of tea onto the table next to her and leaned over closer to him, as if they were about to pray together, as they had done many times while seated in these very same spots.

He nodded and said, "I had breakfast with a man named Benjamin Clark this morning. I thought he was a new member of the congregation." He waited to see if a flash of recognition shot through her. She shrugged *I don't know him* and so he kept going. "I met him for a few minutes last Friday, but we had Abby's program to go to so I didn't get much time with him."

"So, what happened?" she asked. She knew him well enough to recognize he was stalling.

"He said," Thomas tried to articulate the right phrasing without using Benjamin's exact words. "He threatened her."

"What do you mean, *threatened* her?" Linda's voice sharpened to a razor's edge.

He met her gaze. *Really? Tell her what he said, tell her about the choice. Tell her about Emily.*

He prayed silently for guidance and stated, "He said he would..." he swallowed, "I don't know, he just has an unusual fascination with her."

Linda's lips thinned to narrow slits and her eyes watered. "He said that?" her voice quivered. "He said *I have an unusual fascination with her*? Tell me what he said, Thomas."

"He didn't say it like that exactly, but that was the gist of it. I just want you to be aware, is all, and if you see him around, call the cops."

"You think it's a serious threat?"

"Yes I do and so do the police. That's why..."

Her eyes widened. "What? You went to the police? Why didn't you tell me?"

"The guy creeped me out. I reported it immediately and spoke to a deputy at the police station. They're keeping an eye on the house. I didn't want to scare you."

"Thomas, God knows I love you, but..." she placed a hand to her forehead. "Tell me what this man said about our daughter?"

He licked his lips. The evil inside him, that part that no other human knew about, surfaced with jarring mockery and danced around the room jeering. *Tell her about Emily, tell her, tell her, TELL HER!* He wanted to curse out loud, to tell that stupid voice to shut up. *Help me, Jesus, to focus, to keep my mind here with my wife, to deal with Abby.*

"He was just making really creepy comments. I cut him off immediately, of course. Honestly, I wasn't really paying attention to why he was saying it. The whole thing just caught me off guard. It was surreal." The words sounded stupid in his own mind and he felt weak. He simply couldn't allow the exact words to spill out. *Wimp or hypocrite?* that evil voice asked and the good man inside him flinched. He nearly told that voice to shut up, but clenched his teeth, frightened that he'd almost spoken out loud.

She opened her mouth to speak, thought better of it and took a deep breath. She reached out and clasped his hands, holding them tightly; her skin cool and clammy against his.

What's my skin feel like? Hot and shameful maybe? He hoped that voice would stay quiet.

"Okay," Linda gathered her wits as she was so exceptional at doing. "Two things disturb me about this more than anything." She spoke calmly, methodically, and he admired her. "This just makes no sense. Why would this strange man threaten our Abby? And how does he even know Abby?" She took another long, slow breath and gripped his hands tighter, squeezing them.

Thomas nodded, gladly welcoming her placating approach, wondering silently if he'd given the impression that his own way of handling it seemed weak or maybe he'd played things down too much and that's why she wasn't freaking out. He shrugged and said, "I have no idea who he is or why he's fascinated with Abby. I think he's just delusional. Deranged. Psychotic even." Something inside him twisted at that last statement, like a clogged blood vessel suddenly burst open allowing warm blood to ooze through his insides. *I just lied.* Hot nausea spread through him and he swore he might puke.

"Did he give any reason at all? Did he say why Abby? Why not some other girl in town? Why would he tell you this anyway? If he was going to hurt Abby, why would he tell you first? Did he ask you for money or something?" Linda's voice trembled and she clenched her jaw. *She knows I'm not telling her the whole story.*

"No. I don't know, Linda!" Thomas inhaled deeply, checking his frustration. "He just blurted it out. He didn't ask for money and he didn't explain anything." His conscience whispered, but he *did* give a reason, didn't he? Emily. Urgency swelled inside him. *We need to get Abby out of here.*

Linda bent over as if gazing at the floor and her pulse quickened beneath the flesh of her hands.

His palms sweat. Other people had been inside the restaurant when he'd met Benjamin; they'd heard the conversation and they may speak with Linda. The idea of her hearing things third-hand spawned guilt and he swallowed it back. He had to say something more than this; he had to give more details.

"We were just sitting there and he blurted it out, that he wanted to hurt her. I stood up and yelled at him and he laughed and told me he was here for absolution, whatever *that* means." The cynic inside him pictured other people regurgitating the whole thing to Linda. If he got ahead of it, showed he had nothing to hide, he could explain things like that away.

"Absolution?" She focused back on his face.

"I don't know," he shrugged. "It's like he thinks I'm someone else. It's what scares me more than anything, if I'm being honest."

He spoke softly, pleadingly, and said, "I think we need to treat this threat as real, babe. We need to take it seriously. I feel like he might really try to hurt her."

She gasped, then moaned low and deep. The fading recollection of Benjamin's grotesque, changing face shimmered. He considered telling her about the dead stench and the teeth, and opened his mouth to do just that when she asked, "What are we going to do?"

There it was. *What are we going to do?* The chance for Thomas to take over, calm the waters, be the husband. Keep calm, just hold it together. This is about something you did a quarter of a century ago as a young, dumb kid. *God, that was so long ago.* Maybe Emily, in whatever she'd become, had paid this man to scare him. Maybe Emily's dad paid this man.

The threat was real. *I need to tell Linda about Emily… no more secrets.*

"First, we're not going to let her out of our sight," Thomas asserted his words. "Second, we have to work with the police." He paused. "There's something else I was thinking we could do."

"What?"

Thomas flicked his eyebrows. "What if you took Abby with you and left?"

"What? Where?" Linda's face changed from somber to stunned.

"I don't know and don't want to know. What if you just packed her up and went somewhere? Got her out of here."

His statement jarred her silent. Her expression tightened and he knew the gears inside her spun at full speed. She blinked and said, "You don't think that would be overreacting?"

"Yes," he said, "But that's exactly why I don't think Benjamin would expect it. He knows we're rational people and that we wouldn't take chances and do something foolish like try to run. I'd rather you leave and Abby be safe than to do nothing and wish we had."

Linda nodded. "This whole thing feels crazy to me. I don't really understand, but I trust you," she said. "If you think there's any chance we're in danger, I'll do it. When do you think we'd have to leave?"

"Soon. But I'd say by tomorrow night at the latest." He didn't know why he'd said that last part, as if he had any reason to think that waiting until tomorrow would help anything whatsoever, and then added, "And go somewhere totally random and *not* to anywhere we've lived before or to anyone we know."

"What about school?" As soon as the words left her mouth, Linda shook her head and said, "Guess that's not an issue at the moment."

"Nope."

She looked at him. "What about you? What will you do?"

He offered the strongest, most comforting smile he could muster, "I'm going to stay here and deal with Benjamin." Her hands tightened on his. And it felt good.

Nothing could stop him now because God stood by his side. *I can do all things through Christ who strengthens me.*

He and Linda prayed.

Chapter 7

Petey, that faithful black Labrador Retriever who loved the late Donna Johnson, now hated the new man. Love died with Donna and the dogs chewed her bony carcass clean. Petey's innocence faded like sunlight into darkness.

The man brought food. He watched them devour rotted chunks of meat tossed into the pen and then relished the violent fights for the smallest bite. But days had ached by since the man brought anything, even a scrap.

The small pen was the barrier between submission and freedom. If they could just get out of that pen, Petey and the pack could hunt for themselves. Starvation begat hatred toward the man and toward each other. The man watched as Petey killed the small dog with the brown spots and ate him. Petey felt bad about that, but what choice did he have? Surviving to eat another day, that God-given instinct to which even the most amiable succumbs, consumed all of Petey's brain and the taste of warm blood lingered sickeningly sweet.

The other dogs glared at Petey and waited to see what he would do. A band of rogue soldiers prepared to do the unthinkable.

Waiting...

. . . . .

Benjamin stood in Donna Johnson's kitchen, arms folded across his chest, peering out the small window above the sink. The dogs sensed his presence and their hatred deepened. The man laughed. "That's it boys."

Laughter was good in times like these. And hate. Times when duty prevailed and absolution demanded action. The cleansing, as he'd come to think of it.

Fools.

Sooner or later, their payments always came due.

Every window in the old house stood open and the cold wind cut through, lifting the white curtains like ghosts. Mud and snow caked the carpets while dead leaves swirled across the floor, ticking across the worn linoleum like brittle bones.

"Do you want out?" Benjamin said, staring at Petey. Petey didn't hear him of course, but the starving dog stopped just the same, as if sensing that subtle insinuation. "You'll be out soon enough. Then you'll be able to put all that hate to work."

Benjamin unfolded his arms and sauntered to the door. His hands tingled with anticipation as he stepped out into the night and made his way to Petey's cage. To the dogs.

Petey stopped and glared and Benjamin sensed the animal's contempt.

As he walked, he thought of the preacher. The cowardly preacher would choose himself; Benjamin was quite sure of that. He could tell the first time he met the man that the preacher lived in denial. As if time somehow absolved him of accountability. And knowing the preacher's decision spawned anticipation that Abigail would soon belong to Benjamin. He considered, and not for the first time these past few days, that he might be developing an unhealthy fascination with that young girl.

He reached Petey's cage, lost in his own thoughts, eager to do what needed to be done. To get this all over with. *I'm just the messenger*, he thought, *the manifestation of bad choices.*

The consequence.

He shifted his gaze to Petey's crazed eyes and his heart softened. Benjamin understood starvation and the venom it spawned.

He undid the latch at the top of the gate and it swung open with a rusty whine. Petey stood motionless next to the scattered bones of the old woman, distrustful. Benjamin squatted in front of Petey and gently scratched the matted fur under the dog's throat. The madness clouding Petey's eyes cleared as his tongue lapped Benjamin's hand.

"I'm sorry, boy," Benjamin said, "We're just pawns in this game, you and me."

Benjamin sucked in a harsh breath, stood, and stepped back from the gate, leaving it wide open, and smiled at Petey. *Time to do your job*, he thought. *Time to let all that hate loose.*

Don't sweat the small stuff. He'd learned a long time ago that sweating the small stuff only caused confusion and questions for which there were no answers.

"Go," Benjamin said to Petey. Petey was no freer than Benjamin himself was, both pawns of humanities choices. Innocence caught in the cross-fire. "Go on, boy," Benjamin clapped his hands. "Get to work!"

Petey scampered through the open gate, keeping his distance as if Benjamin might kick him on the way out. After a few yards, Petey stopped and twisted back toward the pen; silently calling to the other nine dogs to join him. One by one, they darted out, joining Petey at the top of the driveway. They turned in unison and shot Benjamin one last glare and then disappeared into the night, engulfed by the thick, leafless trees that stood between Donna Johnson's house and the town of Black Rock.

"Go on boys. Make me proud," Benjamin said into the still air.

Chapter 8

Scott's text buzzed around eight, just like they'd planned it.

U still there?

Abby lay on her back with a book propped open, but hardly reading it. A smile curled the corners of her mouth as she responded. Y. Not even grounded.

Sweet. I'm outside. Can u com out?

Her smiled faded. *Damn it.* She slapped the phone against the mattress and growled. *Why did he come here?* Didn't she tell him today not to come over?

Maybe this was a good time to set the record straight. After all, it wasn't fair to lead Scott along. *Just tell him, right now.*

She typed, B right out.

She'd make it clear to him. Friends; we're just friends. *I have a boyfriend,* she wanted to tell him. But that wasn't totally true, was it? *No,* her mind whispered, *someone you're talking to, yes, but not a boyfriend yet.*

Michael and I are *talking.*

Why couldn't things be easy, like they used to be? Back in Texas, everything made sense. Living in this shithole, her life crashed from one catastrophe to the next. It was getting to the point she couldn't keep up. *So annoying.*

Abby hopped off the bed, crossed the room, and delicately eased the curtain open with her finger like a spy gathering intel. God forbid Scott catch her staring out at him. There he stood on the sidewalk, gawking down at his phone. *If mom and dad catch him lurking out there, I'm up shit-creek.* God knows what her parents would assume. Especially with how weird they'd been acting.

She bolted for her door, gripped the knob, and realized she didn't want her mom and dad seeing her walk past. She considered sneaking out the window, but she was already on thin ice. If she did anything else stupid, that might give them enough reason to lock her up for good. She'd sneak and hope for the best.

She swooped down the stairs, paused at the bottom to check that the coast was clear, then crept out the front door without so much as a peep. Awesome, if she did say so herself. She even managed to snag her jacket off the hanger on her way out!

Her dad had told her earlier that he wanted her to stay inside, as if the thought of a fifteen-year-old girl going outside was absurd. *They're hiding something; that's what it is, they're hiding something from me and they think they're getting away with it.*

No matter. She'd gotten suspended from school. Of course they're acting weird. And hey, if she got caught in the driveway, she'd play dumb. Easy peasy.

"I can't believe you didn't get grounded," Scott said.

Abby smiled and said, "I know, right!" At the end of the sidewalk, she stopped as Scott's eyes danced to her body. In the deepest recesses of her brain, in that part that belonged completely to her, there existed a certain fascination with having guys look at her in *that way*, but out here on the sidewalk, in front of her house, alone, with Scott Key, it seemed awkward; she didn't feel desired as much as she felt bare and cold.

"I still can't believe ole' dogface kicked you out of school," he said. "I think it's bullshit."

She folded her arms over her chest and painted a smile. "I deserved it, I think."

"To get suspended?" he looked totally appalled, just a tad over-dramatic, but she knew he was doing it for her, which made it sweet in a nerdy sort of way. "I don't think so."

"You can't swear at the principal," she said.

He shrugged. "Maybe if he'd listened to start with."

"How do you know?" she asked. "Maybe I just lost it in there."

"You didn't." He shoved his hands in his pocket. "Since I've known you, I don't think I've ever seen you *lose* it."

She could've argued with that, but she'd have to dispel some very private situations, ones where she sat on the edge of her bed crying alone, or went down into the basement before her parents got home and screamed at God for being such a jerk for not giving her a normal family, one where it was okay to mess up once in a while or try something tempting, like maybe a small cut to relieve a little pressure.

"It's hard not to sometimes," Abby said and shrugged. "But, I deserved it. I don't blame Mr. Pearson. And besides, it's only four days. Not a big deal really."

"Pearson's a jerk," Scott spat the words, as if thinking of the man caused him physical pain. "He doesn't understand anything about us. He's too old."

An uncomfortable pause fell between them. Finally, Abby said, "What are you doing out here, besides saying hi?"

"Mom said I have to get the salt spread on the sidewalks just in case it freezes tonight, so I gotta do that before I go to bed."

"Ah," she said.

"You know, Abby," he kicked one of his shoes against the dirty cement of the sidewalk. He looked at her. "I want you to know you can always talk to me about your life. I don't want you to think that it's something you have to treat like a secret, not around me."

Something inside her gave way, like a dam that suddenly broke free, and her knees felt wobbly. She didn't want to cry, she really didn't, but in that moment, the sting of tears threatened to spill down her face.

Sure, there was Michael, but Scott was here now.

She stepped up to him and wrapped her arms around his neck. He stiffened, but then relaxed and his arms wrapped around her. She laid her head on his shoulder, her tears soaking his shirt. She wished she knew why his words overwhelmed her, why she was crying. Her screwed up world melted into Scott. A tingle shot through her body. It stopped and centered itself deep in her belly and she found that the harder she hugged him, the better it felt.

She let go of him, quickly. What the hell? Her heart slammed and she breathed heavy. *Jesus.* It sounded stupid, but she wanted to run away, back into her house, and slam the door behind her. She wanted to do that, but she also wanted Scott to hug her again, so tight that she couldn't get away.

"That's sweet," her voice sounded shaky, at least to her own ears, and her nerves sizzled.

"I've just been thinking that for a while, but wanted to make sure I told you," he said. He seemed to be more at ease than she was, that's for sure.

She stood there in awe. What the hell did he do; read a book titled, all the right things to say to a girl? This was Scott Kee for crying out loud, the nerd, one of the biggest geeks in school. Did she care about those things? She heard the laughter that would surely follow, the cruel tweets, the mean pictures on Snapchat - any shred of credibility she'd built over the past year would fall flat, and her stomach felt queasy, as if her insides were held in a slippery trash bag, threatening to give way. Earlier today, she'd pictured him as a stalker, hanging around outside her house.

Am I really this screwed up?

She had a fleeting thought of what this scene might look like if someone she knew drove past and spotted them standing here on the sidewalk – him with his hands in his pocket and she smiling at him. *What if Michael drove by?*

And as quickly as things had gone to being wonderful, they slipped to awkward. Scott had said what he wanted to say. Here he was, opening his heart, willing to take the conversation anywhere Abby wanted to take it, and all she could do was sneak furtive glances at the house or the road.

And why was a cop parked on their street?

"Hey," he said and chuckled, "you want to come over to my place and hang out for a while?" His eyes shot down at the sidewalk and his cheeks flushed. It matched his hair.

"I can't." A strange numbness swept over her as she gazed at the dark cop car. Was there someone sitting in there? Her brain switched to auto-pilot as she said, "My parents won't let me get twenty feet from the house."

His eyes darted to hers and something in his face struck her as odd, the expression etched there was strangely hollow. Embarrassment mixed with something else, something dark hidden behind the fake smile, something she couldn't quite put her finger on. *Quit picking on the poor guy*, she thought. But she wanted to go back in the house. Now. Besides, Scott needed to get salt on the sidewalks. Isn't that what he'd said?

"I gotta get back inside," Abby said.

He didn't answer and she found his silence disturbing as well. She added, "Maybe in a few days, when the smoke has settled around here." His smile reappeared, one that didn't quite touch his face, but there nonetheless.

She felt better about that.

. . . . .

Later, lying in her bed with her hands laced behind her head, staring absently at the shadowed ceiling, Michael's text popped up on her phone. There was no beep or frilly music because she knew better than that. Her parents could hear the chime of an incoming text from ten miles away and that would violate the stupid *no texts after 8 pm* rule. Her phone lit up and casted an eerie, bluish glow across the lamp and stack of books on her nightstand. She grabbed it and yanked it under the covers with her.

Finally!

Sorry I haven't texted you today. Been busy.

She whispered, "You should be sorry." Then typed, No Prob.

The bubble appeared with dots floating and she waited anxiously as he typed.

Finally, so what are you doing now?

She smiled as her thumbs started to type.

Part II
Benjamin

Chapter 9

Let's get back to our summer-night stroll, shall we. It can be a bit disorientating slipping back and forth in time, between *then* and *now* with only me to listen to. Try to relax and let me do the talking. At least it's quiet and there's little worry that a car might barrel through here and plow us over.

There ain't a lot of traffic in this town. Not at this time of night. Not since the Interstate was built in the early '70s, cutting off Black Rock from the rest of the world forever. So now Black Rock is sort of a dead end; which is ironic if you really stop and think about all that happened here. Death and Black Rock pretty much go hand-in-hand.

Hell, the first thing you pass coming into town is a goddamn cemetery!

Just off Richland Heights Road, the Black Rock Cemetery rots while surrounded by woods. Enormous trees tower sparsely throughout the headstones like sleeping monsters with roots spread deep in the ground below them, feasting on old corpses. Many of those graves are over 200-years old and the inscriptions are too hard to read. You'd expect some fading after a couple centuries of Indiana winters. But a few withstood the test of time. One in particular, sits in the northwest corner. It reads:

Jonathan M. Clark
Born 1747–Died 1811

Note that last name; *Clark*. Dear old Jonathan himself isn't relevant, but you may have already started to sense that the name Clark bares relevance to this whole thing.

That stone squats like an emerald among creek rocks. And would you believe, even after all these years, it still sits level? Most of these monuments to the dead lean heavily, sinking slowly into the earth under their perpetual weight. If you made your way through this ancient graveyard and wandered to the back half, the really old section, you'd find several small, flat markers, scattered about like stepping stones. No writing on these. Your feet squish into soft dirt and you might catch the rancid odor of something dead and you might think you wish you hadn't of gone back there.

Enough talk about the dead. We've got more important business at hand. We're heading out to Pastor Loggin's place and we need to get a move on. Hopefully, he's still there. He's a good man.

Was, anyway.

We're getting close.

Which reminds me, I need to finish telling you what all happened three months ago so that you'll understand why we're making this dismal little walk to start with. I'll try not to be so damn long-winded.

After Abby got Michael's text, things got bad.

Real bad.

Chapter 10

The courthouse doors slammed shut and Sheriff Jack Snider basked in the morning sunshine, thankful to be out of that goddamn prosecutor's office. All Jack needed was a temporary detention to pick up a vagrant in Lafayette named Ronnie Castle and ask him a few questions. But to do that, he needed cooperation from Tippecanoe County, which, to do that, he needed the Taylor County prosecutor.

The prosecutor shot him down citing harassment and all sorts of other bullshit. Whatever. Jack decided he'd drive to Lafayette anyway and find Ronnie himself. Too many coincidences pointing to echoes of fifteen-years ago. Archie killing himself kicked it off and then finding that goat all torn to hell didn't help anything. Something about it.

Last night, the night deputy, Wayne Tillwood, had helped Jack drag the goat out of the trunk with its stiff legs clanging against the plastic lining and strewn guts soaking into the tarp (a tarp bound for the dumpster). "What the fuck happened?" Wayne chuckled.

Stupid ass Wayne. Jack would never have hired him if it weren't for the town council demanding that Judge Tillwood's nephew have a job. "Just help me look at it, Wayne."

"Why'd ya bring it back here?" Wayne cocked his head as he shined the flashlight up and down the carcass. "It's a mess. I would'a just tossed in the ditch."

"That's why," Jack had said and pointed. "What the hell would do this? Ripped open. Head nearly torn off."

Wayne squatted and furrowed his eyebrows. "Well, it for damn sure looks like an animal did it." He moved his flashlight beam along the torn belly. "Still don't know why you brought it back here."

Jack toyed with telling him it'd been dark and he'd sensed something was in the woods, watching him. But that wasn't really any of Wayne's business. "I figured it was an animal, but what the hell would tear it open?" Jack lit a cigarette. "Seems unlikely Coyotes would do *that*."

Wayne shrugged. "Who knows. It must've gotten out of someone's pasture."

"Reckon someone might report a missing goat." Jack moved his flashlight along the animal's back noting how the skin had been ripped from the spine and ribs. "Looks like something tried to eat it."

"Yeah," Wayne had nodded as if a vital clue had been discovered, but didn't elaborate.

Jack didn't like it.

He'd been having a conversation with his dead wife right before he saw it in the road, and with a dead old man who'd committed suicide. *And your wife told you to stop before you ran over it. She* told you. Sharing that little detail with Wayne wouldn't help a goddamned thing, so he'd kept quiet and stood there shivering while Wayne examined the goat.

In the end, they'd concluded something was amiss but they didn't know what. Jack had said, "Maybe some big ass wild dog attacked it."

Wayne had huffed, his breath plumed in a white cloud, and said, "Yeah, or a whole pack of them."

And that sparked another horrific memory Jack recalled from fifteen-years earlier. A family attacked by wild dogs out at the old gas station by the new highway. A horrible mess that had been in the midst of chaos.

Chaos.

He'd decided right then, standing in that dark parking lot watching Wayne examine the goat's torn body, it was time to go find Ronnie Castle.

The kid who'd been at the center of everything all those years ago.

.   .   .   .

Jack stopped at the bottom of the courthouse steps, then reached into his shirt pocket and pulled out a red and white box of Marlboro 100's. He lit one and took a strong pull. He still held a shred of hope that all of these strange events; the preacher's daughter threatened, Archie's suicide, maybe a pack of wild dogs running amuck, didn't mean anything. Just a string of coincidences.

And how about that last name… Clark?

He strolled to his car with half a cigarette yet to smoke. He reached inside the open window and grabbed his radio, then strung it out the car window. He thumbed the mic.

"Wayne, you out there?" Jack leaned his elbow against the roof and smoked.

A few seconds later, Wayne came back, "Yeah, boss?"

Jack said, "You find anything on that guy I told you to look into?"

"That Castle guy? Yeah, he's in Lafayette. Sounds like he spends most of his time wandering around and works part-time at a place called Happy Harry's." Wayne went silent and Jack wondered where Happy Harry's was, then Wayne came back and asked, "You get that temp detention order?"

"Nah, but I'm going to Lafayette anyway."

"I don't blame ya." Wayne's staticky voice through the speakers. "Let me know if you need me to do anything."

Jack thumbed the mic. "Will do. Just keep an eye on that preacher's house while I'm out. I think I'll stop by there on my way out of town and chat with him."

"You got it."

Jack flicked his spent cigarette butt to the ground and climbed into the car. He'd grab a cup of coffee at the Shell station, then go chat with the preacher. If all went well, he'd be in Lafayette by lunch time.

. . . .

A teenager named Will Haddenfield noticed the sheriff's cruiser drive past, but didn't raise a hand to wave because honestly, he couldn't give a shit. He couldn't give a shit about a lot of things. Starting with his dad making him do all of these stupid fucking chores on a day he was home from stupid fucking school, sick as a dog. It was bullshit. Three more years, he kept reminding himself. *Three more years and I'm outta here.*

The old hay-barn leaned like a tired dinosaur at the back of the property. He stomped through dead grass until he reached the hay door. He pushed the door open, expecting to be met face-to-face with a stupid cow. For some reason, they liked to stand right in front of the damn door, which meant Will had to kick at them to get back so he could get in. Today, there were no cows. Not one. In fact, they were nowhere to be seen.

Will glanced out the barn door and noticed all ten of the stupid things acting weird out by the fence line, milling about as if they didn't want to be over here. If Will had been paying more attention, he might have pondered that. But the music jamming through the spaghetti thin wires dangling from his ears drowned out all judgment and reason, because fuck being out here.

In fact, had Will been paying more attention, he might have sensed that he was being watched. A pair of hungry eyes peered at him through the slats of the wooden cattle pen. He might have noticed the subtle scent of blood in the air. Had Will been paying attention, he might have heard the soft rumbling growl.

But Will wasn't paying attention. At least not to anything that mattered.

Will was about to toss an armful of hay when something clamped onto his leg and yanked just below the knee. Pain streaked up his body but he screamed more in shock than in agony. He twisted and kicked to free his leg from whatever the hell had grabbed him. One of his earbuds plopped from his ear, the music still banging from the tiny speaker as it dangled beneath him. He caught a glimpse of the black fur. Fear tingled his fingers. This was bad, so fucking bad. He yelled, "Stop it!" as something in his leg tore, something major. Dust kicked up in swirly clouds as the dog's head shook violently and Will slipped and nearly fell.

His arms shot out and caught the barn frame. He cried. He wailed. The bottom half of the door was still closed; if he could hoist himself over and climb inside, he might stand a chance. But he'd need that damned dog to let go of him to do that. He pushed hard. The muscles in his neck protruded. His screams, though loud, drifted unheard in the mid-morning calmness, too far from another human being. *Got to get over the edge of this doorway…*

"Dadddeeeeee!"

Chapter 11

Thomas eased himself into the chair of his study and stared absently out the small window. Sunshine glinted off the damp ground where sparse patches of old snow still refused to melt. He sipped his coffee and closed his eyes. *Thank you, Jesus. Thank you so much for allowing me to see the pureness and wonder of your creation.* Just a quick prayer, that's all. He needed God now.

More than ever. And to be thankful for the little things.

His eyes slowly opened to the hollow thump of feet on the floor above him, and then Abby's muffled voice, angry and loud, cut through the silence, "This is stupid! When are we coming back?"

Linda responded, but he couldn't make out her words. Then more stomping followed by a slammed door. My God, Abby could get so mad. But, at least she'll be safe. A few slammed doors meant nothing, not in the grand scheme of things.

This morning, Thomas's panic had ebbed away, clearing room for calmer thought. Part of him knew that having Linda and Abby leave town was a good thing, but was it the *best* thing? He wondered if they weren't being hasty. What if Benjamin found his wife and daughter and Thomas wasn't with them? What if *no one* was with them?

Thomas had no shortage of unanswered questions. Starting with why this stranger, Benjamin, was taking such an interest in the distant past?

Emily. Or someone in her family. That had to be it. But that would mean someone else out there knew what had happened all those years ago. But that was impossible. Nobody knew. Not even Emily! Thomas had even been careful when he left flowers at her dorm-room door a few days after it happened. His hollow heart oozed guilt and he wanted nothing more than to make things right, which of course, he knew he couldn't. Some things cannot be undone. But there's no way she could've remembered. Hell, *he* barely remembered! So much alcohol. The one and only time in his life he'd ever been drunk. No, it couldn't be Emily coordinating all of this.

Maybe someone had seen him do it. Some voyeur hiding behind a clump of bushes or a random neighbor stumbling upon his vile act while out for a nightly stroll. But if someone had seen him with Emily behind that dumpster, why wait so long before coming forward. Why now?

God, the thought of it caused his guts to clench as that sickening feeling of something slimy and writhing inside him threatened to make him throw up. How many times had he prayed for forgiveness, had he cried alone and cried he was sorry?

Someone knew. Benjamin *knew*.

The choice. *I'm here for absolution.*

Why not just turn me in, tell the cops, and be done with it? Why not ask for blackmail money?

Don't be a moron, Thomas's dad's taunting voice edged its way in, as it so often did when his thoughts drifted to dark places. *You know there's more going on here than just some guy following you. He stank, remember? He stank like rot. And the teeth.*

Had anyone else in the restaurant smelled it?

And how about the fact that Benjamin's face changed, remember that? And not just changed, but transformed... *don't you dare forget that either.* The two things his brain clung to; the smell and the changing face, the two things he'd never tell anyone about for fear of sounding like a lunatic. Not even Linda. If he did, any legitimacy the conversation carried would flutter out the window like butterflies. He pictured the cops, jotting notes furiously as he told them his story, right up until he said, *yeah, and then the guy's face changed into this zombie looking thing, he grew teeth, and he stank like a dead animal*, and the cop would stop writing and maybe a thin smile would cross his face as he'd ask, *you okay, pastor?*

Maybe on some level Thomas didn't want to believe it himself. He wanted to believe this was something... human.

Stop! Don't start thinking like this. It's some crazy guy, that's it.

But what if it was something more than just a man? Thomas could imagine his dad's cruel mockery at something so absurd.

His dad's voice boomed, *I've got no time, squirt... no time to be dealing with your shit or anyone else's.* That had always been one of the old man's favorites. *I've got no time.* Thinking of that phrase always sparked the memory of the old man chasing Thomas and his younger brother, Ralph, out into the winter night and locking them outside after Ralph spilled cereal all over the counter (stale cereal at that) while trying to make himself some supper. Ralph had bawled *I'm sorry, daddy*, as the lock clicked shut and there they'd both stood, out in the cold in their bare feet and pajamas, clinging to each other in a shivering bundle. Thomas had thought, *now what are we gonna do.* He didn't panic, though. Stuff like that happened a lot in the Loggin's house. Everyone knew it too, especially the neighbors, which was how they'd avoided freezing to death on more nights than just that one. And what had his father done after locking them outside in the snow – he'd gone back to watching his television show, whatever it had been, because he'd had *no time for their shit.*

Now the old man lay rotting in a grave and didn't have time for anyone's shit.

What would the old man do if Benjamin's choice had been given to him. *Hey dad, if you had to choose between me or you to die, who would you pick?* No question there. The old man would likely laugh and relish being rid of the damn kids.

Gazing out the window at such a peaceful and serene day calmed Thomas's nerves and stifled those haunting memories. *Jesus, thank you.* Thomas mouthed the words in silence. So thankful. All of those times when life could have gone horribly wrong but the grace of God had swooped in and kept the very worst from happening. Even after they'd found Ralph dead of a drug overdose in Atlanta eight years ago, God had comforted Thomas, His presence strong right there next to him as he'd gazed compassionately at his dead brother lying in the casket inside of an empty funeral home, tears rolling down Thomas's face as he'd thought, *I'm sorry I wasn't there, little brother, I'm so sorry.*

God had been there.

Except for Emily. The one and only time in Thomas's life when he'd gotten drunk. When he'd left that stupid party with Emily, the girl he'd secretly loved since his first day of college. When they'd both hurried toward his dorm, but stopped along the way to make out in the grass. When she'd passed out and Thomas didn't. God didn't protect him on that horrible night.

Thomas sipped his coffee. *Lead me, Jesus,* he said, *lead me in the direction you need me to go because right now, I need you. Because…*

I don't know what Benjamin is.

A hollow tingle spread from his feet to his fingertips at the thought of that — not who Benjamin was, but *what.* That was the brutal, bare-chested truth of it. *I don't know what Benjamin is.* To hell with what the old man might think, I don't know *what* Benjamin is!

A jarring thought popped into his head. *Are you punishing me, Jesus? Are you making my daughter pay for my sin?*

No, Thomas reassured himself, because God doesn't work that way. God would not hurt Abby to get back at him. That's ludicrous: the antithesis of God.

Isn't it?

Of course, it is.

But Benjamin knows.

The doorbell rang and Thomas nearly dropped his coffee cup. Who could that be? He took a deep breath, stood and whispered another silent prayer, then made his way to the door.

As his hand clasped the brass doorknob, he had a frightening image that Benjamin would be standing on the other side. Chill out; don't start jumping at shadows. Still, he checked the peephole and Thomas felt a wash of relief to see the sheriff, Jack Snider, standing at the back edge of the front porch holding a beige and brown cap in his hands. Thomas didn't know Sheriff Snider, but like everyone else in town, knew of him.

Thomas opened the door and forced a smile as Jack caught his eyes.

"Good mornin', pastor," Jack said, "Wondered if ya got a few minutes."

"Absolutely," Thomas stepped outside onto the porch in his house slippers and pulled the door shut behind him. "Can I offer you a cup of coffee or anything?" What else do you ask the sheriff when he's hovering on your doorstep?

"No thanks," Jack said, "I'm on my way to Lafayette and had a cup at the Shell station." He paused a moment and asked, "It's Pastor Loggins, right?"

"Thomas. You can just call me Thomas. We're not too formal." Standing out here in the open, talking to the sheriff, Thomas found himself nervous. It was strange, since the police had been keeping a close eye on the house. A cop car drove past the house about every twenty minutes since he'd called yesterday and reported the issue with Benjamin. But Thomas had not expected the sheriff to show up at his front door.

Did you think you'd get away with it? Your balance is due. I'm here for absolution.

I don't know what Benjamin is.

"I'm Jack Snider. I'm the Sheriff of Taylor County." He stuck out his hand and Thomas shook it.

"Nice to meet you," Thomas said and decided this would be way more comfortable if they were both inside. "Sheriff, would you mind stepping inside? A little chilly out here and I'm not dressed for it." As Thomas said the words, it occurred to him that the sheriff's car in the driveway might as well be a big flashing sign for Benjamin to see. *Don't make any trouble.*

"No problem at all," Jack said.

"Actually, Abby is inside with Linda, and I don't want to worry her. Mind if we go to the garage?" The Sheriff nodded and Thomas led the way and opened the side door to the garage.

The sheriff closed the door behind them, shutting them into a hollow silence. At least the place wasn't a mess. Thomas liked keeping his tools and space organized.

Jack pursed his lips, nodded, and said, "I understand your daughter was threatened yesterday by someone here in Black Rock, is that right?"

Thomas nodded and thought, *he threatened both of us*, but he didn't correct the sheriff. Thomas said, "She was. By a man named Benjamin Clark. I thought he was a new member of my church."

"Is he?"

Thomas shrugged. "I honest to God don't know, but that's why I agreed to meet with him. Guess I just assumed he was."

Jack hesitated, as if debating on how to respond. "Here's the thing pastor, we don't know this guy, Benjamin Clark. Patti, our dispatcher, couldn't find any record of him either. I had her look up the guy's name, see what she came up with. Nothin' from around here. Not even a Facebook page."

"I'd guess it's a pretty common name… Ben Clark. And, like I said, he said he's fairly new to town. He said he came here from the Vincennes area or something like that. Said he worked in construction." Thomas shrugged again. *Stop shrugging,* Thomas thought, *you're acting guilty doing that.*

Jack nodded and took a slow gaze around the garage, like he was waiting for something to happen. The pause seemed incredibly long, growing awkward, and Thomas had the distinct feeling that this Sheriff knew something he wasn't saying. Finally, Jack asked, "So, if ya don't mind, could you go over exactly what happened for me. I read the report, but sometimes it just gets a lot plainer when I hear it from the folks themselves." Jack smiled. *I can read your mind,* that smile said, *and if you lie to me, I'll know.*

Thomas cleared his throat, unease creeping into him, and he said, "I guess it all started with Benjamin Clark. He'd requested a meeting with me…"

Jack politely interrupted with, "Did he say what he wanted to meet with ya about?"

Thomas shook his head, "No, just asked if I'd have time for breakfast sometime."

"That's pretty common, folks asking to meet without givin' a reason?"

Thomas said, "Yeah, I'd say so."

Jack nodded and stayed silent. Thomas wondered if the sheriff thought something was wrong with meeting people without a reason, but continued, "We met over at the Red Barn Café. We've met twice, actually. First time, that was a short meeting, and Benjamin seemed nice as can be, but even then, there was something odd about him." Thomas explained as best he could the uncomfortable aura Benjamin emanated, stopping short of the distorting face and rotting smell. Jack asked a few questions, but remained relatively quiet throughout, listening and nodding, occasionally raising an eyebrow, his face portraying his surprise and concern at points along the story.

"… and that's when he threatened Abby." Thomas threw it out there, hoping it would be enough, but knowing better. *Please don't ask me what Benjamin said.*

"Exactly how did he threaten her, pastor? What words did he use?"

Thomas suddenly felt trapped. "I, I don't remember exactly how he said it. He just said it."

"He just said it?"

"That's right. He said he would kill her." *Please, just let it go. Let's move on to how you're going to go arrest this man and keep my daughter safe.*

"He just said he'd kill your daughter?" Jack furrowed his eyebrows. "No reason? No demands? No discussion? That's damned odd. He didn't threaten you? Just her?"

"Yeah, he just threatened her," Thomas said and looked away. The sheriff was considerably older, but the man's sharp eyes missed nothing: clear, crystalline; the eyes of a man who'd *seen* things.

Jack nodded and Thomas watched him as he absorbed the words, processed them, and finally said, "This man obviously thinks you did something to him. That you wronged him in some way; otherwise, he'd have no reason to threaten you or your family. Now, I'm not saying you actually did anything to him, but he *thinks* you did. So, given that, you've got no idea what that might be?"

Thomas shrugged. "I really have no idea."

"You have no idea?" Jack rubbed his chin. "Well, I've got to be honest with you, pastor. I think this man is just having a bit of fun with you. I don't think he's really a threat at all."

What? This is not how Thomas wanted this conversation to go. "I'm convinced he's a real threat, sheriff." Thomas remained calm. Collected. Don't overdo it. "He really frightened me."

The sheriff paused. His eyes narrowed. "This man, huh?" The sheriff's gaze remained locked onto him. "Have you heard from this man since then?"

"No, not since breakfast yesterday."

"Let me make sure I've got the timeline right, pastor. You met this man at the end of last week for breakfast. Nothing out of the ordinary. Then you met this man again yesterday for breakfast. At about what time did you meet this man?"

Thomas shot a glance at the ceiling, considering the question. Something about the way the sheriff asked questions bothered him, but he couldn't pinpoint why. "Abby had been in school, so it had to be after 8 AM. Maybe around 9 or so, I'd say."

The sheriff nodded. "And then afterward you drove straight to the school to pick up your daughter?"

"Yes."

"Immediately after speaking with this man?"

Thomas realized what bothered him about the sheriff's questions. He wasn't using Benjamin's name, which seemed odd. "Why do you keep saying it like that? *This man*?"

The sheriff shrugged but his eyes seared into Thomas's. "What else would I say? He's a man, right?"

"Why would you ask me that?"

The sheriff shrugged again, but said nothing.

Thomas shot a glance out the window. His fingers tingled and his heart picked up pace. Where was this going? He toyed with saying, *I don't know*, but how preposterous would that sound? That trapped feeling reared its head again and Thomas shifted his weight nervously from foot to foot, then realized he was doing it and stopped.

I don't know *what* Benjamin is.

Just say it.

The sheriff broke the looming silence. "Don't take this the wrong way, pastor, but do you know if your daughter's had any contact with this man? In any way?"

No way. There's just no way Abby would be in contact with a man like that, especially since Benjamin was considerably older. "No," Thomas said, but wasn't sure the confidence touched his voice, and then added, "Not that I know of."

"Is Abby aware of what's happening?" Jack asked.

"We haven't told her, no."

"Do you plan to?"

"No. She and my wife are leaving town today and I don't know where they're going."

Jack raised his eyebrows and Thomas couldn't tell if the gesture meant the sheriff agreed with that approach or if he found it shockingly stupid. "Hmmmm," the sheriff didn't say anything at first. The silent garage was marred only by the muffled chirping of a bird outside. "I'd recommend you tell her." The sheriff glared right at him. "She's fifteen-years-old. If she's in danger, she should be aware of it. Might keep her from steppin' into the line of fire, so to speak, and gettin' burned if she knows the fire's there. Right now, you've got her blindfolded and stumblin' around."

The first thing that popped into Thomas's head was, *I think I know what's best for my daughter*. Don't get defensive. The sheriff is here to help. Thomas nodded. "Guess I was hoping to avoid it. She's not been herself lately."

"How's that?" Jack asked and immediately, Thomas wished he hadn't said it. The sheriff would assume the worst.

No reason to hold back now. This was information the sheriff could get easily from other people. "She had some problems at school yesterday, mouthed off to the principal and got expelled. Definitely not typical of her." Guilt at talking about her behind her back gnawed at his conscious. How sardonic.

Jack leaned against a small table and cast a dubious stare at the floor, apparently finding this information of particular interest, and Thomas did not like that at all. He could handle Abby. He wanted the Sheriff to handle Benjamin. This entire conversation, Thomas had felt like the sheriff didn't believe a word he said.

Thomas needed to move the focus from Abby and back onto Benjamin, where it belonged. "You've got to understand," Thomas said, forcing desperation into his voice. Gaining peoples' trust was Thomas's gift. God's purpose for his existence. "Moving here was difficult for Abby, but you don't need to worry about her," Thomas said, "It's Benjamin we need to worry about. For whatever reason, he's fixated on my daughter and he's…" Thomas realized he came frighteningly close to saying *he's a monster*, the memory of the distorting face and rancid smell surfaced, but he stifled the words. "...he may be capable of anything, God knows what, and Abby might not be the only one in danger."

Jack stood silent, as if considering his next words carefully. "Mr. Loggins, just being honest here, I have no idea how dangerous this man actually is or what his intentions are, or why he's chosen your daughter. But, what I *do* know is that parents are blind when it comes to their children." He paused and Thomas prayed silently for patience. The Sheriff was on his side and one thing that Jack possessed, that single element that could potentially be the lifesaving variable in all of this madness, was objectivity... something Thomas himself couldn't possibly harbor since Abby was at the heart of it. *Fools delight in their own opinion, but wise men listen to others before forming their own.* How utterly true.

Thomas nodded his hesitant acceptance. He rubbed the heels of his hands against his eyes. God, this was all so messed up.

The sheriff said, "I don't know anything about this Benjamin Clark." Jack's eyes locked onto his and Thomas once again felt the Sheriff suspected something he wasn't saying. "So, I want you to be doubly cautious, mind where you're going, and definitely let me know if you hear from him again. I'll have a deputy in this area at all times, so we can get here quickly if you need us. In the meantime, I'm gonna see if I can find out where this guy's living."

"Thank you," Thomas said and he hoped he sounded as sincere as he felt. But the sheriff's next question plucked a twinge of unease in his guts, perhaps due to its unexpectedness.

The sheriff placed his cap back on his head, glanced around the garage as if it looked familiar to him, and said, "Before I go, I gotta ask you somethin' and I want ya to be honest, no matter how crazy you might think it sounds." His expression reminded Thomas of someone fluctuant, as if scared to say what he needed to say, which appeared oddly out of place on a man like this. "Did Benjamin ever do anything that made you think he... that he might be capable of doing things beyond just scaring you?"

This man. You mean like his face changing shapes, his teeth growing, or smelling like a dead animal? Is that what he's asking? Surely not, no one would believe that. What about how Benjamin knew about Emily? Or how ten minutes had passed while I'd sat there in that diner and cried (according to the waitress), only to discover Benjamin had left without me knowing it? Were those the types of things the sheriff was asking for? *I don't know what Benjamin is.*

Thomas pondered the question. "He had an aura about him," Thomas said. "When he talked, he spoke things so as-a-matter-of-factly, like he did things like this all the time."

The sheriff nodded and what Thomas found most off-putting was the lack of surprise on the Sheriff's face. As if he expected he might hear this.

Thomas continued. "He also..." goodness, how should he say this, "When I was sitting there, right at the end, his face changed." Thomas gave a couple of dry chuckles and shook his head. "He also smelled horrible, like a dead animal, and I didn't know he left. I just sort of snapped out of it and Benjamin was gone. I mean, with everything he'd just said about Abby, it was probably all in my head, but it sure seemed strange."

He waited for Jack's stern face to crack into a smile, maybe even an all-out laughing fit, perhaps followed by some technical cop language like, *it's not uncommon for people in intense stressful situations to imagine things.* But the sheriff said no such thing. His face slackened and his eyes seemed to age in seconds. And something else darkened the big man's face; something Thomas couldn't put his finger on.

The sheriff nodded and that strange expression deepened. What was it? "I want you to be careful of this man. I also want you to consider having your wife and daughter stay here rather than leave."

"You think they should stay here?"

"I'd seriously consider it. If it truly is Abby he wants, he'll be stalkin' *her*, not you."

"Alright," Thomas said, "I'll talk to Linda about it and tell them to stay here for now."

The sheriff nodded and shook Thomas's hand. The big man's grip swallowed Thomas's fingers. "Anything else you need me to know, pastor?"

Thomas said, "Just anything we can do to keep Abby safe." *And me,* Thomas thought and felt sheepish for thinking it.

The sheriff moved quickly to the door, hastily opening it up and hurrying to his car. Thomas followed and stood shivering on the driveway as Sheriff Snider climbed into his cruiser and sped away without so much as a wave.

And then it hit Thomas what that strange expression on the sheriff's face had been, that look that didn't fit.

Recognition.

The sheriff kept wording things strangely. How he'd kept saying, *this man*. As if goading Thomas to admit something.

Does that sheriff know Benjamin? That was absurd. Of course he didn't. But the question kept lingering.

Chapter 12

Five minutes prior to the sheriff showing up at the door to greet Thomas...

Abby stood in her bedroom doorway and leered at her mom. "This is stupid! Why do we have to leave?"

Her mom's mouth dropped open, a stupid expression if Abby had ever seen one, and said, "I have no idea. I don't have this all planned out."

God! *I could just scream!* Abby twisted away, stomped down the hallway to her room, and slammed the door behind her.

She flopped onto her bed and checked her phone to see if Michael had responded. Nothing. Last night he had been so perfect. They'd traded messages for hours. He was like a real boyfriend. But now this morning, he'd apparently thrown his phone away. Maybe he was still sleeping or something. Or maybe he'd gone to school and left his phone at home (wherever home was) but that didn't *feel* right either. What it felt like was that he'd forgotten about her and just the thought of him forgetting about her sparked despair.

Michael was the only good thing in her life. Someone to talk to, someone who understood her, someone who *wanted* to talk to her, and she loved that. And after last night, her boyfriend.

At least, she thought so.

And right now, she needed someone to talk to because her stupid parents decided she needed to leave right away. Right out of the blue!

Punishment for her little outburst at school, they'd said. *You are grounded to me, young lady.* Her mom's exact words meaning that Abby had to go wherever her mom went. How stupid.

Sometimes she hated them.

Don't I get to have my own opinion on things?

She rolled her eyes and murmured, "They think I'm crazy."

I'm not crazy. I just couldn't take anymore.

Where would they go? Maybe to Austin? That would be fine. More likely, they'd send her to some mental institution. She clenched her teeth thinking about it. She heard parents did that kind of stuff sometimes with teenagers. She'd watched an entire Youtube video about it.

She looked at her phone again. Still nothing. She needed something to get her mind off Michael. Music. Something loud. Something bad. Something with cuss words.

Why *can't* we all move back to Austin? *Because you have no voice. You're just a silent puppet moving whichever direction the puppet-masters want.*

Abby, get ready for church. Abby, get ready for school. Abby, you're wrong. Abby, don't talk that way. Abby, don't dress that way. Abby, give me your phone. Abby, go to bed. Abby, do your chores.

She hit play and closed her eyes, relishing the thrum blasting into her ears. Tears flowed and she let them run freely down her cheeks. *Where is he?*

That's when her phone rang.

Michael. *Holy shit. He's calling?*

Her heart stopped, she swore it did, and even the roots of her hair tingled. *This is crazy*, she thought, *I'm acting like a little kid.* A few months of emails, online chat, and texting, but she'd never actually spoken to him. That was the one thing that was really stopping him from being her *real* boyfriend.

She didn't want to sound desperate when she answered, even though she was. *Hello? Oh, thank God you called!* She needed to stop worrying about how she sounded. They knew each other well enough. She just hadn't expected a real conversation to happen at this very minute!

God, how stupid.

She sat up, pushed her hair behind her ear, exhaled a calming breath, and answered.

"Hello?" She'd need to keep her voice down. Her mom or dad overhearing the conversation wouldn't help anything.

"Abby?"

"Yeah."

"It's Michael. Didn't you see on the caller ID?"

"OMG, sorry! I didn't even look. It's so nice to hear your voice!" Good grief, she sounded so dumb.

"Hey," he chuckled, then said, "Last night was so perfect, I had to talk to you. I was gonna wait until this weekend to call you, but I just couldn't."

"Cool." She felt like a three-year-old being told that she'd get to start using the *big* potty. Why did her brain pick now to become socially inept?

Silence dangled on the phone and terror swept over her as she realized he might hang up. Finally, he said, "Is now a bad time?"

"No!" She took a deep breath. Calm the fuck down. "I was just laying here." Finally, a coherent sentence.

"Like, in your bedroom laying down?"

"Yeah," she smiled and twisted a strand of hair through her fingers. "Just wasn't feeling the greatest."

He laughed and she loved that laugh; throaty and deep; strong. She relaxed into the conversation. He sounded older than seventeen, but she liked that.

"What are you up to?" she asked. Maybe he had one muscled arm tucked behind his head as he spoke to her.

"I just finished some school work." He paused, then added, "Sucks."

"Yeah." She giggled. Not sure why. Something about the way he said it.

"What are *you* up to?" He asked.

"Honestly," she said and chuckled. "Wondering why mom and dad have gone totally psycho this morning is all."

"Psycho?"

God, he was so easy to talk to. So easy, in fact, that she just laid it all out there, telling him everything. Like pressure bottled up suddenly released. And Michael never interrupted her, not once. He just let her talk, throwing in the occasional *yeah*, or *uh-huh*, or *that sucks*.

"You could always just wait and see what happens," Michael said. "Maybe nothing will come of it."

"Are you serious?" her mouth dropped open. *Is he insane?*

"I don't know." Michael spoke so calmly, so matter-of-factly, as only someone who'd understood things could do.

"Nothing is easy in my life right now," she said. Stupid thing to so say, but it's all she could think of. She closed her eyes feeling the whole weight of everything. As the thoughts roiled in her head, a reflection splashed across her wall, a signal that a car was pulling into the driveway. She slipped off the bed and stepped toward the window and gazed out, keeping a safe distance so she couldn't be seen. A cop car.

"I'll try to help make things easier," Michael said.

She wanted desperately to get lost in this moment, but that cop car outside bugged her. Did this have something to do with her? More shit stemming from yelling at Principal Pearson?

"You'll make things easier, huh?" She asked.

A knock on the door drifted dully through the house, barely audible from where she stood. Any moment she expected someone to yell, *Abby... come down here please.*

Michael's soothing voice settled into her ears. "After last night, I feel so close to you. I have to see you."

"Like, hang out?" She heard her voice speak the question, but also listened as her dad answered the door, unable to make out the muffled words from downstairs.

"Yeah," he said. "Hang out."

Her attention snapped completely to Michael.

Excitement shot through her. It surged up her spine, spread through her body like some special power igniting every part of her, every piece, every cell. It sparked in her belly and seeped through her skin where it caused goosebumps.

"That would be pretty cool," she said. Her voice sounded calm, rational, at least it did to her own ears. Her brain immediately kicked into *how can I make this happen* mode.

"What about tomorrow?" Michael asked.

Oh shit, she may not even be here. He'd understand, she knew he would. "I'd love to," she heard herself saying, "I can't tomorrow. My mom's making me go with her."

"Oh yeah, that's right. You have no idea where you're going?"

She shrugged. "I have no clue. Seriously, no idea where, why, or how long. This just pisses me off."

"Well," Michael seemed to ponder thoughtfully, then said, "Then I have to see you today."

Michael's words soaked into her brain. Something suddenly didn't seem totally right, yet it didn't seem totally wrong either. She said, "I don't know," and shrugged while gazing down at the cop car.

"Maybe you could beg them to stay?" He chuckled after he said it and she smiled against her phone.

"Yeah, like that'd do any good." She watched her dad and the policeman stroll out to the garage. This was so weird.

"Let's pick a place to meet."

Her eyebrows furrowed despite her excitement. He wasn't screwing around. "I can't leave, my parents are all freaked out. It's like I'm grounded or something.

He hesitated, then said, "Then I'll come to your house."

She cocked her head as her dad and the cop disappeared into the garage. "I can't," she giggled. "Are you crazy?"

Another hesitation, a little longer this time, which stoked her excitement, and then he said, "Text me your address."

"Okay," *God, and I don't even know what he looks like!* "But it's got to be tomorrow. I can't get out of the house today."

"But you said you'd be gone tomorrow."

"I know, but maybe I won't be." She knew he wanted her to say today. Seemed odd that this came up out of nowhere, him wanting to come see her. They'd been talking for over two months and now all the sudden. "I'll try to talk them out of it."

"Perfect," he said.

The lie she'd tell her parents required thought. Planning. *You can do this, Abby. You can make this work. This is all you. Do it.*

"I'll send you my address, okay?" she said and shocked herself at the sound of her voice. Was she breathing heavy? Did she sound nervous? The small voice of reason inside her struggled to be heard, to scream *wait just a damn minute here*, but she couldn't help it. She *needed* this!

"Cool," Michael said. "I'll wait right here."

He hung up and she stood in her room and lowered her phone from her ear. Was this really happening? Was she actually doing this? She licked her dry lips and relished the thudding of her heart.

A text buzzed on her phone: Waiting.

She smiled.

. . . . .

Benjamin Clark held the phone in the silence of the dead house. Abby's sweet voice lingered in his ear.

The most beautiful thing we can experience is the mysterious.

Chapter 13

Benjamin sensed anger buried in the man, like catching the stench of rot, and the anger was good.

Benjamin sat at the end of the bar, allowing a cup of coffee to cool in front of him. He had no use for such things, but knew the pleasure people derived from it. His hatred for these people stirred in his gut as they stuffed the shit into their loathsome faces, chewing like pigs. Benjamin cringed at the thought. But he needed one of them and *that* was the only reason he was here.

And that someone was Jesse England. Jesse stepped into the bar with his hands shoved into the pockets of his dirty jeans. His brown and gray-streaked hair hung wet across his neck and face. A nauseating aroma of stale alcohol drifted from his breath like smoke clinging to cloth. The stench of hate, of anger, is what drew Benjamin to Jesse. To anyone else in the room, it was impossible to notice. But to Benjamin, it was overwhelming. Benjamin smiled as he watched the man stroll stupidly through the poorly-lit room and park himself on a stool, about two down.

The bartender meandered over to Jesse and said, "You're up early."

Jesse blinked, shot the bartender a shitty look, and said belligerently, "It's 11:30, Bill, what the hell you think I'd be doin' at 11:30?"

The bartender forced a smile that said, *oh, you stupid son-of-a-bitch.* "Guess I didn't realize it was that late," Bill said. "What do you want?"

Jesse laughed in a strange, irritating huff, and bobbed his head as if the world were finally turning his way, and said, "You got any biscuits 'n gravy left?"

"Yep, we have some."

Jesse pointed a finger and said, "Well, that's what I want."

Bill's jaw tightened and he sauntered away. Then Jesse turned and gawked directly at Benjamin and said with a goofy smile, "I wouldn't have asked if he had any left if that ain't what I wanted," and he laughed.

Simpleton, Benjamin thought, but only nodded and smiled back. This was exactly the kind of guy he needed. He'd wait a few minutes before striking up a conversation. Idiots like Jesse possessed the intelligence of a primate - getting him to do what needed to be done would require very little finesse. Just tell people what they want to hear. Trying to keep a low profile while at the same time, stirring a stinky pot of chaos could be tricky. Plus, that goddamn sheriff was already poking around and that could be a problem. Benjamin spotted the sheriff's car parked at the preacher's house earlier. Benjamin hadn't counted on that big, stupid motherfucking sheriff to still be around here after fifteen years. Oh well, a mere speed bump in the scheme of things.

Benjamin studied Jesse thoughtfully. The simpleton rested both elbows on the bar and puffed a cigarette in quick, successive movements. Only in Taylor County can a person still smoke in a bar. How does a man this stupid and lazy survive?

Within a few minutes, the bartender plopped the plate of biscuits and gravy in front of Jesse. "There ya go Jesse. Don't choke on it."

Jesse nodded and said, "Thanks." A second later he shoveled the first dripping bite into his mouth.

The time had come.

"Looks good," Benjamin said and smiled.

Jesse shot him an odd stare, then his eyes darted to Benjamin's cup of coffee. "How come you ain't got any?"

Benjamin shook his head. "Not hungry, I guess."

"It's good shit," Jesse said and shoveled more of the slop into his mouth. Benjamin grimaced at the wet smack of chewing.

"Yeah," Benjamin locked eyes with Jesse. "You seem to like it."

"Yup." Jesse stuffed in another shovel-full, scrunched his eyes, and asked, "Haven't seen you in here before. You live around here?"

"It's been a while since I've been back." That was true. It'd been fifteen years at least, maybe longer. The exact year eluded him. Time gets away.

"Why would you come back to this shithole?" Jesse packed in another bite.

"I had a good friend who lived here. You might know him; Ronnie Castle?"

Jesse swallowed his last bite and clinked his fork down on the plate. "Ronnie Castle?"

"Yeah," Benjamin said. "You know him?"

"Fuck," Jesse said. He wiped his hands with a napkin. "I ain't heard that name in a long time. You talkin' about the Ronnie Castle who went and killed his girlfriend a long time ago?"

Benjamin pointed a finger at Jesse. "Not sure they proved that."

Jesse shifted his gaze down to his food-smeared plate. "Hell if I know. I just know he don't live here no more. I think a preacher lives there now."

A preacher. A preacher who was talking to that shitbag sheriff.

"Goddamn," Jesse rubbed his chin thoughtfully. "I ain't sure we're talkin' about the same guy. The Ronnie Castle I'm thinkin' of ain't been around here for years. They ain't never found that girl. Goddamn, that shit was a long fuckin' time ago. If it's the same guy."

Benjamin said. "We all make choices. Who are we to judge?"

Jesse looked toward the end of the bar. "Hey Bill, you remember Ronnie Castle?"

Bill stopped and rested one hand on the bar, then nodded and said, "Yeah, I remember him. Crazy kid. Killed his girl."

"See," Jesse laughed hysterically. Benjamin had no idea what was so damned funny.

"Why the hell are you asking about Ronnie Castle?" Bill asked, walking back toward their end of the bar.

"This guy asked about him. Said they was friends," Jesse said and shot a thumb at Benjamin.

Bill picked up Jesse's empty plate. "Ronnie moved away a long time ago, mister. Pretty much got run out of town. Said some monster kidnapped his girlfriend. But everyone knew the fuckin' nutcase killed her himself."

Benjamin nodded. "Is that so?"

Jesse belted out that same annoying laugh. "See," he said, "'Ole Bill knows everything about everything. You ask it, he'll answer it. Ain't that right, Bill?"

"Fuck off, Jesse." Then Bill turned to Benjamin and said, "I'll ask you again; why are you in here asking about Ronnie Castle?"

Benjamin glared at him. He clenched his jaw. He tensed and tightened both hands into fists.

Bill's nostrils flared; the contempt palpable in his narrowed eyes. "I got no use for strangers looking for trouble around here. You understand me, friend?"

Benjamin smiled. *Be patient with them, they're fools.* "I'm not looking for trouble. Just looking for an old friend."

"Well," Bill nodded. "Trouble's about to find you if you ain't careful."

Jesse's gaze shifted between the two men, as if hoping they'd go to blows.

Benjamin said, "Whoa, like I said, I ain't looking for trouble. I'll just pay my check and get on my way."

"That sounds like a plan to me," Bill waited, not moving.

Benjamin dug out four dollars from one of his front pockets and plopped it on the bar. It was four dollars he'd found in a jar shoved to the back of one of Donna Johnson's cabinets. Came in handy for little things like this.

"That enough, friend?" Benjamin asked.

Without looking, Bill mumbled, "Close enough," then scraped the dollar bills into his hand and walked to the other end of the bar.

"Well perfect." As Benjamin slid off the barstool, he clapped Jesse on the shoulder. "Good meetin' ya my friend." He leaned close to Jesse's ear and spoke quietly. "Despite that asshole bartender giving us shit, it was good talking to you. I'll bet that bartender knows better than to fuck with you." Benjamin backed away. "Enjoy the rest of your breakfast."

Jesse twisted around and stared at him, as if he'd just met the most amazing man he'd ever come across, and he nodded, "Hell yeah he knows better."

Benjamin said, "You're the man to know around here, Jesse. I doubt anyone messes with you." He gave one last clap on Jesse's shoulder, one in which he felt Jesse's ego swell. "Take care, Jesse. We should go have a beer and shoot the shit sometime." And with that, Benjamin made his way through the dimly lit bar, happy to leave the stench of stale cigarette smoke and disgusting mouths.

Benjamin strolled about twenty feet down the sidewalk when he heard the door to Ada's bar open and close and then Jesse's voice drifted over his shoulder, "Hey, wait up."

Benjamin halted, a smile stretching across his face. *Just tell them what they want to hear and the magic happens.*

Jesse caught up and lit another cigarette, smiling and shaking his head. "Goddamn," he said, "Guess you pissed 'ole Bill off."

Benjamin laughed. "Guess I did."

Jesse bobbed his head in that same, stupid way he did before, and said, "I ain't never liked that fucker anyway." He drew on his cigarette and exhaled a cloud of smoke. "Hey, you wanna go have that beer?"

And just like that, the deal was sealed.

Chapter 14

Jack's cell phone chimed about ten minutes from Lafayette. He glanced down and saw Daisy Howard's name splashed across the screen. He grunted, "Shit," and pulled into the deserted parking lot of FRED's ICE CREAM.

He tapped the green ANSWER button and said, "Hey there, Daisy."

"Oh," her voice warbled. "Didn't know if you'd answer." At the sound of her voice, Jack pressed his palm against the steering wheel and tightened his grip on the phone.

"Daisy. What's up?"

"Well," she acted hesitant, unsure. "I found some things while cleaning out Archie's room. His chest of drawers and whatnot. Not sure what to make of them or if it's a big deal."

"What did you find?" Jack gazed through the windshield. Did he really have time for this?

Daisy didn't answer at first, then she said in that same diffident tone, "Pictures Archie drew. He had them stuffed in a drawer." She took a shaky breath, "I mean, they may be nothin', but they're strange. Thought maybe you'd wanna see them. I don't know."

He opened his mouth to say he was busy today and he'd try to get in to look at whatever she'd found tomorrow, if he could. But waiting didn't feel right. She clearly thought they may be important or she wouldn't have called. "Pictures of what, Daisy?"

He heard papers rustle through the phone and Daisy said, "Pictures of a person. Yet, not a person. I don't know. Like a shadow with wings."

A chill burrowed into Jack's spine. "How many pictures?"

Her voice warbled, "Well, I don't know. Stacks of 'em. Dozens. Some look like scribbles, but some are more intricate."

Pastor Loggins' description of Benjamin echoed. The rotting stench the pastor described. The changing face. The threat.

Jack asked, "What's the picture look like, Daisy? Anyone you recognize?"

"There's not really any faces," she said. "Just shapes. Sounds silly, but it's like a demon." She hesitated, then added, "Or an angel maybe."

Jack swallowed and he felt a dry click in his throat. Just pictures drawn by a crazy old man. *Yeah, keep telling yourself that, Jack.*

"Listen," he said. "You did the right thing, callin' me. Hold on to 'em. I wanna see 'em." He rubbed his hand against the rough stubble of his chin, and added, "I'm headin' into Lafayette today..." He considered telling her his plan to find Ronnie Castle. Daisy would certainly remember him. She would remember everything from back then. She might even draw the same similarities between what had happened in those days to what was happening now, especially with the timing of Archie's suicide and the pictures she'd found.

"You want me to bring them into town?" she asked.

"Nah," he said, "I'll come get them."

Jack remembered fifteen-years-ago when he'd found Archie out by the cemetery on Richland Heights Road, sitting in a daze, his maddened eyes wide with shock. Old Archie, the lawnmower man who kept all of the cemeteries in Taylor County mowed, just sitting there alone by the road, his eyes blank, his shirt torn, and his mouth hanging open in a silent cry.

I want to see those pictures.

Jack cleared his throat and said, "Tell ya what, since I don't know when I'll be back today, I'll send Wayne over to pick those pictures up. Might be later this evening since he doesn't get off until 8 or so, but he'll be there."

"That sounds fine, Jack," she said. "I'll put them in a box for him."

"That'll work." He said and rolled down his window. He needed fresh air and a cigarette. "Call me if anything else comes up."

"Oh, I will," she said.

"Bye, Daisy." He waited for her to say goodbye then hung up and sat in the silence of the car. The cool outside air drifting in through the window felt good and he blew cigarette smoke out in a plume.

You okay, baby? Amy asked him from the passenger seat.

Jack let his cigarette dangle from his lips while his fingers crept down to the wedding ring he still wore. "I think I might be losing it." He chuckled and thought, *and not only because I keep talking to my dead wife.*

She said playfully, *no one would ever think you're losing it.*

He gazed out the windshield, at the deserted ice cream stand. "You remember that kid, Ronnie Castle and his girlfriend? How he'd said a man abducted his girlfriend, Sherri Hensley?"

I do, she said.

"I've always thought that kid was full of shit." He shrugged, "hell, maybe I still do. But I just won't ever forget that call Ronnie made and the way he looked when I got there that day. The way that lying little shit swore up and down someone kidnapped his girlfriend."

What's this got to do with anything? Amy's voice was so patient. So soft. Jack's heart yearned for her.

He chuckled again and plucked the cigarette from his lips. "I'm starting to feel like I'm chasing the boogeyman."

The boogeyman? She giggled.

"I know, sounds crazy." He flipped his spent cigarette out onto the gravel and rolled up the window. "But I have to talk to that kid Ronnie again." Jack supposed Ronnie wasn't a kid anymore. "I'm not saying I've changed my mind about him, I still think the sonofabitch had something to do with Sherri's disappearance, but I need to try and make sense of this shit; starting with the fact that they both had the same last name."

Maybe Benjamin's some kind of monster, Amy giggled again. Jack loved that giggle.

"I ain't sayin' that," Jack said and almost added, let's not jump to silly conclusions. But in his heart, he knew he was well past jumping to conclusions.

He shifted the car into Drive and stomped the gas.

At least he had Amy to keep him company.

Chapter 15

Thomas called his assistant pastor, Tim Turpin, from his study about an hour after Jack Snider left and asked if he could run the services on Sunday. Thomas knew there was no way he could preach an effective sermon, not with all this craziness going on. Tim preached well and he'd been asking for more involvement anyway. It didn't hurt that he was young and absolutely on fire for God.

"Everything okay?" Tim asked. *Do I not sound okay?* Thomas grew suddenly worried he'd said too much.

"I hope so," Thomas avoided an all-out lie. "I'm distracted and there's just no way I'll be able to prepare, and I may need to leave unexpectedly."

"Woah," Tim said, "That doesn't sound okay. You sure there's nothing else you need?"

"No, no." Thomas forced a chuckle. "I'm good."

Tim paused, as if he sensed that there was more to this situation and Thomas feared he might start asking more questions. More questions Thomas didn't want to answer. Finally, Tim said, "Don't worry about the service. I got it covered."

Thomas smiled, "Speak whatever God lays on your heart, my young padawan."

"I'll make it so, Obi Wan" Tim said and chuckled. "Anything else?"

Thomas's phone beeped – someone else was trying to reach him. He quickly checked the face, saw that it was a local number, and put it back to his ear. He hoped they'd leave a voicemail.

"No, that's all I need." Even as he spoke the words, Thomas wondered if that was true. Easter Sunday loomed only a few weeks ahead and he had a whole series planned starting Palm Sunday. Surely this mess would be over by then. Wouldn't it?

"Okay," Tim's enthusiastic voice projected a man at peace with himself in a way Thomas had never experienced; a peace only achieved without evil in one's past. "Just let me know if anything changes or you need me to do more. I'm open."

"Thanks, Tim, I really appreciate it. Sorry for the last-minute notice."

"No problem. Call me if you need anything else."

Anything else, Thomas thought. *You mind coming over to my house with your shotgun?* "Will do and God bless." He tapped the red icon and ended the call.

His phone buzzed in his hand, startling him as if he'd grabbed a bee. "Good grief," he mumbled. That same local number. He tapped the answer icon and put the phone to his ear.

Before he could say anything, the familiar voice crept into his ear. "Hello, pastor."

Cold, prickly fingers pierced his chest and grasped his heart. Thomas pressed the phone to his ear, unable to speak, dimly aware his hands were trembling.

"You've been a bad boy, pastor."

"What? What do you mean?"

"Have you made your choice?" Benjamin's voice carried a nauseating wetness.

Thomas closed his eyes, hating this… this thing. He wanted to scream *leave me alone*, but couldn't. His terrified mind simply wouldn't allow the words to lurch from his throat, as if an unseen hand had grasped his throat and choked off the air. Dear Jesus.

"And why was the sheriff at your house this morning, pastor? What did I tell you about causing trouble?"

Thomas squeezed his eyes shut. *Help me, Lord Jesus.* Time for a long shot; he decided to lie to Benjamin. But what if Benjamin already new? What if he could sense the false words coming out of Thomas's mouth? Crazy as it sounds, it seemed possible. Maybe probable.

Thomas spoke as calmly as he could and fought a hitch in his breath. His heart ka-thudded and he felt the pulse in his neck. He licked his dry lips. "Abby got into trouble earlier this week at school with the principal. She got suspended."

"Are you lying to me pastor?" Benjamin's question hung in the air like a sharp dagger.

"I'm, I'm sorry," Thomas said. "I was scared."

"You should be scared. Emily was scared, I can tell you that." A long pause where Thomas thought shamefully, *Emily wasn't scared, she didn't even know*, then Benjamin continued. "Here's the thing pastor … there is nothing the cops can do for you. This is entirely in your hands. You get to decide who pays."

Thomas nodded and plopped down into his chair, placing a hand on his head and allowing the tears to flow freely. The words, *take me*, danced on the edge of his tongue, but his mind wouldn't let them slip out. Not yet. Not while there was still time to track Benjamin down. "How do you know Emily?"

Benjamin ignored him and said, "You can't avoid this. You have to choose. If you let them leave," his voice thickened with cruelty. "I'll kill them both. Your wife and your daughter. Then I'll come for you. That what you want, pastor?"

"How did you…" Thomas stammered. *How does he know they're leaving?*

"Don't you worry about how I know. I know the same way I know about you. The same way I know about Emily. I just know."

Thomas wiped briskly at his forehead with a shaking hand as anger and terror roiled and mixed together like an unholy concoction. An unpleasant memory surfaced of his drunk father cornering him in his bedroom, slipping off his belt, preparing to teach him a lesson in manners because *I got no time, boy* and Thomas's heart galloped like an animal fighting its way out. That memory and this situation shared an intimate similarity – in both he was trapped.

He tried to focus his thoughts on Jesus. Trust in Jesus.

Thomas squeezed his eyes shut and prayed silently; *I lay it all at your feet, Jesus, help me combat this evil, take control, allow me to –*

"Someone has to pay pastor. And you have to choose."

And then Benjamin was gone.

. . . . .

Someone has to pay.

Thomas's eyes flew open.

You have to choose.

He climbed back up into his chair. He wanted to pray, but it suddenly seemed so useless. What he needed were answers. He needed help. He needed to talk to Linda and tell her the plan had to change; that she and Abby must stay for the time-being, because Thomas sure as hell thought they should. At least here, they'd all be together.

He opened the laptop on his desk and the screen flickered to life. What was he looking for?

He popped open a Google Chrome search screen and typed Benjamin Clark. Over 5 million results. Useless. He typed Benjamin Clark in Black Rock, Indiana. Still nothing useful. Maybe this was a waste of time. Benjamin's voice lingered heavy in his ear, like an ugly worm wedged deep inside. *You have to choose.* He typed Murders in Black Rock, Indiana.

Several hits popped up and Thomas's fingers tingled for fear of what he was about to find. He clicked the top link and shortly after, the screen filled with the black and white image of a news article. He gasped and sat back in his chair as one hand crept up to his mouth. His eyes absorbed the words in icy gulps.

FROM THE INDIANAPOLIS HERALD; May 13th, 2008

Black Rock teenager missing. Father killed in dog attack.

Tragedy struck Black Rock, Indiana on Saturday when teenager, Sherri Hensley, was abducted. Circumstances surrounding the abduction were not immediately clear and local police confirmed that the boyfriend of the girl, Ronald Castle, was not a suspect at this time. A stunned community gathered at the Black Rock Christian Church on Saturday evening for a candlelight service where shocked and tear-stained faces filled the sanctuary.

When asked to provide details, Taylor County sheriff, Jeff Lardo, only offered this: "Our hearts go out to the family of Sherri Hensley. We're doing everything we can to find her. The citizens of Black Rock have been instrumental at coming together for support during this awful time and all of Taylor County joins them in their suffering. Our officers will work tirelessly to find her."

Details were not provided. One resident of Black Rock said, "It's that damned highway out there," referring to the four-lane highway built in the early 1970's that runs North to Chicago, "always strange people going up and down that highway. God knows who might've come through here." Sheriff's officials said they couldn't rule out anyone without an alibi at this point.

When asked if there was anything the public could be doing to assist, the sheriff only said to pray for the citizens of Black Rock and Taylor County, giving the impression that he believes the kidnapper is no longer in Black Rock, or anywhere near Taylor County. Sheriff Lardo didn't confirm this, but didn't deny it either.

At the same time, another tragedy struck the community out by the abandoned gas station when father of two and husband, Lewis Hoskins, was killed by wild dogs. The family, while traveling North, pulled off the highway for a restroom break and discovered...

"Oh my God," Thomas whispered just as Linda stopped in the doorway and stared at him.

"What now?" She asked..

He looked at her. "What was the name of the people who owned this house before us?"

She stepped timidly into the room. "Castle," she said. "Joe Castle. But didn't the real estate guy say that the place had been empty for years?"

Thomas recalled how the sheriff had glanced around the garage; how Thomas had had the distinct feeling the sheriff had been in there before. He struggled to make the connection to Emily, especially if all of this turned out to be related. His incident with Emily occurred nearly 25-years ago down in Texas and he couldn't fathom how that could have anything to do with an event that occurred here in Black Rock fifteen-years ago, but still, he couldn't rule it out. God, he should really tell Linda about that. He *needed* to tell Linda about that. A secret dangling between them no longer dormant.

Thomas rubbed his temples in long, slow circles and said, "I think this Benjamin has been here before. I think he was here fifteen-years ago and for whatever reason, he's back." He glanced up at Linda whose face said, *what in God's name are you talking about.*

He said, "I need to talk to that sheriff again."

Part III
Ronnie

Chapter 16

Ronnie Castle gawked out the small order window and cringed when Jack Snider sauntered through the door with his silver badge dangling out of the front pocket of his coat like a silver tongue. Holy shit. What was that asshole doing here?

He turned back to cleaning the plates stacked up on the sink ledge. This was bad. Real bad. He debated slipping out the back door. A brief surge shot through him; *did they find Sherri?* His fingers trembled as he picked up a plate and sprayed it, then slid it neatly into the dishwasher rack. The small kitchen didn't offer many options if he had to run.

Of course, part of Ronnie knew his paranoia was illogical. The cop was probably coming in for coffee and a donut with no idea Ronnie lurked in the back washing dishes. But this was not just any cop and when you've been through what Ronnie had been through, it changes your mind. Changes your perspective. The world becomes a hostile place and your only goal is to survive.

Run.

At least no one could see him back here. Hidden. For now.

The sheriff stepped up to the bar and plopped down onto one of the round stools. *Oh Jesus, it's a bad vibe.* Why would Jack Snider be here except for something bad? How long's it been... ten years, at least. Ronnie loaded the remaining plates, but didn't push the green START button. With that dishwasher running, you couldn't hear a goddamn thing.

Ronnie mumbled to himself, "I haven't done anything." And that was the truth. He repeated it. "I haven't done anything, I haven't done anything…" *Shhhh, don't be too loud.*

He slipped a small bottle of Old Crow Whiskey out of his pocket and drank the last swallow then plopped the empty bottle into the trash. Better. But now he was out of whiskey. Nothing was working out.

From out in the lobby, Ronnie heard, "Howdy sheriff. What brings you in today? Business or pleasure?" That was Harry. Fuckin' Happy Harry. No mistaking that prick's voice. The owner and resident son-of-a-bitch. Harry took pride in demanding the shitters be cleaned or the front sidewalk be scrubbed, always barking orders with his arms crossed over his ample belly and a cigarette dangling from his mouth.

"I'm afraid today it's business," Jack said.

Tingles shot up Ronnie's feet and legs and his hands numbed. *I haven't done anything.* Ronnie clamped his teeth tight, straining to control his heart beat. *Oh God, don't let me have a heart attack.* He leaned against the sink counter, just in case he passed out. People passed out when they had heart attacks. *If I fall face-first… if I fall face-first I'll hit…*

"Watch ya got?" Harry asked. Ronnie pictured Harry, the stained apron covering his fat gut while standing behind the bar with his arms folded.

"Lookin' for Ronnie Castle."

Oh God, there it was. Jack *was* after him. He whined, "I haven't done anything. Just leave me be." *Quiet, you goddamned idiot.* He paced back and forth. His sneakers splatted on the wet floor. He slapped his hand against his forehead. *Oh Jesus, Oh Jesus…*

Ronnie squeezed his eyes shut. A tear popped out and slid coldly down his cheek. *Why me? Why won't they just let this go?* He knew that nobody had believed him about Sherri, but there's a reason they never charged him with a crime. *I didn't do anything.* He knew they all wanted him locked up, not walking around free. *But am I free?* If this is freedom, Ronnie would take prison.

They'll never stop!

And he was out of Old Crow.

"Ronnie Castle, huh?" It's a wonder ole' Happy Harry didn't sell him out. *Here's my chance… run now.* But he didn't. Instead, Ronnie made a fist and jammed it against his mouth, biting down on one knuckle. Get to the church! He had to get to the church.

Harry asked, "What do you need 'im for?"

"Nothin' big." Jack's deep voice seeped into the kitchen. "He here?"

Nothing at first, then Harry's voice echoed through the empty dining space, "Hey Ronnie, sheriff is lookin' for ya."

Breathe. Just Breathe. Control. Don't pass out. His heart thudded and he winced. Ronnie knew a few cops, and most ignored him. But Jack *knew* him. And hated him.

"Be right there," Ronnie tried to yell, but his voice warbled. *Guilty, my voice sounds guilty. But I haven't done anything.* But was that *really* true?

Ronnie clamped his hands together and hissed through his teeth.

He's from Black Rock, Ronnie. They found Sherri, buried and rotting somewhere, and your balance is due.

Ronnie whispered, "They'll never find her. He'll make sure of that." Although part of Ronnie wished they would find her body. Even though it might shine the light of justice back on him, at least he'd have some closure. *As least it would be over.*

Ronnie looked up at the small order window. Jack's face glared through at him with scrunched eyebrows and slack jaw.

I'm gonna need whiskey after this. So much so that Ronnie's cheeks already tingled with anticipation. The calmness.

"You alright?" Jack asked him.

"Like you care, sheriff."

Jack eyed him, a perplexed expression strewn across his face as he chewed fervently on a toothpick, undoubtedly one he picked up from Harry's counter.

Ronnie blinked. His hands trembled.

Jack's gaze remained fixed on him. "I need to talk with ya. That's all."

Ronnie twisted away and shoved his hands deep into his pockets. *Stop judging me. I haven't done anything!*

Wait.

The aftertaste of alcohol wafted up from inside him. The thought of liquor on his tongue. God would speak to him, but he needed to get the distractions away. He needed Harry to float him a few bucks. He needed —

Why is Jack here?

Harry said, "You'd best get out here, Ronnie."

"I just wanna talk." Jack stood, scooting out his stool with a short scape on the floor. "Right now." His eyes locked onto Ronnie's. "You got a sec?"

Jack's tone implied something was wrong. He thought again that they must've found Sherri and Jack was here to arrest him.

Run, now!

Tell him no. *No, Jack, I don't have a sec.*

He pictured the sidewalks outside, the grass along the edges of the bench out front, and of the church. He needed to get to the church. After a drink. And a cigarette. He shifted his weight from foot to foot. Keep moving.

Jack stared. Ronnie stole a few glances at the man's face, at the furrowed eyebrows and the confused twist of the mouth. Why was he here?

Why are you here, Jack?

Ronnie pressed his fist against his forehead and said, "Okay, but I only have a few minutes. I gotta be somewhere."

"I only need a few minutes." Deep lines cut Jack's face. *He looks old.*

Ronnie's eyes darted to the back door, then back at Jack. The choice. For the rest of his short life, he'd reflect often on what might've happened had he chose to run out that door.

He reflected often on so many choices. *You or her, Ronnie. Your choice. Your balance is due.*

"Jack?" Ronnie asked. The word shot from his mouth before he even realized it was there. "This about Sherri?"

"Sort of."

Ronnie turned away from the window. His heart slammed. *Settle down, just settle down.* "I'll be out in a sec. Can you meet me out back?"

"Yep," Jack said. "I'll meet ya back there."

Harry's voice, "I'll show ya the back door, sheriff."

Beautiful perfume. Sherri's. He could have collapsed right then, just fallen flat on Happy Harry's wet floor and laid there as Jack and Happy Harry shuffled out, and Happy Harry would probably come back in and ask, *why in the fuck you just layin' there?*

Unpleasant memories flooded him and he didn't need that shit right now. Once he got out of this damned kitchen and out into the open air, he'd feel better. A drink would calm his nerves. If Harry could float him a few bucks, that is.

The back door to the diner slammed shut and Ronnie's eyes darted up. Happy Harry said, "You'd best get out there. He's waitin'."

. . . . .

Jack leaned against a rusted dumpster smoking a cigarette. Ronnie stepped cautiously out the door and kept a comfortable distance. He didn't like people standing too close to him and especially not Jack Snider. The chilly air bit Ronnie's skin and he crossed his arms.

"How'd ya find me?" Ronnie stared at Jack's feet. Scuffed boots.

"Wasn't hard," Jack said.

Ronnie rubbed his hands over his bare arms. "What do you want?"

Jack took a long drag on his cigarette and exhaled the smoke in a steady cloud. Ronnie sensed the sheriff's sharp gaze searing into him and hated it. He felt exposed out here. Accused.

Finally, Jack said, "Something's goin' on in Black Rock. I think Michael Clark might be back, but calling himself Benjamin."

Ronnie's eyes shot to Jack's. "What? Michael?"

Jack nodded. "And, he's threatening another girl there."

Ronnie's ears grew hot and his pulse quickened. Anger flared. "You didn't believe me about him." He unfolded his arms. "You blamed me, Jack. Goddamn it, you blamed me!" Ronnie jabbed his finger into his own chest. His eyes watered.

Jack's eyebrows raised and he glanced away. "Yeah. Well, I ain't sayin' I believe you had nothin' to do with Sherri disappearing, but this Benjamin Clark's got me shook. I think he's a dangerous man – "

Ronnie pointed his finger at Jack and growled, "I told you he's no man. I told you that!"

Jack shifted his eyes to the ground. Not what Ronnie expected him to do. He appeared almost, sorry.

"I know," Jack said and flipped his cigarette onto the dirty asphalt.

Ronnie's lip quivered and he wished he could stop it. "Did you find her. Did you find Sherri?"

Jack shook his head. "That's not why I'm here. I need your help."

"*Now* you need my help?" Ronnie flipped his hands up and then down. "What the fuck am I gonna do, Jack? What the fuck am I gonna do?"

"You know him," Jack said.

"No!" Ronnie yelled. "No, goddamn it! You didn't believe me. *YOU* didn't believe me." He pointed his finger at Jack. "This is not my problem." Ronnie turned away and paced a few steps. Michael. Fucking Michael. Icy fear crawled into him. He turned back to Jack. "You wanna start somewhere? Start with whoever it is Michael is talking to. Ask them what they did. Ask them what they did to deserve it."

Jack's eyebrows scrunched. "What who did? To deserve what?"

Ronnie shook his head and glanced down. He'd forgotten all about being cold. He pictured Michael. Sherri screaming. *I didn't do anything. I didn't do ANYTHING!* His insides wrenched at the thought of ever seeing Michael again. He couldn't. He wouldn't.

"I can't," Ronnie said. "I just can't."

"Tell me what you mean by deserve it." Jack stepped toward him and stopped.

Ronnie's hands trembled. "He only comes for you if you've done something." As he spoke, he suddenly pictured Michael hunting him down later, maybe slithering out from beneath his bed while Ronnie slept, descending on him, taking him. *I'll know if you cause me trouble. I'll KNOW.* "That's all I can tell you," Ronnie crossed his arms again. He wanted to be away from here. Away from Jack Snider. Away from everything. "I have to go."

He turned and plowed through the back door, back into Happy Harry's, gasping. He pressed his back against the door, hoping to God Jack wouldn't come barreling through chasing after him. Jack didn't.

Alone inside the back kitchen, he bent and braced his hands on his knees, and cried.

Chapter 17

Ronnie trudged the six blocks to the Lutheran Church on South Street. It was the only one that would let him enter and the pastor there would actually speak to him.

The asshole, Harry, didn't float him a dime. "Advance?" Harry had said with a sneer. "You want to leave town for a few weeks. Fine. I can replace you as easy as anyone else. But I ain't givin' you no advance. Hell, I suspect I'll never see you again, Ronnie."

You won't. That's the whole point.

Just gotta make it to the church. A dull throb in his head annoyed him and he wished it would go away. Thinking about Jack Snider and that whole conversation prompted memories he'd spent years trying to suppress. *You or her.*

Your balance is due. Absolution.

Sherri's screams as he hid…

Stop it! He pushed his hands into his pockets.

Ronnie spoke aloud as he walked, as he often did. It helped him think. "Why'd he come here?" Pause. "Jack Snider. No way! Just no fuckin' way. How'd he find me?"

Good damn question. But, Jack was a cop and finding people is what cops do.

He reached the church and had a quick cigarette (a half-smoked butt abandoned on the sidewalk) before plodding inside. He entered and the familiar aroma engulfed him; something between the smell of old books and fresh carpet. It was the only place that reminded him how bad he stunk.

The doors to the huge sanctuary are *eternally open,* as Pastor Gregg would've said, and Ronnie slipped through and plopped down in a pew toward the back. He rubbed his palms against the coarse fabric of his dirty jeans. Finally, some peace and quiet. His fingers tingled and the aching in his clenched teeth faded to a dull thrum.

Pastor Greg's voice echoed from another dimension when he said, "Mr. Castle! Always good to see you. How are you?"

Ronnie glanced at him. The pastor's pudgy hand rested on the wooden pew arm and a tender smile touched his lips.

Pastor Greg asked, "Mind if I join you?"

Ronnie nodded and turned his eyes toward the front of the church. No one understood, could ever possibly understand, the relevance of today, of knowing who Michael Clark was. Of *what* Michael Clark was.

The pew creaked as the pastor settled in. The scent of soap and cheap aftershave wafted the air. Pastor Greg said, "You seem distraught?"

Ronnie stared at his grimy hands.

"You mind sharing it with me?"

Ronnie asked, "Have I ever told you about where I come from and about my girlfriend?"

"Yes," Pastor Greg said. His eyes narrowed. Troubled. "You've mentioned Black Rock and how she was abducted when you were young."

Ronnie huffed, "I don't even remember telling you that. How shitty is that?" He stretched his lips into a painful smile. "So today a cop from Black Rock shows up. Shows up where I work."

"Someone you knew?"

"Oh yeah," Ronnie said, "A guy named Jack Snider. He wasn't the sheriff when I lived there, but I guess now he is. He told me that Michael Clark may be back there."

The pastor folded his arms and asked, "Michael Clark?"

Ronnie rubbed his palms together. "Michael Clark kidnapped Sherri. Except this cop, Jack Snider, always thought that I had something to do with it."

"Sherri was your girlfriend, I assume?"

Ronnie nodded. "Michael Clark took her."

The pastor paused, as if contemplating his next set of words, then said, "Well then, I guess I'm not understanding," Pastor Greg spoke with honed patience, "Isn't it a *good* thing that they might have found the guy *you* think did it?"

Ronnie gazed forward at an enormous cross hanging above the alter. Sherri would have marveled at the sight of it. She'd always wanted to go inside the big churches to see if they were like the movies. *They are,* he wished he could tell her. She'd been gone fifteen-years. My God. "You'd think so."

The pastor drummed his fingers against his elbow but didn't say anything. Ronnie stared at the cross at the front and said, "Here's the thing, pastor; Jack's right. I did have something to do with it but not in the way Jack thinks I did."

The pastor's fingers stopped. He stiffened, then said, "Go on."

Ronnie rubbed his hands against his jeans and thought, *what's said cannot be unsaid.* "Michael gave me a choice, but it wasn't really a choice."

"What do you mean, a choice?" The pastor's voice hardened.

Ronnie gazed down at his hands. "He told me to choose." Had he ever told anyone this? *I don't think I have.* Because this was somehow worse than people thinking he kidnapped Sherri. Worse than anything. "I could've saved her." He said flatly. "But I chose me." Ronnie jabbed a finger into his own chest. A cold tear slipped down his face. "I'd give anything to take it back, I swear I would." He swiped his cheek. "I let him take her while I hid."

"I'm confused," the pastor said. "A choice for what?"

Ronnie closed his eyes. "Something I'd done when I was eighteen. Way before I met Sherri. Way before any of this happened." He looked at Pastor Greg who stared at the front of the church. *Oh God, do I tell him what happened?* Ronnie had gone too far to pull back now. "It was just a stupid night and I had sex with a girl, pastor. That's it. I ain't sayin' it's right, but that's all that happened. I didn't even know her and like I say, it was before I met Sherri."

"That's it?" The pastor's incredulous voice said, *you're full of shit, Ronnie.* "People have adulterous sex all the time. So why isn't this Michael Clark hunting them all down? Why just you?"

Ronnie shrugged. "I've asked myself that a million times. Why me?" He stopped short of telling the pastor the girl had only been fifteen-years-old, which Ronnie had *not* known. But somehow, Michael Clark *had* known. It still didn't answer the question of *why me.*

The pastor inhaled deeply and Ronnie sensed a coldness that had not existed prior. *Pastor Greg suspects me now. Well of course he would. You just told him you had something to do with it.* Maybe's he's deciding whether to call the cops – *hey, a guy just confessed to knowing something about a kidnapping.* But despite that, Ronnie actually felt better. Lighter.

Pastor Greg asked, "So, what are you planning to do?"

"I don't know." Ronnie thudded his forearms against his thighs. "I don't know!" His voice raised and echoed.

Pastor Greg touched his arm and said, "Easy. It's just us here."

Ronnie clamped his eyes shut and nodded. *I can do this.* Another tear slipped down his cheek.

Ronnie's voice hitched as he spoke. "I had my chance to prove myself and I messed it up. You always see yourself being the hero, fighting the bad guys to save your girl, but then the moment comes and I came up short." Another tear slipped down his cheek. "That's why I'm doomed to live this shitty life."

Pastor Greg cleared his throat and said, "I believe you Ronnie. I do." The edge in the pastor's voice dulled. He patted Ronnie's forearm and said, "So this policeman…"

"Jack Snider."

"This Jack Snider traveled here from Black Rock?"

Ronnie nodded.

"To find you?"

Ronnie nodded again.

"He didn't slap handcuffs on you. He didn't yell at you or threaten you?"

Ronnie shook his head.

The pastor said, "It almost sounds like he *believes* you too."

Ronnie blinked. "What are you saying?" He recalled Jack's expression as he'd leaned against that dumpster. Desperate maybe? "I haven't been back there for at least fifteen years, maybe longer. I didn't even return for my dad's funeral."

"I didn't say you should," Pastor Gregg said. "I just said it sounds like maybe he believes you."

Ronnie leaned forward and rested his forearms on his legs, hanging his head low.

Pastor Greg took a breath and said, "Ronnie, I've always welcomed you into this church and I've always listened to you. Wouldn't you agree with that?"

Ronnie nodded. Damn right he agreed with that. This church and Pastor Greg were his only refuge.

"And in all the times that you and I have talked, you've never spoken more clearly on a specific thing than you are tonight."

Ronnie sat up, still listening.

"I don't know that I believe in the monsters from your hometown, but I believe that *you* believe in them. And now I hear you talking about *doing* something. Taking action." The pastor clenched his fist on the word *action*. "God knows, I don't want you to hurt anyone or yourself, but in all of the times you've told me about Black Rock, and please don't take offense at this, you've told it like a frightened child might explain a bad dream to his mother." The pastor chuckled humorlessly.

"It *was* a nightmare," Ronnie interjected.

"Maybe so, but my point is, whatever is happening; it's got you thinking about things bigger than you."

Ronnie listened. Thoughts bounced within him like lightning shooting between clouds.

"Said a different way," Pastor Greg folded his hands and leaned forward, his face exuding a dark excitement. "You sound motivated. And that's a *good* thing. God puts things in our path, Ronnie, that forces us back to Him. He places those obstacles there so that we must turn and go around them, and then He places Himself at the edges so that He becomes the best option. Some people hit the obstacle and stop. They just give up. That's what you did all those years ago."

Ronnie shrugged and thought, *if you only knew what you were encouraging me to go back to.* Monsters are real. "You think I should go back?"

"Yes!" The enthusiasm in Pastor Greg's voice was palpable, the enormous room seemed to fill with it. "I'm not saying I wouldn't miss you here, but honestly Ronnie, you don't belong here. You belong home."

"A lot of people there hate me," Ronnie said. "They blame me for Sherri." The accusing glares; *they don't believe you.* Part of the reason he'd left.

"You may never change that, but you could at least get back to who you are."

"And who am I?"

Silence sprang between them and Ronnie frightfully thought the pastor might answer with *hell if I know.* But instead, he said, "I can tell you what you're not. You're not a bum. You're more than a poor man working at a lousy hamburger stand and living in a trailer park. I've always thought that. I'm nothing but an old fool who's never done anything remotely dangerous. But you are more than this, Ronnie. I know it."

Ronnie stared at his clasped hands with no idea how to respond.

Pastor Greg heaved himself up and shuffled into the aisle. "I'll be right back." His footsteps echoed in the sanctuary and once again Ronnie sat alone.

A dormant excitement stirred deep in his gut. It swirled and mixed with dread as he considered what it might be like to once again set foot in Black Rock. Would everyone gawk at him? Perhaps with blank expressions where disgusted thoughts lurked. Would he run into anyone he knew?

And Michael Clark, calling himself Benjamin now, where was that sonofabitch? What had Michael done? What if I got the chance to face Michael again? *Take me.*

His palms sweat and he rubbed them on his jeans.

Pastor Greg returned and plopped back down. He handed Ronnie a white envelope. "There's $50 in there," the pastor said, "something to help out." Then he handed Ronnie a blue metal crucifix the size of his palm. A blue polished stone stuck in the middle. Heavy.

Ronnie nearly dropped it. "What's this for?"

"The money's to help out. Get something to eat," the pastor said, "That cross is to remind you that I believe in you. That God believes in you."

Ronnie swallowed. "Thank you," he said, his words felt small and lame.

"You don't need to thank me," Pastor Greg said, "Just don't make me regret it!"

. . . . .

Back out on the street, Ronnie's feet carried him faster than they had for years and the crucifix rubbed in his pocket. Could people tell it was in there? *No one knows I have it*, he told himself. No one knows, so just keep walking.

Where in the hell am I going?

He walked. Could he leave the solace of invisibility? If he remained hidden, he'd continue to have no expectations. No responsibility. Freedom lived at its most primal level. Imagining life outside of this ten-mile radius frightened him. Go back to Black Rock? Back where his life derailed?

"What would I do?" he muttered. He pictured Michael Clark's sunken eyes and gaping mouth. He pictured himself standing before Michael once again. "Take me," he muttered and fresh tears burst down his cheeks.

Sherri. Screaming...

STOP!

Ronnie reached the liquor store on Main Street and didn't hesitate to go inside. Just a small drink and some smokes. To get his mind straight.

Sherri screaming as Michael dragged her away.

As I hid.

The bell dinged over the door as he entered and he gazed at the bottles covering the shelves. His cheeks tingled.

Chapter 18

Wayne Tillwood stopped at the edge of the tall grass behind the Taylor County Home and inhaled deeply. Nervous. Darkness so thick you could lick it.

No moon and the star splattered sky offered nothing for light. Blacker than a coal miner's ass and Wayne didn't like it. Not at all. Like stomping around Ft. Hood at midnight hoping like hell a goddamned rattlesnake wasn't coiled up, poised to bite.

Only this was worse; something lurked out here with him and judging by the growl he'd just heard, it was way bigger than a goddamned rattlesnake.

Jack and his bright ideas. *Hey Wayne, can you swing by the County Home after your shift and pick up some pictures from Daisy?* Sure. Why not. Like Wayne had nothing better to do than to pick up shit from old ladies. And now here he was stomping around in the weeds because the little old lady is scared and thought she heard something out here. Christ.

Before stepping into that tall grass, he turned back to see if Daisy was still standing by the back door, watching him. Her small frame silhouetted by the back-porch light seemed dreadfully distant from here, but at least someone could see him. He'd told her earlier it was probably just a dog wandering around, but she wanted him to make sure. She swore up and down she'd heard a person back there. Old lady is probably going senile.

Shut up, dumbass. Get in there and get it over with.

He strode into the hip-high grass, his shoes crunching stupidly loud, and then stopped.

Off to his left, something rustled, something big. Wayne swung his flashlight and gasped when the light caught two glowing eyes. The animal, what looked like a dog, shot deeper into the weeds and then movement startled him a few feet the other way. He darted the light around, looking for anything, but finding nothing.

He should not have come out here.

Whatever was in these weeds, they were all around him. *Run! They're surrounding you!* Christ, how many were there? He drew his pistol and stepped backward, certain that if he whirled and ran, they'd descend on him and tear him to shreds. The sweat soaking his palms caused the grip on his pistol to feel slippery and unsure, and he hated the feel of it.

Jack's words haunted him. *If anything weird happens while you're out there*, Jack had pointed his finger and glared down at Wayne like a father scolding a son, *and I mean goddamned anything, you call me immediately, you understand?*

At this point, Wayne knew. *I should have called Jack as soon as the old lady said she heard something.* But damn it, who would've thought *that* was weird? Just a little noise outside.

A pack of wild dogs. Jesus. *I should've called Jack.*

Wayne yelled back to Daisy, "There's dogs out here, Daisy, stay up where you are. If you've got your phone with you, call Jack." His voice blasted through the darkness with startling loudness.

Daisy's hand shot to her mouth and she scrambled inside.

If he could at least get out of this tall grass, away from the underbrush, and out into the openness of the back yard, at least he'd be able to see movement. So many mistakes in the last three minutes.

More movement off to his right, only this time it sounded so close he could reach out and touch it. His heart hammered and Wayne decided to hell with it. *Run. Just get to the back yard. Then you can use the flashlight to scare them. Then you can use your gun.* God knew how many dogs were out here. By the sounds of it, several.

Wayne whirled and broke into a dead sprint. The tall grass slowed him down, like running on a mattress, and the rough ground threatened to twist his ankle.

He focused on the back-porch light where Daisy burst out the door holding the phone to her head. Her eyes swelled open and she yelled out, "Wayne, run!"

"Get in the house," he hollered to her. "Get in the house!"

The fierce growls gained quickly, and the sounds of large animals tearing through weeds sparked panic. *Stumble now, it's over.* The clearing opened up, but God help him, if he stopped and turned to shoot, they'd be all over him. He'd never make it to the back door. Sweet Jesus. He'd never make it.

The picnic table. Wayne realized if he could just make it to the table, he could use it for cover. *A couple of seconds, is all you need.*

Blind panic consumed him, seizing every thought, every action. Wayne Tillwood, former high school track star, ran for his life. His strong legs launched him forward and his arms pumped like pistons. The flashlight slipped from his grip and spun toward the ground. Wayne didn't even look down. *Picnic table.*

Wayne felt the weight before he felt the pain. The dog's teeth clamped onto his side, and the 70 additional pounds sent Wayne sprawling forward in a flailing mass of arms and legs. *"Fuckinnnooooo!"* His words drowned out by the tornado of man and animal.

In the tumble, Wayne managed to scrambled to his knees, but the animal held tight, its teeth buried into the soft flesh just below his ribs. Then the dog yanked hard. Wayne thought miserably of a puppy playing tug-of-war. Another yank. Wayne felt his flesh tear loose, and he screamed. He kicked wildly at the ground, searching for any way to get purchase so he could run again. Then pain seized his leg and he knew another dog was on him. Jesus, they're killing me!

Your gun.

He rolled hard to his right just as another dog latched onto his back. Thank God, he could raise his shooting arm. Shadows descended on him from the darkness. Too many. His thumb released the safety and he fired at the dog on his leg. A wounded yelp rang out, and for an instant, Wayne found hope. He fired at another. *Shoot anything that moves.* One wasted shot, and they might get a hold of his gun hand. He hit a second dog square in the throat, but the bullet blasted straight through and blew part of Wayne's left foot off. He felt the slug hit him, like having someone slam his foot with a hammer. Wayne's mouth opened wide. *You're going to die out here.* He was going to die out here and that realization penetrated his brain with terrifying surety, like the anticipation of a needle piercing flesh, and he thought of his mom and sister and what they'd do when they found out.

Wayne fired again, hitting another dog in the leg. But it kept coming. That was the last time Wayne's bullets would find a target. Every shot thereafter hit nothing, until finally, a hot, wet mouth grasped his throat.

Chapter 19

Thomas stepped into his study and found Linda staring blankly at his computer screen with a folded newspaper perched on her lap. In the twenty-three years he'd known her, he'd never seen an expression like that etched on her face. Distant. Cold. Her face no longer gentle. Only hard angles and rigid.

"What is this?" she asked. Her voice low. Frightening.

The words *I have no idea* danced on his tongue and he knew that's what he was going to say as he strode across the room. *But something feels so wrong here.*

He acted shocked when he reached her and peered over her shoulder. His eyes caught the newspaper laid open atop her thighs. Scrawled in red marker: *Make your choice.*

Oh my God.

He read the date at the top of the paper – twenty-four years ago. Then the headline: **Rapist on Campus.**

No one knew about him. No one. *Where did she get this paper?*

His heart fluttered and he suddenly felt he may pass out. His eyes crawled to the computer screen where an email sat open. The same article was pasted into the body of the email, but at the top, it read: Your husband is a rapist. Ask him if he's made his choice.

No, no, no…

The sender name was Jesse England; someone he'd never heard of. A hollow void bubbled in his chest and the world turned dreamlike. This couldn't be happening. No, this could not be happening. Disgust swallowed him and control slipped away. He was a feather caught in a windstorm.

Linda spoke through clenched teeth. "I asked you, what is this?"

His knees weakened and he knelt before her. As a preacher, it's okay to have problems, *little* problems, but nothing major, God no. Other people did the big things, the ugly things, because they're other people; other people had drug addictions, abuse problems, sexual perversions, and the list goes on, because that's what other people do. That's why we have pastors; to help other people.

In that few seconds that he knelt on the floor before Linda, he saw himself losing his job, his friendships, his family; all of it fluttering out the window like an awkward black butterfly.

"I was planning to tell you," he said and felt stupid and had to look away from her.

"Oh..." and her face crumpled as her hand shot up and covered her mouth.

"I don't know why," he said and swore this was the closest thing to an out of body experience he'd ever had. "I've never known why. I was still in college. I barely remember it, I just know I was drunk, and I..." Oh my God, this sounded so dumb. So ridiculous. Like admitting it was him who forgot to put the toilet seat down versus admitting to a rape he'd committed twenty-four years ago and never gotten caught.

Her lips pressed to a dark, thin line.

He touched her hand and she pulled it away and tucked it under her chin. He said, "Linda, I'm -"

She slapped her hand down on the desk. A pencil rolled across the surface, as if fleeing, and fell off the side with a *plink* onto the floor. Thomas's mind still reeled with *how did this happen? How did she get this paper? This email?*

Linda stood, took a deep breath, then stormed out of the room with one hand still pressed to her mouth and left him sitting like a fool on the floor. God, why was this happening? This was the worst way possible for Linda to find out about Emily. The absolute worst. How in God's name?

He crawled up into his desk chair. She'd taken the old newspaper with her; the one with the red words, *Make your choice* written across the front. Once she settled down and absorbed the shock of learning she'd married a rapist, she'd be asking what that meant. *Make your choice.*

He needed out of this house. Away from all of this!

He launched to his feet and hustled across the room, out the door, and down the stairs. *Gotta get out of here. Now.* It was like moving through a fog. A dream. His life had just changed. Everything had just changed.

He grasped the doorknob, heaved it open, and stumbled out into the chilly air. He pulled the door shut behind him and stood, gasping, and wondering what to do. Where to go. Anywhere but here. Disappear.

He marched toward the garage. He could be alone in there. Hide.

Alone.

.　.　.　.　.

Thomas sat in the darkness, engulfed in a cloud of his own misery, wondering what on earth Linda might be doing inside the house.

She'd never understand.

Things had never been more wrong. What if Linda called the police? Calling the police prompted all sorts of implications, not to mention the death of his career. The accusatory people who would most certainly judge him.

Abigail's hateful glare.

One single decision he'd made almost a quarter of a century ago, an act taken in seconds, distorted his entire life forever. Hot tears fell in rivulets down his face as he careened down a path of self-destruction, his entire life in upheaval, destroyed as the truth crashed through his paper walls, revealing the ugly creature behind those weak facades.

He'd avoided Emily at all costs all those years ago, often taking the long way to classes or events, even in bitter cold. Guilt consumed him and he'd left her flowers on random occasions and watched her from afar to ensure she was okay. She was!

Thomas had done his best after committing an unforgivable sin. He'd been so good at avoiding responsibility. Better than good, he was a master. It was the alcohol. Someone had drugged him. Emily had been willing. Thomas had forgotten about the event entirely. Moved on. Thomas guessed Emily herself didn't remember. God, he hoped not.

So how on earth, how in *God's* name, had it happened that Linda had gone into his study and there it all was; an old newspaper and an email splashed across his computer screen? The only story ever published about the rapist at Greenville College who'd never been caught. A story that Thomas knew existed, a story he'd read several times when it originally published in the Greenville Circular because it was written by Emily's sister who was hell-bent to find the truth. Who could blame her?

Why in God's name was Linda reading it? *How* in God's name had she found it?

Benjamin.

Benjamin had given her the newspaper, somehow. Benjamin emailed her. Benjamin *knew*.

Thomas couldn't even pray about it. The guilt inside him squeezed out everything good, even Christ. He felt stupid praying about something so self-inflicted, like asking God to please remove your fat as you gobbled down the double Whopper with Cheese and large fries.

"Stop it!" Thomas hissed into the darkness. He didn't want anyone to know he was out here. To stay hidden forever would be divine. He may never go inside again.

What if Linda told Abby? Had she called anyone and told them?

Did she call the police?

I'm such a coward.

. . . . .

Thomas crossed his arms, walked over to the garage window, and stared out into the young evening wondering what to do next. Praying seemed so deceitful and fake. Could he claim to have ever been a man of God, truthfully? A good man might turn himself in. A righteous man definitely would.

He could see the lights on in the upstairs bedrooms and he knew Linda was up there. He turned away and paced. His breaths echoed in the small space and the scrape of his shoes on the concrete floor carried a forlorn emptiness he'd never noticed before. *I'm hiding in the damn garage.* Was Linda even looking for him? His phone had not dinged, so he assumed not.

They'd been so unified dealing with this Benjamin Clark threat. Working together. Protecting Abby from whatever Benjamin was.

And now a great divide had formed, a bottomless cavern, and God no longer intervened. *He's dividing us. Benjamin was turning them against each other.*

"You bastard." His voice reverberated and fell dead in the room. *Divide and conquer.*

Thomas dropped to his knees and prayed in that dark garage. "I can't get any worse," he said, "I can't go any lower. Help me protect them; that's all I ask. After that, I'll face whatever you ask of me."

Make your choice.

Thomas stood and took a breath. He had no idea what would come next. Being exposed brought a degree of freedom. His darkest truth screamed from the rooftops, but this was beyond just a spilled secret. Benjamin had raised the stakes. Admitting his sin wasn't enough. *The choice is yours; you or your daughter.*

And he knew, with absolute certainty, there was only one way out of this. Only one way to save Abby and himself.

He'd need help dealing with Benjamin. Help beyond just God. He needed muscle. Firepower. He'd call that sheriff again.

He'd do whatever he had to do, starting with the courage to step back in his house and face the music.

Chapter 20

For over an hour, Ronnie laid in the old shower room, staring at the ceiling as a retched headache throbbed in his skull. *Stupid, stupid, stupid! Get a few bucks and go buy alcohol, like an idiot. If Pastor Greg could see you now.* What a terrible investment he'd made. Ronnie wiped a dirty hand across his mouth. The best thing going for Ronnie right now was having this damn shower room to himself. Nothing but the hollow plink of dripping water and the smell of old soap. For a filthy truck-stop off of I-65, he couldn't bitch about the accommodations. It beat his old, broken-down trailer by a mile!

Ronnie's eyes drifted shut and he lay there, listening to that monotonous water drip. *God, just let me sleep a little, that's all I need.* A little sleep. Black Rock awaited him and he needed a clear head, if that were even achievable.

Fear engulfed him like a giant cloak. Returning to Black Rock meant facing far more than Jack Snider; though Jack hadn't acted hateful or hell-bent on tossing Ronnie in jail like he had all those years ago.

Returning to Black Rock meant stepping back in time and reliving *that* day. The day that Ronnie had made his choice.

Did Sherri know? Did she know that I chose myself over her?

These questions haunted him more than anything. They'd been a plague on his conscience since the day he hid behind the counter and listened to her screams fade away – did Sherri know what he'd done? Had Michael told her before he committed God knows what to her? *I didn't mean too!*

"I didn't mean to," he hissed. The methodic dripping of the shower head, echoing...

.   .   .   .   .

"Call the police," Ronnie said. "Tell them we're heading to your house now. We'll be there in a few minutes."

Sherri sat in the passenger side of the pickup truck; her knees pulled up to her chest. Her eyes brimmed red from crying. Ronnie hated seeing her scared like this.

He loved her so much and would die before letting that son-of-a-bitch hurt her. He had to get to Black Rock. It was the closest place.

"I thought you said he wouldn't find us," Sherri said, her voice stuffy.

"I didn't think he would." Ronnie licked his lips. He reached over to touch her hand, but she leaned away, shaking her head.

"What does this guy want with me?" Her relentless questions tore through him.

"I don't know, baby," he lied. He knew exactly what Michael wanted. Ronnie knew because Michael had told him. It's either you or her, young man, *Michael had said.* It's that simple and it's your choice.

But of course, he couldn't tell her that because that would mean coming clean and he couldn't fathom doing that *at this moment. They just needed to find help and Sherri's house was closest.*

He slowed the truck to make the turn into her driveway.

Sherri dug her cell out of her pocket and dialed 911. She said into the phone, "This is Sherri Hensley. We need help!" A pause, then, "We're at my house on Richland Heights Road right outside Black Rock. Can you please send someone out here?"

She listened, then said "Yes, a man is following me and wants to hurt me." More listening, then she said, "I don't know him. His name is Michael Clark," her eyes darted to Ronnie for confirmation and he nodded. She paused, then said, "Yes, I'm with my boyfriend, Ronnie Castle." She chewed nervously on a fingernail then said, "Thank you. Please hurry!" She dropped the phone on the truck seat as he stopped abruptly.

"What'd they say?" he asked.

She didn't look at him and spoke as she yanked her door open. "They're sending someone here now."

"Goddamn it, dad's not home." Sherri's eyes gleaned tears and her expression reminded Ronnie of someone lost. It was her father's consoling she sought now, not Ronnie's. His jaw clenched as he wrapped his arms around her. She twisted away and opened the front door. They both hustled inside and locked the door behind them.

Sherri said, "It'll take them at least ten minutes to get here. You think that man's out there, that he followed us here?"

"I don't know. He's close," Ronnie said and thought, I wish it was just a man. "Real close. I saw him when we came out of the school." Ronnie would never forget that; Michael standing at the edge of the parking lot, gawking at him, then Michael pointed at his own wrist, the place where a watch would normally lay, and mouthed the words, it's time.

Sherri said, "How will we know?" Her gaze shifted to the window. "What's he driving?"

Ronnie shrugged. He didn't know. He wasn't sure that Michael drove anything at all.

Her eyes narrowed and settled on him. Did she think he was full of shit?

"Listen," he said, his words suddenly feeling wrong and silly. There's no way any of this made sense to her. It wouldn't make sense to anyone unless they knew what Michael had said. "I'm not lying about this. He told me he wanted to hurt you. That he was going to hurt you. I can't let that happen." Ronnie shuffled to Sherri who slunk away from him as if he carried the plague. Was she pissed? Dumb question. Of course she is. You're scaring the shit out of her. He asked, "Do you guys have a gun in here anywhere?"

Her mouth dropped open. "Are you serious?"

He nodded.

She crossed her arms, as if cold, and said, "We have a shotgun in here." She led the way into the first bedroom and Ronnie followed feeling scolded, like a puppy who'd shit on the carpet.

Less than two minutes later, as Sherri handed the gun to Ronnie and he checked that it was loaded, a dog started barking outside. Ronnie looked at Sherri and she gazed back at him; her eyes wide.

They hurried out into the dining room.

"He's here." Ronnie stuffed spare shotgun shells into his pocket and dropped two of them on the kitchen counter.

Sherri's eyes shot to the window. "The police are on their way."

A crash boomed outside and the house shook, rattling glass. Sherri's face stiffened and she said, "What was that?"

Ronnie caught shadowed movement outside the front window, the lumbering gait as Michael closed in. The massive wings expanding and Michael's roar. The dogs surrounded him, charging the house, and Sherri's voice, "Oh my god... oh my god!"

And in that moment, he almost said, *I'm so sorry. It's all my fault.* His chest ached and he hated himself. He would tell her everything once she was safe. Just get her safe.

"Call the police again! See where they are," he said. She didn't respond. She swiped her eyes and nervously shook her left hand.

Finally, she said, "What if my dad comes home and that... thing... is out there?"

He felt small and wrong. Tell her.

"He'll be okay." Ronnie said. "Michael only kills what he came for. Now call the police." He forced himself to add, "Please, Sherri."

She asked, "How do you know that?"

He checked the back-door window and didn't see anything out there. Looking back on this moment, as Ronnie would do in the years to come, he wished to God he'd have kept driving into town, straight to the sheriff's office. In nightmare after nightmare, he'd repeat the same, wretched mistake that only the alcohol would let him forget.

Sherri didn't move and glared at him. "How do you know that, Ronnie? How could you possibly know that?"

He caught her gaze and the words *because Michael told me* danced precariously close to his lips. But he'd explain after she was safe.

She turned away from him, her eyes puffy and red. She dug her phone out of her back pocket. Ronnie peered out the front window. The afternoon sun hung lazily, hardly giving way to the slightest breeze. Huge trees stood motionless, as if in a painting. The woods beyond were silent.

She tapped the buttons and as she pressed the phone to her ear, she said to him, "You're lying to me."

Ronnie had no idea how she could possibly be so focused on him right now, but the guilt she induced tore at his insides.

Outside the door, a deep and thundering voice boomed, "Ronnie!"

Ronnie watched, unable to tear his eyes away as dread consumed him. Oh Jesus, Ronnie thought, oh Jesus… it's here.

"You can't run, Ronnie. It's time to choose." Then Michael banged on the door and one of the pictures on the wall fell and shattered.

Sherri cried out. Why did we stop here, he thought, we should've kept going! Where are the damned cops?

Ronnie grabbed the phone from Sherri's hand and she gaped at him.

"Taylor County Sheriff," a female voice answered.

"We called 911 a few minutes earlier! Where's the police?" His voice trembled and his hand shook.

Sherri paced in the dining room, glaring out the front window. She chewed viciously on her fingernails.

The woman asked. "Who is this?"

"It's Ronnie Castle. My girlfriend Sherri called you a few minutes ago… Someone is trying to kill us!" Ronnie huffed as Sherri stood next to the window, gazing out. He yelled to her, "Get away from the goddamn window!" She snapped back as if the glass tried to sting her.

"One sec," the woman on the phone said, followed by excruciating silence, and Ronnie waited, gripping the phone so tight that his fingers ached. Finally, she came back. "Ronnie?"

"Yeah."

"Sheriff said they're on their way. Should be there within a few minutes. Are you still at the Hensley house?"

"Yeah," Ronnie answered. A few minutes seemed like forever.

"Are the people that are after you in the house with you?" she asked.

"No. Not yet." He felt like a mouse in a test lab; in control of nothing.

"Is Sherri Hensley with you?"

"Yes, she's here!"

"Is the person chasing you armed?"

"No." He didn't think so.

"Do you know who it is?"

Ronnie hesitated, then lied, "No."

"Okay, I want you to…"

Ronnie dropped the phone as the front door crashed in and Michael stepped inside. "Time to pay up, Ronnie." The smell of rot wafted through the house and he retched. "Guess you made your choice."

Ronnie clambered away and ducked behind the counter. He listened, frozen in place, unable to block out the horrid sounds of scuffling and screaming as Michael grabbed Sherri and dragged her out of the house and away forever.

And Ronnie cowered there hiding, his mouth dropped open, slobber drooled, and his sobs echoed. I'm sorry, I'm sorry, I'm sorry…

.   .   .   .   .   .

A voice, muffled and hoarse, "Hey! You need to get the hell outta here."

Ronnie's eyes snapped open and he stared at a dingy white ceiling. The shower room at Ned's Truck Stop offered little more than the stink of mildew and old soap. His chest heaved and sweat coated his forehead. His first reaction was to yell out, but he couldn't draw enough breath to speak.

Sherri. Oh god, I'm sorry.

"What the fuck ya doin'?" Someone stepped into the shower room. A thin-haired man, older. The man's shoes squeaked on the tile floor. "You ain't allowed to sit in here, dipshit."

"Jesus," Ronnie muttered. "Water's shut off at my place and I needed to clean up a little. What time is it?" He blinked and gazed at the man. The tag on his shirt said: Dave, Assistant Manager.

"You goddamn bums ain't supposed to sleep in here, ya know," Dave sneered at him. "Get the hell out or I'm callin' the cops." Dave shook his head and left the shower room, and Ronnie heard him mumbling on his way out, "I'm callin' the cops, so you'd best get out," and then the door shut, leaving him in sudden and wonderful silence.

He heaved himself up and lingered there. He'd considered a few times that he should've gotten Sherri out of town, but he knew in his heart it wouldn't have done any good. Michael would have hunted him down wherever they went.

Michael's words from fifteen years ago, "It's simple, Ronnie. You or her. Make your choice. Did you really think you'd get away with it?"

Yes, Ronnie admitted to himself, he thought he'd gotten away with...

His heart fluttered and for a horrible moment, he thought it might stop beating. *Gotta get moving, just gotta get moving. Gotta get it started to get it done*, his dad used to say.

He checked his pocket and felt the metal crucifix in there, then breathed a sigh of relief. At least he still had that. And he had a few bucks left. What he hadn't spent on booze and smokes, anyway.

He lit a cigarette and smoked it in the shower stall. Dave might get even more pissed, or the cops might show up before he was done, but damn it, *I just need to get my mind straight; plan my next move.* He stuck the cigarette between his lips and pulled in the smoke.

He relived the day Sherri was taken from him every day of his life, but in his own distorted version, he bravely launches himself from behind that kitchen counter, hands raised, and saying, *Take me! Take me, you sonofabitch, and leave her alone!* And Michael turns to him as Sherri's confused gaze falls upon Ronnie, her savior, and Michael grabs *him* and drags *him* away leaving Sherri safely behind.

But life's a bitch and there are no do-overs. We're always the heroes of our own stories, aren't we? Of our own bullshit, more like it.

The cigarette burned down to the filter and he dropped it onto the shower floor and stepped on it, twisting the toe of his shoe until it was good and out. He glanced around to see if that bottle of Jack Daniels he'd purchased last night might still be sitting somewhere. *Just a small sip to get my mind straight.*

But no such luck. He wondered if they sold any liquor here at the truck stop then chuckled dryly; a truck stop that sold whiskey to truck drivers.

What the hell time was it, anyway?

He stood and stretched, then picked up his few belongings – a small, canvas bag and long-sleeved shirt, and shuffled out of the shower stall and into the truck stop lobby. A clock over the door read 9:40 AM; later than he guessed.

He made his way to the front doors and trudged out into the early morning sun. Thank God he was outside. The fresh air helped. And thank God he hadn't seen Dave while strolling through there.

He cast his eyes to the horizon, in the direction of Black Rock. It wasn't that far away. A mere forty-five-minute car ride.

Could it really be happening to someone else now, fifteen-years later? In the same goddamned little town? What were the odds?

Jack Snider acted clueless when Ronnie had told him, *ask them what they did to deserve it.*

Someone had a secret to tell, that was for damn sure. The question was who.

But another innocent girl being taken sparked rage and if Jack Snider was right, that Michael was back in Black Rock and this shit was happening again, that meant Ronnie had a chance to see that sonofabitch again.

And this time, he'd kill it. He'd kill it or die trying.

He popped four Motrin into his mouth, chugged a drink of water, and then started to walk in the direction of Black Rock.

Time to atone. Time to make things right.

Chapter 21

Dead leaves swirled across Donna Johnson's living room carpet. The once clean, shaggy surface was now tracked with mud and grime, dank with mildew. The stench of rot infested the air.

Benjamin stood motionless in front of the dark television, his arms folded across his chest, staring blankly as the cool breeze wisped the curtains and circled the leaves around his feet. The gears of his ancient mind creaked slowly, in no rush, and he was pleased. He knew the hearts of men and what choice the preacher would make.

Benjamin whispered to himself in the silence of the room, "I always play my part. My purpose. To make things even." He sought no inner peace. Who needs it? These weren't *his* choices. The choices he gave these men – to choose courage or weakness; those were choices they brought on themselves. Truth be told, he kind of liked it when they proved themselves weak – it meant an added prize. Oddly enough though, he *craved* the preacher's girl like a ravenous animal craves meat; more than just a hunger, far more, and Benjamin wondered if she hadn't become an obsession, perhaps a dangerous one. He chalked it up to anticipation – he knew her father would choose to save himself, thus sacrificing his daughter to Benjamin. And what the preacher didn't realize was that not choosing was also a choice. And if the preacher wanted to go that route, it still worked out in the end.

Benjamin hated people like the preacher; two-faced, self-righteous cowards who always believed they could get away with their sin, hauling around baggage they didn't know they had; that age old addiction to sex. Nothing but animals undeserving of the divine love bestowed upon them.

Fools.

They stank. Had he not had Jesse England deliver that newspaper to the preacher's house, who knows what may have happened. That's all it took to set chaos in motion. Benjamin cracked a crooked smile thinking, *that and a forwarded email.*

Outside the living room window, the Friday morning sunrise splashed the trees. A new day. *The* day. Benjamin licked his lips. He dug in his pocket and pulled out his cell phone.

"You can use a friend, sweet thing," Benjamin said as he dialed Abby's number. "Daddy's time has run out."

Chapter 22

A stalker? I have a stalker?

It explained her parent's oddness lately. Well, sort of. But hearing her dad explain that some weird old guy might be following her around had opened up a wealth of other questions. *Why me?*

Abby knew this wasn't the only thing either. A coldness lived between her parents now that had not been there before. A cavern capable of swallowing her family whole. And most irritating was how fake her mom and dad were about it.

Like she couldn't tell when they were fighting, like everything's hunky-dory and they're just one big happy family. It's why living in this world sucked sometimes; why people like dogface Pearson tried to act like her dad and then preach about how she's not applying herself. It's why living in *this* house was like living in a convent, because everything had to be perfect. She was a round peg shoved into a square hole.

She sat up, stretched, and hopped off her bed. She'd slept decent for a change. God only knew how *that* happened, but first thing this morning, her parent's arguing seeped through her door and woke her. "It makes no sense!" Her mom's voice. Then, Dad's voice, "I didn't plan it!"

God, they were lame sometimes.

She stepped over to the window and glanced out. Nothing unusual. Last night she'd spotted a police car driving past, but nothing today. No creepy old guys either. When she'd asked her dad why someone might be stalking her (though her dad had never actually used the word *stalker*), he'd smiled in a way that looked totally fake to her, and said, *probably some weirdo who knows me, knows I'm a preacher here, and is trying to cause trouble. Just be aware, sweetie, and stick around here for now.*

Really? Just be aware? She'd thought, *this is kind of a big deal, dad,* but didn't say anything. Maybe it wasn't.

Guys creeped her out on so many levels. She'd started to wonder if she even liked guys. If she'd *ever* like them.

Honestly, it angered her more than anything. Everything about it angered her; both the creepy guy having nothing better to do than follow her around and that her parents provided such sketchy details.

If Abby had it her way, she'd definitely –

Mom's voice cut through the door like a razor, "You disgust me! Stay away from me!"

Abby froze. She'd never heard anything like that before. Ever. A tingle of dread spread through her. Maybe the issue was bigger than she thought. Worse. A world where her parents fought was as foreign as the surface of Jupiter and she didn't want to deal with that.

What if things kept getting worse?

Mom's feet banged on the hallway floor as she stomped past the door. Abby pictured her scowled face and clenched fists; her house-robe trailing behind her like the cape of Darth Vader.

"Please talk to me about this." Her dad. His weak words deepened her fear. His pleading voice. A desperate certainty, as if whatever had been done could not be undone, and the result was a gaping, festering wound. A coldness that she'd never experienced.

She tiptoed to her door and pressed her ear closer. Dad was still out there in the hallway.

"I was a dumb, drunk teenager, Linda."

What? What on earth were they fighting about?

Deep in her heart, she knew this was something bad. Real bad. She listened helplessly as it went on, a dreadful weight growing inside her. Dad said, "I know that's a lousy excuse, but I don't know what else to say."

"That's your argument? You were a teenager and that's it? So, you get a free pass because you were just a drunk teenager?"

A long, uncomfortable pause ensued. *I need to do something.* But what?

She could yank the door open and yell *Stop*. But then what? She squeezed her eyes shut. *Say something, dad, say anything.* She wanted to scream it through the door. What was wrong with him?

Mom said, "I'm done." Abby's breath stopped. "I can't be around you and I don't want Abby around you either."

A cold chill raced through her. *I can't be around you?*

Divorce.

The word had a sticky, foul taste. It couldn't be. Not her parents. They loved each other. Stop jumping to conclusions! Open this stupid door and ask, *what's going on*. But she couldn't.

Her mom's footsteps echoed down the stairs and she was gone. Her dad still stood out there, alone. What the heck was he doing? Then he came back from the stairs and creaked the board outside her door. Terror gripped her as she pictured him suddenly opening her door and then she'd have to talk to him about uncomfortable shit. But his footsteps finally echoed away and his bedroom door closed.

She released a breath she didn't even realize she'd been holding. *Oh. My. God.* She stepped back to the edge of her bed and plopped down. She tucked a strand of hair behind her ear. She needed to talk to someone.

She slipped her phone out from under her pillow and noticed she had two text messages. Both from Michael.

First message: Hey, you there?

Second message: Can't wait to see you tonight!

Abby grimaced. Did she want to mess with him right now? He'd be great to talk to, but this issue felt more private, almost sacred. But she needed someone.

Besides, Michael would be a welcome distraction.

No way she'd try to explain her family's crisis in a text message, if she tried to explain at all.

The face on her phone lit up immediately with Michael's number flashing across the front. She didn't answer it and let it buzz silently, then texted: I'll call you right back.

She bounced off the bed, pulled on a pair of sweats, and snuck out the door. She'd call Michael back from the garage, where they could talk in private.

.　.　.　.　.

He answered on the first ring.

"Hey," he said.

"Hey." She licked her lips.

"You okay?"

His question hung in her ear like a magic riddle. *No! I'm not okay! My parents sound like they hate each other. My school never wants me there again. And some creepy old guy is stalking me.* She said, "Well, things are a little weird here, but I'm okay."

"You sound sad or something."

"Tired, I guess. I just got up." Tell him something. She glanced around the garage. What if *the stalker* was hiding in here? Not sure why, but she suddenly wished Michael hadn't called her. She actually didn't want to be talking to him.

She asked, "What are you doing up this early?" Lame question.

"I always get up early. Just one of those people."

She shuffled to the door and flicked on the lights. The windows didn't let in enough light. *Maybe I should not have come out here.* No one knew she was out here in this gray and lifeless place where terror lurked in dark shadows.

"Hey," he said, "Are you excited about tonight? I can't wait. I was thinking we could go to Lafayette for a burger and then catch a movie."

"You know," she twisted her hair in her fingers as she spoke, "I don't think I can." She hated that all this stuff had to be happening now, like planning a major sleepover and then someone's mom gets the flu.

"What? Why not?" he asked.

She sensed something in his voice. *Disappointment? Agitation?*

"Like I said, things are a little weird around here."

"You serious?"

"Yeah."

"Getting away will help. Take your mind off things."

She shrugged and said, "Just too many things. Parents fighting and stuff like that."

"About you?" He seemed genuinely interested and she loved that.

"I don't think so." Her dad's words echoed, *I was a dumb, drunk teenager*. No way it was about her.

"Well, maybe it ain't that serious."

"Maybe not," she said.

"People fight."

"I guess." She flipped her hair back. It felt good to talk. "I've also got some weirdo following me around."

"Really?"

"Yeah."

"Lucky you."

"Aren't I lucky." She smiled. "Creeps me out."

"I can come over and hang out with you?"

Weird, but now she actually did want him to come hang out with her. To just be here. "It's got my parents freaked out. They're not letting me leave the house."

"I get it."

"Maybe another night. There's just too much going on right now."

"How about I just pull up on the street in front of your house? I can say hi to your parents. We can just stand by my car in plain sight from the front window and shoot the breeze."

Shoot the breeze?

"It'd be fun," he said.

"I don't know. Not the best time to introduce you to my parents."

"C'mon," he said. "I've been looking forward to tonight for three days now. Plus, I'd feel way better knowing you're okay."

She scrunched her nose and let the thought bounce around her head. So many things to go wrong.

"We'll be in plain sight. Everyone will see us the whole time. I'll come in and meet your folks, if you want."

Folks? Something troubled her, but she had no idea what.

"Oh yeah," she chuckled. "They'd love that. I'm not even allowed to date yet."

Just then, she caught the reflection of the front door of the house opening and closing. She peeked out the small window facing the house and spotted her dad standing at the edge of the porch. Could he tell the light was on in here? His hands were shoved into the pockets of his lounge pants, his head hung low, and he looked shockingly old.

"I gotta go," she whispered into the phone.

"So I'll see you tonight?"

She hesitated. She needed to end the call. Now. But saying *I told you I couldn't* felt like things may drag out more. Like he may not take no for an answer and then she'd have to hang up on him if her dad decided to come in here. She blurted, "Sure," and shook her head. She'd have to figure it out. "But park a few houses down from mine so that no one gets weird about it until I tell you to pull up."

"Okay, see you tonight."

"Yes, yes," she said, "okay." That's when her dad shifted his gaze, ever so slightly, and stared straight at the window she was peeking out of. She quickly hung up the phone and stuffed it into her pocket. *Good god.* But he turned away, apparently not noticing anything.

He looked so defeated and broken; so unlike how she'd ever seen him before. Like watching a stranger.

Oh dad.

But hey, she had Michael to think about and that was good. Wasn't it? To finally meet him in person, even if it was just standing out front on a sidewalk. But something nagged at her. Something he'd said. She couldn't put a finger on it. Maybe not what he said, but *how* he said it? God, everything had her freaked out. Every little thing.

"Just in your head, crazy girl," she said and forced a smile.

Of course, she'd think of it later, after it was too late; that bothersome thing he'd said.

Chapter 23

Jack unfolded his arms and eased himself onto a worn bench behind the Taylor County Home. He gripped the edge with a trembling hand to keep from losing his balance. "Christ ah'mighty," he huffed. He tore his eyes away from the bloodied spot where he'd found Wayne Tillwood last night.

He just needed to sit here a bit. Maybe a long bit.

A tad chilly this morning.

He keyed the radio snapped to his shoulder harness and said, "Howard, you still out here?"

A quick blurt of static, then Howard's voice, "Yep."

Jack glanced around and didn't see anyone. An hour ago, the place crawled with people. He lacked the energy to stand up and take a stroll to the front. He said, "Can you meet me out back of the County Home? I'm sittin' back here."

"You got it."

He refolded his arms and gazed across the back pasture of dead grass, still barren from Winter. Trees had yet to sprout leaves. A pack of fucking dogs roamed out there, somewhere.

"Christ ah'mighty," he said again and closed his eyes.

A minute later, Howard Laughlin, another of Jack's deputies, stepped around the corner and walked solemnly with his hands stuffed deep into his pockets. Howard's gray hair peeked from beneath the brim of his hat and the lines of his face seemed considerably deeper today.

He reached Jack and stood there gazing at the blood caked grass.

"How in the hell did this happen?" Jack said.

Howard shook his head and shifted his gaze toward Jack. "You okay?"

"Fucked if I know. Are you?"

Howard shrugged.

Jack folded his arms across his chest and spoke as he glared out across the pasture. "This remind you of anything?"

Howard nodded, "I was thinking the same thing."

Howard had been Jack's partner that day out at the old gas station. *What a mess.*

"Yep," Jack pursed his lips. "A whole goddamned pack of dogs, remember? We had to clear the damned things out with shotguns. Remember that?"

"Oh yeah." Howard nodded again, "That old gas station out by the four-lane. Scared the shit out of me."

"Me too," Jack said. He'd never forget having to go into that abandoned gas station with flashlights to hunt those damn things. The growls in the dark. "If you recall, that was the same time the Hensley girl went missing."

"Yeah, it was," Howard glanced at the ground.

Jack recalled his meeting with Ronnie Castle yesterday; of seeing what Ronnie had become and Ronnie's reaction when Jack told him what was happening here. *You didn't believe me.* Jack ran his tongue across his teeth. "Someone sure as hell took her."

"Yeah, I know you always thought that Castle boy had something to do with it," Howard said.

"Or he knew who did."

"Yep." Howard pulled his hands out of his pocket and crossed them. "Ya goin' somewhere with this?"

Jack leaned forward and rested his forearms on his thighs. He wished he had Ronnie Castle here with him right now to talk to about this. "I don't know. Maybe." He considered keeping quiet until he actually had something concrete to go on, but he also needed to get this out. See how crazy it sounded to someone else. Ronnie sure as hell wouldn't think it was crazy. "Doesn't it seem odd that we've got this Benjamin character stalking the preacher's daughter and now we've got wild dogs again?"

Howard shrugged. "I suppose so," he spoke nonchalantly, but his eyes narrowed as they always did when he started thinking and putting pieces together. "But, I reckon a guy could use whatever name he wants; a name like Clark. But why would he be *here* again?"

Part of the mystery revolved around that very question. "Hell, why was he here the first time?"

Howard scrunched his eyebrows. "Damned if I know. We all assumed to stalk that girl."

"Yeah, but Ronnie Castle knew something. I know it, Howard, plain as I know my own shoe size, that kid *knew* a hell of a lot more than he let on." Jack grimaced and glared at the spot where Wayne died. "Like the fact he raped that girl."

"That wasn't proven," Howard quickly added. "She never pressed charges, nor did her folks."

"Yeah, but we both know that's because her parents where religious assholes who didn't want the attention of it." Jack remembered having those conversations as well.

Howard said, "Not sure what all this has to do with anything, Jack; I ain't sure I agree with ya on Ronnie. They were both young. Ronnie was a good kid for the most part, from what I remember, that is. Why's this comin' up now?"

Jack clasped his hands together and said, "Do me a favor; do a little diggin' on that preacher, Thomas Loggins. See if he's got anything in his closet."

"What's this got to do with Wayne gettin' killed by dogs?"

"Goddamn it, Howard, just do it," Jack snapped, then said, more calmly, "Please."

Howard nodded. "Alright, Jack. I'll look." They both remained silent for several long seconds, then Howard asked, "Anything else?"

Jack shook his head. "Nah, that's it for now. Make it a priority. I wanna know."

"You got it." Howard paused, then asked, "What are you gonna do?"

"Try and find out where all these fucking dogs came from. By the looks of things, there's a bunch of 'em. Wayne emptied his clip." Jack rubbed his chin. "Think I'll start by checking up in Black Rock at that old gal's place, Donna Johnson. Daisy knows her and said she had a shit load of dogs up there."

Howard stood for a moment, as if about to say something, then turned and headed back around the building. Jack sat alone, again, staring at the dried blood.

He scanned the pasture and woods beyond. Goddamned dogs. Somewhere out there, most likely huddled up in some abandoned barn somewhere, or perhaps just huddled together in a pack.

He'd dispatched last night to everyone in the area and informed them that a pack of dangerous dogs were loose and to stay clear of the woods. Two dozen volunteers were out hunting for the damn things right now and the State Police agreed to help in the search as well, though no one had shown up yet.

And then Patricia Haddenfield called into the station this morning, distressed and ranting that her son, Will, was missing and that all these dogs running around had her terrified. Tom Haddenfield volunteered to go out hunting, but wanted to stay close to home, just in case Will might be out there, somewhere. Jack didn't know what to think of that whole situation – he prayed to God that Will Haddenfield hadn't ran into those dogs, but the way things were going, who knew?

Shit was unraveling in a hurry and he couldn't slow it down.

Chapter 24

Thomas awoke to silence and gazed at the ceiling. For a hopeful moment, he thought he might have dreamed everything. Maybe the argument with Linda had only occurred in his head. He'd had dreams like that before and woke up thankful that his world hadn't changed.

He blinked and realized he couldn't recall what day it was. Friday? Had to be.

He frowned lying there at the absurdity of it. The longer he laid there, the more reality sank in, and he wished he could fall back to sleep.

Maybe sleep forever.

The house was silent. No one was talking, at least not that he could hear. Perhaps that was normal in a house where everyone hated each other.

He closed his eyes. How had it came to this?

Me. That's how.

Me.

He considered praying. But praying made him feel hollow. The portrayal of an inauthentic self. We convince ourselves that God forgives all. But does He? There was a time when Thomas thought himself a good man.

Absolution, pastor. That's why I'm here.

But he could do something now. He could stop more bad things from happening. Couldn't he? To protect Abby from whatever this thing was. This thing called Benjamin.

Absolution. *You or your daughter, pastor. Make your choice.*

There had to be another way to deal with Benjamin. Even if Benjamin took him (whatever *that* meant), then could Thomas trust that Abby would be fine, that Benjamin would just disappear? What if Benjamin came back and hurt Abby? Thomas couldn't take that chance. Not in a million years. He'd be abandoning his family.

He placed his hand on his forehead. "Please help me find a better way to deal with this," he whispered.

Information. He needed information. About Benjamin. *What am I dealing with here?* Not a who, but a *what.* And, an even bigger question – *am I the only one?*

Thomas sat up as if summoning a sense of motivation and commitment. *Protect Abby. No matter what.* Even in a world where his family hated him, he'd protect his little girl. It was the only redeeming possibility he had left.

These thoughts as hollow as prayers.

You're no hero.

Linda. I'm so sorry. I don't know how it came to this.

He needed to check that Abby was in her room and that Linda was… well, who knew where Linda was. Down on the sofa, drinking coffee, planning their divorce? If she'd only talk to him. Listen.

To what, that I accidently raped a girl? Jesus.

Time to pay the piper. *The balance is due.*

He hoisted himself off the bed and pulled on a pair of jeans. He plucked a t-shirt off the floor. *The same one I wore yesterday.* Who cares? He put it on and stepped lightly down to Abby's room. Her bedroom door stood cracked open and he pushed it open another inch to see her bed. She wasn't in it.

He opened the door and stepped inside.

"Abby?"

Nothing.

He opened his mouth to yell and then heard the thump of footsteps downstairs. A muffled voice. Then another. Linda and Abby. *Oh, thank God.* He whooshed an exhale.

He strode across Abby's messy room and lifted back the curtain to gaze outside. A police car happened to be driving past right then. His thudding heart slowed to a small gallop and he breathed a huff of relief.

He glanced down at the garage's roof and face, obscured by a tree branch stretching across the yard. He'd prayed in that garage last night and determined he needed help. *I need to call that sheriff this morning.*

And say what?

Maybe the truth?

But first, he wanted to see if he could find out anything on Benjamin. Anything at all.

He left her room and stopped in the hallway, careful not to creak the floor. More muffled talking. He cocked his head and tried to listen, but couldn't make out the words. Oh well, none of his business. Though he couldn't shake the possibility that they might be talking about him.

Focus on something else. Do a little research. See what he could find out. See what he could dig up on that trusted information super-highway; Google.

He continued his stealthy trek to the spare room where his computer lay on a desk like a lonely novel. The seared memory of finding Linda in here reared its ugly head. As he'd stepped in and found her staring at that email. That look on her face with that old newspaper on her lap. The red letters scrawled across... *Stop it!*

He slipped into the chair facing the desk and opened the lid on his laptop to wake the machine up. The computer screen blipped to life as he watched in a fog of jumbled thoughts, waiting patiently for it to finish its routine so he could actually do something with it.

The screen finally reached the "ready" point and he clicked the Chrome icon to fire up a search screen.

He recalled the last time he'd searched Benjamin Clark on the computer. He'd found nothing useful on the name. But he *had* found that article about the teenager and his girlfriend; how she'd been kidnapped.

He typed: Benjamin Clark supernatural

Nothing but a bunch of hits about some weird show called Supernatural.

He rubbed his chin. Damn, he sucked at this. He debated on what to search for. Something more precise. Location maybe? He'd found that last article about the kidnapped girl by googling Black Rock.

He typed: Black Rock, Indiana.

The screen blipped again, then a list of hits listed themselves in blue letters with short descriptions. Most were just generic things like maps, the Black Rock cemetery, or the Taylor County Home. He scrolled down and something caught his eye:

Black Rock Public Library: Black Rock Historical Registry

Hmm. He clicked it and the screen filled with a newspaper article dated June 4th, 1912. *Just a few months after the Titanic sank*, he thought bemusedly. He read it as if in a trance.

23 men gathered at the Black Rock Courthouse for the trial of Samuel Osborne. Osborne was arrested in March, 1911 for rape. Osborne denied the charges and claims the perpetrator kidnapped his only daughter.

Osborne's daughter has never been found and prosecutors believe Osborne may have some responsibility for her death.

The Taylor County prosecutor said, "It is unfortunate that Samuel's infirmity has cost innocent lives, but his claims are preposterous, and only due to his standing in this great community, will we seek leniency in his sentencing, asking the jury to give him a life sentence to the Indiana State Mental Institution in Logansport."

Neighbors of Mr. Osborne continue to support him, stating that a stranger had settled in Black Rock about three months before the girl's disappearance and that prosecutors and the town Constable turned a blind eye to what was happening here.

Thomas rubbed his chin. What did *a stranger had settled in Black Rock about three months before the girl's disappearance* mean? He wished there was more about that.

He clicked back into the search bar and typed in:

History of crimes in Black Rock, Indiana

Good grief. Several articles popped up. Which seemed odd for such a small community. He spotted the one he'd found a few days earlier from The Indianapolis Star titled, *Black Rock Teenager Missing. Father killed in dog attack.* That was the article about the teenage boy and the kidnapped girl.

But there were more. One article was dated March 25th, 1942, titled, *Black Rock suffers loss during time of war*. Another was dated March 12th, 1959, this one titled, *tragedy strikes small community of Black Rock*. The last article was dated April 29th, 2008, titled, *Black Rock tragedy*.

Thomas clicked on the most recent 2008 article *Black Rock tragedy*.

Taylor County sheriff, Dave Lardo, expressed sorrow at the loss of a man's life at the abandoned gas station near highway 63, just outside of Black Rock, Indiana. The deceased man named Lewis Hoskins was killed tragically when attacked by dogs after exiting his vehicle. His wife, Kimberly, daughter Lori, and infant son, Caleb, survived the attack after the sheriff and Deputy Jack Snider arrived and destroyed the animals.

The family was traveling from Florida back to Chicago over Spring Break when they pulled off the highway at the abandoned station for a bathroom stop.

Sheriff Lardo called the incident a tragic loss of life in one of the most horrible days in recent Taylor County history with the abduction of Sherri Hensley occurring on the same day.

Thomas sat back in his chair and moved his hand slowly to his mouth. Fear snaked around his heart. *So much violence.*

"Oh my God," he whispered in the silence. Something was wrong with this place. As if the roots of the town itself had bored themselves into rotted soil. Is this town evil? Haunted somehow?

Shame gripped him. *Or does this town draw evil people toward it?* People like him.

And somehow, Benjamin Clark rested at the center of it all.

Thomas rubbed his temples where a dull throb threatened to engulf his skull. *Tell them, why don't you? Tell them what this man actually told you – tell them the choice he gave you.*

Thomas pictured himself strolling right up to Benjamin and saying defiantly, *take me, you bastard. Leave my daughter out of this.* But doing so answered nothing and left no guarantees. How did Benjamin know about Emily? And what if he did tell Benjamin, *take me*? What did that even mean?

Sure, he could sacrifice himself, but deep down he knew it would do no good. Benjamin would do whatever he set out to do and if something happened to Thomas, then there'd be no one here to protect Abby.

You or your daughter, pastor. Make your choice.

The balance is due.

Yeah, right. No way he was falling for this trickery.

Thomas closed his eyes and prayed. *The prayer of the damned*, he thought. Hear me, my blessed Savior. Thomas needed the light in a world consumed by eternal darkness.

And as the words poured out of him, he felt… nothing. Just words. As if he were praying to a lifeless tree, barren and rotting.

"Lord Jesus," Thomas prayed. He clenched his fist. Is this what it's like when your faith dies? Why was this happening now, in the midst of his collapsing life, his daughter's danger? "Lord Jesus, give me strength."

Nothing.

Perhaps God decided to abandon him.

He clenched his teeth. He hissed the words.

Please.

Thomas opened his eyes and fought the tears that threatened to spill down his face. He whispered, "But God is faithful, He will provide a way out, so that you may stand up under it."

Choose me.

.   .   .   .   .

Abby snuck up the stairs to get a sweater, having just received a text from Michael saying that he would meet her outside. She'd planned to ask her dad, but as young people often do, she decided not to waste the time. He'd just say no anyway. Besides, his door was closed to his study and when the door was closed, he hated to be interrupted.

She thought, *No big deal. I'm going to stand out on the front driveway, for crying out loud, where the cops and everyone can see me standing under that street light.* She then tiptoed back downstairs to the front door and stepped outside, careful to close the door softly behind her.

Chapter 25

Ronnie stood at the corner of Highway 28 and Richland Heights Road, staring at Black Rock, and fighting the urge to turn and run. Chirping birds and the occasional bellow of a hungry cow sparked a familiarity he could do without. Even the air whispered *welcome home* with the scent of smoke from spring yard fires and the awakening winter sleep. Goose bumps pebbled his arms. He closed his eyes.

God almighty, what am I doing here?

Everyone called this intersection Cactus Junction, though he had no idea why, and in a town where change occurred about as often as an ice age, seeing a brand-new gas station struck him as shockingly out of place. It was nothing but a field when he lived here. Miracles never cease.

What else had changed around here? Likely, nothing. Returning to Black Rock would be like stepping back in time. A community of people who still believed life peaked fifty-years ago and the world had gone to shit ever since. He hated this fucking place.

What to do next; that was the question. He didn't want to take another step closer. Everything here haunted him. The mirror he was terrified to look into.

The price of always choosing to save ourselves. *You or her, Ronnie. It's simple. Your balance is due.*

Sherri. Her screams echoed as Michael dragged her away.

While I stood there and watched.

He clamped his eyes closed.

He slipped his small bag off his shoulder and gently settled it onto the dirty asphalt of Richland Heights Road. It'd be dark soon and far too cold to be standing out here. His grand plan of reaching Black Rock and calling Jack Snider sounded better before leaving Lafayette. Shit was getting too real now.

Ronnie recalled Jack's defeated look while leaned against that dumpster. The way Jack's eyes had cast down when Ronnie yelled, *you didn't believe me.* No argument. No defense. Acceptance.

Is that what made me come here? That look on Jack's face? *Indeed, that's exactly why I'm here.* Because something changed Jack's mind. And Ronnie needed to know what it was.

Ronnie squatted down, opened the bag, and dug through it carefully. Just a little nip was all he needed. He set the bottle of Jim Beam on the aged asphalt of the road, popped the cap, and took two gratifying gulps to steady the nerves. A slow, calming warmth flowed through him, splashing into his belly and cascading out through his arms and legs, even dissolving the tingle in his fingertips.

Much better. Now he could get his mind straight, which was really all he needed to do. Thank the lord he no longer smelled like a shithouse and his clothes were decent, courtesy of the good Pastor Gregory. He sipped another quick nip from the bottle, then twisted the cap back on and stuffed the bottle into his bag.

The sun had set. He hoisted the bag over his shoulder.

Okay, time to get this shit over with.

. . . . . .

The sight of this new gas station still awed him as he made his way across the pavement. The bright lights of gas pumps, the yellow and red SHELL sign on the front, was like discovering a UFO parked in the desert. So damn weird.

Only one car sat at the pumps where a heavy woman stood pumping gas. She peered at him as he trotted across the parking lot. People here don't like strangers, never have. *But I'm not a stranger.* Nope, you're the guy everyone thinks killed Sherri Hensley. The guy who saw monsters.

Which means they'd like him even less.

He focused on the front doors and shuffled inside. A little ding echoed as he stepped through. An older woman, forties or early fifties perhaps, sat behind the cash register reading a newspaper. She glanced up nonchalantly, then went back to whatever she was reading. He didn't recognize her.

Eventually though, someone would recognize him.

"Help ya?" the woman sitting behind the cash register asked without looking up.

He glanced at her nervously. He hated talking to people. He cleared his throat and said, "Yeah."

She stared at him, then scrunched her eyebrows and asked, "Alright, what do ya need?"

"Uhm," he scratched the corner of his mouth and avoided her gaze.

The door dinged and the heavy woman who'd been pumping gas walked inside with that hateful look still etched on her face. Ronnie didn't like that woman, not one little bit, and he wanted out of this place. Everyone here hated him. *You just need a sip*, his mind whispered, *just a sip from the bottle to get your mind straight.*

"You want anything or not?" the woman behind the counter asked him.

I should not have come in here.

The heavy woman glared. The cashier glared.

The cashier shrugged and turned her attention to the heavy woman. "You're comin' through here late," the cashier said.

"They got us workin' twelve hour shifts," the heavy woman rubbed a chubby hand across her forehead. "It's a sweat shop down there."

"Don't know why you're still there."

"The money's good and I can sure as hell use it." The heavy woman handed over a twenty and the cashier took it and stuffed it into the register drawer. Then the heavy woman said, "I'm gonna go home and get some sleep."

When the heavy woman finally finished, she bid her farewell, and walked out the door, leaving Ronnie alone once again in the wake of that little ding over the door.

"I guess it's your turn again," the cashier said and she peered at him. "You ever decide anything?" When he still didn't answer, she shook her head and said, "You ain't from around here, are ya?"

He decided to lie. "Nah," he mumbled.

She raised her eyebrows and said, "Well, be careful if you're out walkin'. There's a pack of wild dogs runnin' around. Heard they killed a deputy early this mornin' out at the County Home."

"Wild dogs?"

She nodded with pursed lips.

Ronnie shook his head and said, "This might sound strange, but could you call the sheriff to come get me?"

Her eyes narrowed. "Why don't you call 'im?"

"I don't have a phone."

"Sheriff Snider?"

"Yeah."

She eyed him, then asked, "What's your name?"

"Ronnie Castle."

"Castle?" her eyes, perceptive and leery, crawled over him. Perhaps she recognized the name. In a small town, everyone's bound to know you in some way.

She stepped away cautiously to make the call.

. . . . .

Sheriff Snider arrived twenty minutes later as Ronnie sat in the small dining area of the gas station's lobby. The flimsy plastic chairs and Formica tables, along with a floor badly in need of sweeping, felt right at home. Like being in Happy Harry's diner.

He stared out the windows and watched Jack Snider unfurl from the police cruiser like a giant awakening from a deep slumber. It was almost full dark, but in the station's outside lights, Ronnie caught Jack's eyes lock onto him, peering through the window. *Hope he doesn't hate me for leaving yesterday*, Ronnie thought.

He expected his nerves to jitter as Jack approached the door, but they didn't. An odd calmness swept over him as he watched the sheriff walk through the doors, those eyes, always quick and knowing, finding him immediately. Jack's lips pursed. He sauntered over to Ronnie's table and eased himself into a plastic chair. Ronnie glanced at the cashier. She watched Jack enter then went back to her paper.

"Wasn't expectin' ya," Jack said and removed his hat. He placed it on the table.

"Yeah," Ronnie said.

Jack nodded. "I'm surprised."

"Yeah, sorry about yesterday. Freaked me out when you showed up." Ronnie shifted his gaze down at his plastic plate of food, now containing only chicken bones and the smeared remnants of ketchup.

Jack said, "I don't blame you. Like I say, I'm surprised ya came." Jack folded his arms over his chest.

Ronnie shook his head slowly. "What choice did I have?" He lifted a quick finger and scratched at his ear. "If that asshole is back, I want to find him."

Jack glared at him. "If you're serious, which I'd guess you are since you're here, I can use your help. Let's get down to it." Jack tapped a finger on the table. "What do you think he is?"

"Michael?"

Jack nodded. "Michael, Benjamin, whatever. Doesn't matter what name he uses."

Ronnie raised his eyebrows feeling as if he were sitting here in a dream where he might wake up at any moment. A nip of Beam never sounded better than right now. He leveled his eyes with Jack. "You're never going to believe me."

"Try me."

Ronnie shifted his gaze down and shook his head. He remembered how this went all those years ago outside the Black Rock police station, the night Sherri was abducted, and Jack Snider hissing into his ear, *I know you, you little shit, and even if you didn't kidnap her, you know who did and you know why.*

But Jack looked different now. Fifteen-years is a long, long time.

"I think he's some kind of demon," Ronnie said and felt hot tears welling under his eyelids. Goddamn it, he wished tears wouldn't happen. He waited for Jack to bellow laughter.

"What makes you think that?" Jack's eyes never smiled.

Ronnie shifted his gaze out the window and stared into the darkness outside. He'd come all this way. He was back in Black Rock. He was here for Michael (or Benjamin now, apparently). Another chance to avenge Sherri.

Sherri was why he was here. For her.

And to do that, he needed to come clean. Once and for all.

He turned to Jack Snider and said, "Well, for one, you were right, I did lie to you."

Jack leaned forward and rested his forearms on the table.

"You remember how I told you and Sheriff Lardo that Michael threatened Sherri?"

Jack nodded.

Ronnie scooted his empty food tray away and placed his hands on the table. His palms sweat but he didn't tremble. "Well, it was a little more than that. I met Michael about a week before he took Sherri."

Jack's eyes narrowed.

"I walked home from work that night. Michael was at the park, just standing in the dark. Scared the shit out of me." Ronnie recalled the shadowed shape and how the shape had startled him. "Michael had a hat on, like one of those old gangsters hats they wear in the movies."

"A fedora." Jack leaned back and crossed his arms.

"Yeah, whatever it is. And a long jacket. But I could tell he was old. He didn't look threatening. Then he said to me, *I need to speak with you Ronald Castle.*"

Jack glared him, but kept quiet. Ronnie's heart beat harder as he considered what he was about to say. A secret set loose.

Ronnie shifted in his seat. "I wasn't sure what to do, ya know. I mean, he knew my name. Then he says to me, *Sherri Hensley is in danger.*" Ronnie clasped his hands together on the table, both slick with sweat. "Then Michael said to me, *come sit a moment, this won't take long.* So I did. I loved Sherri and if she was in trouble, I wanted to know about it."

Jack nodded, but still maintained that steely glare.

Ronnie kept going. "So Michael says to me, *Did you really think you could get away with it?*" Ronnie swallowed hard. "I asked Michael what he meant by that. Michael said to me, *rape, young man. Two-years ago you raped a girl. Don't act coy.*" Ronnie waited for Jack to react, though he had no idea what that reaction may be. But Jack still said nothing. Ronnie continued, "So I just stared at him, ya know, I had no idea what to say.

There's two kinds of rapists in this world, Ronnie, Michael said, *the ones who are blatant and violent. The cops typically take care of them. But then there's the ones who get away with it. People like you. Do you know what you've taken from that girl?* I stammered that I'd done no such thing, but I also remember that I just started shaking so bad and I felt something; something weird. Like, I knew this guy was something more than just an old man, ya know."

"This why you think he's a demon?" Jack asked.

"Well," Ronnie nodded and said, "Yeah, but there's more to it. Then Michael told me, *my name is Michael Clark and I'm here to make things right. Your balance is due, young man. It's time to pay the piper.* I told him again that I didn't rape anyone, that he had the wrong guy, but he waved me off." Ronnie stopped and took a deep breath, hating this next part. "Then Michael told me right there, *I'm going to give you something you didn't give that girl. A choice. I'm going to take either you, or that girl you love named Sherri, out of this world forever.* Michael held his hand up to me in a fist and then popped it open, spreading his fingers, and said, *poof, just like that, one of you will no longer exist in this world.* And then I just stared at him like an idiot."

Jack asked him, "Did you rape someone? Was Michael right?"

Ronnie leaned back and gazed at the ceiling. "I knew you'd ask me that." He shook his head, wondering at what point Jack would walk out of here. "Technically, yes. I know this'll sound like bullshit, but I was drunk at a party and there were a million people there. This girl asked me to her room and I went." Ronnie kept his voice low. No need for the cashier to hear this shit. "I was so goddamned drunk that night."

"Like now?" Jack sneered. "I can smell it a mile away."

Ronnie shook his head. "I had no idea she was fifteen. I swear to God I don't remember her telling me anything like that, if she ever did. I swear to Christ I didn't know!"

Jack kept his glare locked on Ronnie's face. "You ever tell Sherri Hensley about that?"

"Of course not," Ronnie said. "I wasn't even dating Sherri when that happened."

Jack nodded and his face softened. "So what happened with Michael after he told you to make the choice?"

"I didn't know what to say to him, ya know. And then he… well, this next part will sound even crazier, but Michael started to change into something while sitting there."

Jack cocked his head. "He turned into something?"

"I know how crazy that sounds, but he did. It was like he grew wider and his face stretched into something with teeth. I bawled and asked him to please go away. *Your choice*, Michael said to me, *your balance is due. It's time for absolution!* And I sat there crying like a fucking baby alone in that park. And then, it was like I woke up or something, because I was sitting there by myself at that table. No one else around." Ronnie felt a cold tear slip from his right eye and slither down his cheek.

"So, you think he's a demon?" Jack asked.

"Have you heard anything I've said?" Ronnie huffed a dry chuckle, "Yes, I think he's a demon."

"Sounds like he thinks he's doing the world a service. Maybe he's an angel."

"Yeah, well, if he's an angel, then he's a fucked-up angel."

Jack nodded and said, "Can't argue with that."

Silence dangled between them. Jack's jaw clenched, unclenched, and he tapped a finger against his arm. The door dinged from across the dining area as someone entered and approached the counter, an older guy, filthy and likely on his way home from work. As he paid, he shot a quick glance at Ronnie and Sheriff Snider seated at the table, and then the man left.

Ronnie said, "Not sure if you believe me, but that's what happened."

Jack unfolded his arms and leaned forward. "I don't know what to believe, but I know what's happening here isn't normal."

Ronnie shook his head. "Don't you get it? I chose me." He jabbed a finger into the middle of his chest. Nausea washed over him. Tears swelled. He felt hollow. "I chose me!" A sob lurched out of him and he clamped his teeth together. "That day in the house, when he took Sherri, I…" he swallowed, hating this. "I hid behind the counter. I hid! I hid and listened to her screams while he dragged her away."

Another long pause spread between them, then Jack said, "So let's say this shit is true, you got any ideas of how to deal with him?"

Ronnie leaned back in his chair and shook his head. Another shameful tear slid down his face. "I want to kill it," he said. "I want to know what it did with Sherri and I want to kill it."

"I'm sure that preacher would appreciate that."

"That's another thing I was thinking about," Ronnie grabbed a napkin from his empty food tray and wiped his nose. "If Michael is after this preacher's daughter, I'll guaran-*goddamned*-tee you that preacher is hiding something."

Jack's eyes narrowed. "You mentioned something like that yesterday."

"Michael's not some blind killer. He believes he's doing the world a service by making people like me pay."

Jack grumbled, "By taking innocent people to pay for other people's sins?"

Ronnie shrugged, "Not exactly. It's more about giving them a choice."

Jack nodded and glanced around the dining area, then settled his eyes back on Ronnie. "There's also a bunch of wild dogs runnin' around out in Black Rock making a goddamn mess. Same as last time. Ain't no way that's a coincidence either."

"I heard. That cashier told me. Yeah, no way that's not related."

Jack focused his gaze out the window. "Goddamn things killed Wayne Tillwood, my deputy. Good guy. Also killed a young kid named Will Haddenfield." He took a deep breath, as if to gather his thoughts. Ronnie remembered the Haddenfields. He used to work for Jim Haddenfield as a kid, walking beans and putting up hay. Jack said, "I looked into past incidents around here and there's similarities dating back at least a hundred years. Some of them mentioned dogs."

Ronnie thought about it and nodded.

Jack asked, "What about Archie Winthrop killin' himself. What's that got to do with anything?"

"It's gotta be all related," Ronnie said. "Somehow, that bastard leaves nothing but misery in his wake. Archie saw Michael that day the sonofabitch took Sherri. Archie was retarded, ya know. Maybe he just snapped or something."

Jack smiled dryly. "Yeah, maybe."

"You know what I think it is?" Ronnie leaned forward.

Jack's eyebrows shot up.

"Chaos," Ronnie said. "I think that sonofabitch spreads chaos wherever it goes so everyone's attention is focused on the wrong shit."

"Decent theory." Jack rubbed his chin. "That's sure as hell what's happening. We got several folks out huntin' those damn dogs, but no one's seen one yet. Someone told me that there's a lady out by Black Rock who's got a lot of dogs…"

"Donna Johnson," Ronnie blurted. He remembered the place well. An old house on the edge of town, not far from where he'd grown up. He remembered riding his bike past there as a boy, always having to build up speed in case one of her dogs decided to chase you. "That old house on the hill close to my old place."

Jack nodded. "Yep. Daisy mentioned her too."

"Daisy Howard?" Ronnie looked at him. "She still at the County Home?"

"Yep," Jack said and cast his eyes down at the table, as people with horrid memories often do, and Ronnie thought, *he hasn't slept for days.*

Ronnie said, "You said that the preacher spoke to Michael?"

Jack nodded. "Said his name was Benjamin."

"Anyone else?"

"Not that I know of."

"Is it too late to go over and talk to the preacher?"

Jack nodded. "I don't see why not."

"I say we start there."

"Let's head out there then." Jack hoisted himself out of the plastic seat. "It's still fairly early. Can't imagine they wouldn't still be up."

Ronnie nodded, holding his small satchel and stole a quick glance at the cashier, who pretended to still read her paper, though she hadn't turned a single page since he'd arrived, not even when that guy paid for gas a little bit ago.

"That all you've got?" Jack asked, shooting a thumb at the small bag.

"Afraid so," Ronnie shrugged.

"My trunk's full of propane tanks and road flares," Jack raised one eyebrow as if to say, *don't ask why*, then pointed at Ronnie's bag hanging off his shoulder, "but that'll fit in the backseat."

The temperature had dropped at least ten degrees, maybe more, since the sun went down. The warmth of the sheriff's car, as well as the smell of aged vinyl and gun oil, reminded him of his dad's old truck.

Guess we gotta start somewhere, Ronnie thought and felt good about it.

Fifteen minutes later, everything went to shit.

Chapter 26

Do not leave the house, they'd said.

Like that made any sense given they hated each other for whatever reason. At least, that's how they acted. Then this afternoon, they decided that having Abby and her mom leave town was a bad idea. *So, I guess now we're staying?* God, if they could just make up their mind already. The stalker must not be *that* dangerous. Everything was weird and she didn't want to be around her parents; if they caught her sneaking out, then so be it.

Abby's tennis shoes scraped against the concrete driveway as she checked every shadowed nook and cranny. She'd feel safer if it was daylight, that's for sure. She dipped down to peer under the car. The crazy old guy might be hiding under there and it'd be foolish not to check. Irresponsible. Men screwed up the world and now here she was, checking under cars for one.

The front driveway felt safe enough. The bright street lamp helped and it seemed like a cop was driving by every ten minutes, though she hadn't seen one since she'd snuck out. She pulled her jacket tighter and buttoned the front. Chilly out here. She walked past her dad's car and stopped. Far enough. She leaned back against the trunk and stuffed her hands into her jacket pocket.

And waited.

She and Michael agreed over text that he'd pull up in front of her house and she'd slip into his front seat. In the two months they'd been talking, she never asked what kind of car he drove. Not that it mattered. She'd recognize him regardless. He'd sent her enough pictures to fill up a yearbook! Her jitters sprang from not knowing how she'd react when she actually saw him. What would he expect? What if she didn't like him in *that way*?

What if she did?

What if he didn't like her?

She blew out a long breath and leaned her head back to gaze at the stars. Too much to process. Too much to worry about. Did she even like guys? Frankly, they scared the crap out of her.

If her dad caught her out here, she'd simply tell him the truth. She hated being in that house with them. *You and mom act like you don't even like each other. What did you do, dad?*

What did I do?

She had the distinct feeling that whatever the issue, it was partially her fault. Likely the trouble at school. A shameful weight, but for the life of her, she had no idea what to do about it since no one was talking to her.

And where on earth was Michael?

She reached down to dig her phone out of her pocket and caught a glimpse of movement. She gasped and froze. Her heart thudded.

Scott Kee lingered at the edge of her yard, straddling a bicycle, and smiling at her. In the streetlamp light, he appeared horrifying.

"You scared the shit out of me!" she hissed.

His cheeks blushed. "Sorry," he said, "What are you doing out here?"

"I'm meeting a friend."

"Oh, really? I figured your parents had you on lockdown. Who are you meeting?"

"It's nobody you know. A friend of a friend."

"I haven't seen you for like three days. Did you get my texts?"

"Yes, but I'm not allowed to text right now," she lied. She wished he'd leave. Why'd he show up now, anyway? "I'm actually not supposed to be out here, but I had to get out of the house for a minute." *Please don't let Michael pull up right now.*

"Any idea why the cops keep driving through here?" Scott shot a thumb toward the street.

She debated on whether or not to say anything to him about the crazy old guy, then decided what the heck, her parents never said not to tell anyone. "There's this weird guy following my dad around."

Scott's eyes grew wider. "Weird guy?"

Her eyes darted up and down the street. "Yeah, I don't know him. I've never even seen him, but my dad says I have to stay close to the house."

Scott stood with his mouth open. She looked away and folded her arms across her chest. Scott said, "Good idea to stay in your house until they catch the guy."

She nodded. "Look, Scott. I have to go. I'll text you later, okay?"

His eyes slipped down. "Sounds good," he said, then turned on his bike and peddled away.

A text from Michael dinged on her phone: Pulling up now.

Headlights glinted from the other end of the street and she watched the car approach and roll to a stop in front of her house.

That's him!

She grinned and suddenly felt she was showing too much teeth. The passenger window hummed down a crack.

"Abby?" A soft voice. Different.

She nodded and painted on a smile. "Michael?"

She stepped closer, then stopped. Something didn't feel right. She should have told her parents she was out here. The hairs on her neck stirred.

He shifted the car into park. The driver's side door swung open.

It suddenly dawned on her what Michael had said on the phone the other night, something that hadn't been quite right. *"We can just stand by my car in plain sight from the front window and shoot the breeze."* How odd *shoot the breeze* had sounded.

But that wasn't it at all.

How did he know we have a front window? How could he know that? A hundred justifiable reasons shot through her head. *It's no big deal.* But it was and she knew it. Trust your instincts.

Run, Abby!

A leather clad boot settled heavily onto the road. A man hoisted himself out.

An old man.

The space between them melted away. The hand shot out and seized her throat, cutting off her air, and then yanked her forward like tossing a rag doll into the front seat of his car. A brief and horrid weightlessness caused a hiccup in her chest, and then her head slammed into something immovable. Her neck cracked. Pain, piercing and sharp, shot down her shoulder. Realization sank in. She couldn't scream, she couldn't breathe, she couldn't do anything. Her strength seeped away into the seats of this god-forsaken car.

Help! Somebody help me.

She twisted herself up so she could get a door open. The terrible sounds of him climbing back into the car sparked panic and she flipped onto her back, kicking her feet at him. She caught a glimpse into the backseat.

The shocked eyes of her mother gazed back at her as she lay across the backseat with her mouth taped and hands twisted behind her in a contorted way that Abby couldn't process because her mind simply wouldn't accept it. The car lurched forward.

Michael spoke. "Your mother isn't part of the plan. She came outside and saw me a little bit ago and I had to do something quickly." He shrugged. "Just bad timing." He shrugged again. "Terrible timing, if you really stop and think about it. Makes everything more complicated."

Abby opened her mouth to scream, knowing she *had* to scream, gasping for air. She sucked in a harsh breath, ready to belt it out, when his fist slammed into her soft stomach, cutting off any intent she had to make even the slightest peep. Pain blossomed and spread with absurd intensity, locking her breath. She choked out a garbled moan, and the sound escaping her frightened her and reminded her of something dying.

She curled up and puked. Her lungs would not work, no matter how hard she tried. *I'm dying. He killed me.* If she could only breathe. Her head...

The darkness swallowed her.

. . . . .

Soft whimpers drifted over his shoulder as Abby's mother cried. Benjamin couldn't blame her. But in the scheme of things, she didn't matter. Just bad timing for the woman to be nosy. The trunk would've been better, now that he thought about it. Oh well, split-second decision and only a little complication, nothing big. Not that it mattered. Only Abby mattered. His unhealthy fixation amplified by her father's cowardly choice to save himself.

She would be Benjamin's forever.

He glanced at Abby lying on the seat next him. Close enough to touch. Her head hung limply off the edge of the seat. Her mouth gaped open. He was glad she'd passed out; glad she was missing this. "I'm sorry," he said hoarsely. He really hadn't meant for her to hit her head that hard.

Timing was everything for things like this. So many things can go wrong, even with the best laid plans. What if Abby had decided not to come out? Or if that cop had driven by in the 12 seconds it took to snag Abby? This would be an entirely different situation.

Only one more stop to make to give the preacher his final chance.

.   .   .   .   .

No one saw Abby's abduction.

But someone heard it.

Scott Kee halted his bike and gawked behind him as the car in front of Abby's house pulled away. Something sounded strange. A hollow *thunk* then a slamming car door. *Something about that sound...* An uncanny sense washed over him that something was wrong, way wrong, and his heart raced as the car sped past him.

What the heck?

In his fantasies where he rescued Abby countless times from terrorists, or a school shooter, or a gang of thugs, he possessed the strength of ten men and fought like a ninja. But right then, heart thumping and palms sweating, he was useless.

Maybe it was nothing.

Maybe it was everything.

He walked his bike to the edge of the road and strained to see the front of Abby's house. He wanted to see if she was still out there. *There's this weird guy following my dad around*, she'd said. Scott didn't know what that meant, but he *did* know that the grey car looked like Donna Johnson's old, grey car.

He couldn't see Abby. Maybe she went inside.

Or maybe she got in Mrs. Johnson's car. But why? This seemed damned weird. He'd never seen Mrs. Johnson out of her house past dark.

The gray car's taillights were nearly out of sight. What to do, what to do. Where was that damned cop that always drove through here?

Adrenaline kicked in and Scott's hands shook. *Call the cops.* On what? Call the cops on Mrs. Johnson? If Abby was with Mrs. Johnson, she had to have a reason. Strange as it sounded, maybe Abby was helping the old lady with something.

He could follow Mrs. Johnson's car to the end of the street and see where it went. No harm, no foul. Not being nosy, just seeing what they're doing. If anyone asked, he could just say he decided to take a ride on his bike. In the dark.

There's this weird guy following my dad around.

Fuck it.

He broke into a rapid peddle and turned left onto Richland Heights Road. The cool, evening air wisped his hair and his breath puffed out clouds of mist.

As he passed by Abby's house, he cast a sideways glance to make sure she wasn't standing out there. He dug his cell phone out of his pocket and typed out a quick text (something he'd grown surprisingly good at – riding a bike and texting) to Abby: You Okay?

Please answer, Abby.

The grey car's brake lights flashed at the end of the street and then it whipped left. What the heck? They're going to Mrs. Johnson's house.

Should he call the police?

Why do I keep asking myself that? It's Mrs. Johnson.

He didn't want to start a bunch of shit only to learn Abby had simply gone back into her house. Or that she was helping Mrs. Johnson carry groceries or something like that. Abby would really hate him then. And if she was with Mrs. Johnson, she had to have a good reason. Didn't she? Abby was so smart and everything she did had purpose, even if it was just standing there.

He coasted around the corner. The cool air wisped his hair. Mrs. Jonson's long, tree-shrouded driveway loomed ahead of him.

He heard car doors open and shut from up at Mrs. Johnson's house. Definitely more than one person.

Wait until you know more, he thought. He hoped like crazy Abby wouldn't hate him for following her. If she only knew how much he loved her. He just needed to know she'd gotten into Mrs. Johnson's car.

My spidey sense, he thought as his bike left the asphalt and entered the gravel driveway. He pedaled toward the house.

Chapter 27

Thomas called out, "Abby?", then stood in the hollow silence. Was he alone in the house? It seemed impossible that Abby and Linda could've left, but he had to admit, he'd been distracted all day. Maybe Abby and Linda left together while he'd been sleeping, or maybe while he was surfing the web for information. A quick run to the store or to grab a sandwich, nothing big. Nothing to worry about. They'll be right back.

He called Abby's phone. No answer.

He called Linda's phone. No answer.

He shivered. He didn't like this.

He stepped halfway up the stairs and stopped, hoping to hear a shuffle or muffled phone conversation. Nothing. He opened his mouth to yell for her again when the doorbell rang.

Now what?

He glanced at the top of the steps, then quickly made his way back down and went to the front door. Maybe it was Abby; perhaps she accidently locked herself out. Though God knew why she'd be outside alone to start with.

For the second time in two days, he opened the door to find the sheriff, Jack Snider, standing on his porch. Only this time, he wasn't alone. A man stood next to the sheriff shifting his weight nervously from foot to foot with his hands buried deep in the pockets of his jeans. The man's disheveled hair and scraggly beard sparked unease.

"Mr. Loggins." The sheriff's piercing gaze bothered Thomas and his initial thought was, *did Linda tell him anything?* Thomas's eyes darted away and he felt stupid for thinking it. "You have a minute?" the sheriff asked.

"Sheriff." Thomas glanced around outside. "Did you see my daughter, Abby, or my wife Linda outside by chance?"

The sheriff shook his head and looked at the bearded man next to him who said nothing.

"You can't find 'em?" the sheriff asked. His eyes narrowed.

"Abby was just here," Thomas said, then added with a nervous smile, "She's gotta be here somewhere." *Was she?* He needed to run upstairs and check there.

The sheriff asked, "Your wife's car still here?"

"I'll check the garage and upstairs," Thomas said, "I'm sure it's nothing." *Why did I say that?* This didn't feel like nothing.

The sheriff shot a thumb at the man next to him. "This is Ronnie Castle. He might be able to help us out with Benjamin Clark."

Thomas settled his gaze on Ronnie. *Ronnie Castle.* He'd been mentioned in one of the articles he'd read earlier. "You've seen Benjamin?" Thomas asked.

Ronnie nodded. What did this man know?

"Can we come inside Mr. Loggins?" the sheriff asked. "We have some questions and some things to share with you. I'd like to speak with your wife and daughter as well."

"Sure," Thomas said. He had a million questions. He stepped back from the door and allowed them to enter. "I need to run up and check on Abby real quick."

The sheriff stepped in first. He ducked his head as he passed through the doorway, then Ronnie followed. The stench of alcohol touched the air as Ronnie passed by and Thomas thought of his own father, so many years ago. *I got no time, boy!*

"Want me to check the garage for ya?" The sheriff asked as he entered the house.

"Nah," Thomas glanced outside and noted the garage door was closed. Linda always left it open if she pulled her car out and left.

Thomas closed the front door. He turned and said, "I'll be right back down." He pointed through the archway into the kitchen. "Feel free to take a seat in there. I shouldn't be but a sec."

He left the men standing there and shot up the stairs two at a time. The sense that he would reach Abby's room and find it empty dwarfed everything. *Lord, please don't let that be so.*

But it was.

Abby's room was empty. He hustled down the hall to his and Linda's room. Nothing. "Abby?" His voice fell flat as if spoken in a tomb. "Linda?"

He snapped his attention to the bathroom, hoping to see a light on, but found it dark. "Abby! Linda!"

They're not here.

Which meant they'd most likely gone somewhere together. Maybe Linda decided to take Abby and flee after all, even after they'd decided that Abby should stay put. *Maybe Linda has had enough of me.* Would things ever be normal again between them?

Or maybe they're just down at the diner for some hot chocolate — don't panic. *At 8 o'clock at night?*

Too late in the evening for that; hasty conclusions invaded every cell. Thomas plowed back down the stairs to find the sheriff and Ronnie seated at the table.

"They're not up there," he huffed.

The sheriff hoisted himself back to his feet. "Did they leave like you and I discussed yesterday?"

"No," Thomas shook his head, "I don't think so. They wouldn't have left without telling me." *They wouldn't, would they?*

His eyes darted to the back door and he moved swiftly to open it. He pictured Abby and Linda huddled together outside on a chair wrapped in a blanket, just hanging out. He scanned the backyard, checked the swing up by the porch, then the bench closer to the yard. He called out, "Linda? Abby? You out here?"

Nothing.

He closed the door and turned to the sheriff. "They're gone."

The sheriff raised a hand and said, "Okay, let's not lose our heads. If they're both gone, then they're likely together and that's a good thing."

Thomas nodded. That sounded all well and good, but something was not right here. He said, "Abby was *just* here. I don't know when she left. I honestly haven't seen Linda since earlier today."

The sheriff shot Ronnie a quick glance, the two of them exchanged a look, and then the sheriff set his gaze back on Thomas.

"What?" Thomas asked. "Shouldn't we be leaving right now to look for them?" He sure as hell thought they should.

The sheriff said, "What we need…"

"Did he give you a choice?" Ronnie blurted.

Thomas locked eyes with him. *He knows.*

"Michael, or Benjamin, I guess he's calling himself Benjamin now." Ronnie's face grew red. "What choice did he offer you?"

Despite his best effort to stop it, a fake and stupid smile spread across Thomas's face, and he said, "Choice? I'm not sure what you mean. He threatened my daughter."

"He's lying," Ronnie said, turning toward the sheriff.

Thomas's ears grew hot as he glared at Ronnie. Who was this guy?

"Hold on," the sheriff said. "Ronnie, just hold on." He turned to Thomas. "Pastor, this isn't the time to hold back anything. You have to tell us everything, so we can help you."

"How, how is this going to help?"

"Pastor, has it ever occurred to you that Benjamin might be…" The sheriff looked up, as if the words he was seeking might be written on the ceiling.

"A demon," Ronnie Blurted.

He knows everything, Thomas thought. Guilt swept through him. The sheriff's gaze bore into him and Ronnie started to shift his weight again, wobbling back and forth. *Just tell them. Tell them!*

"We're wasting time here, Jack," Ronnie said. "Donna Johnson's place is right up the road. We need to go see if…"

"Okay," Thomas spat the word. *What's said cannot be unsaid, remember that.* "Okay. Yes. He gave me a choice."

Both men gawked at him. He wanted to scream, *I'm a minister! A man of God!* But even in his own mind, the words felt fake. Pride's last stand.

The sheriff's eyebrows furrowed. "Go on, pastor."

Thomas gripped the back of a kitchen chair and gazed down at his feet. Oh God, where was Abby? If she'd show up right now, no harm, no foul. He didn't need to admit anything. But she wasn't here and that made all the difference.

Your balance is due.

"Years ago," Thomas's voice quivered, "I… uhm…" he breathed deep. "I had sex with a woman that wasn't consensual. I'd been drinking heavily and while walking her home she… uhm…" he struggled. His breath hitched and his palms sweat.

Ronnie said, "You raped her."

"I didn't set out to do that!" Thomas thundered. "I never intended to do that. I just…"

"He gave you a choice for it, didn't he? Your life or your daughter's." Ronnie gazed at him and finally stopped that ridiculous wobble back and forth. "Told you your balance was due."

Thomas nodded.

"You chose to save yourself." Ronnie shook his head.

Thomas snapped his eyes to Ronnie. His first impulse was to yell, *I did no such thing!* But his heart fluttered and a tear slipped down his cheek. Thomas's words warbled, "I don't know how he knew, but he did."

"He did the same to me," Ronnie said. "A long time ago. I'd guess he has your daughter." Ronnie shrugged. "He's probably long gone now."

Thomas let go of the chair. He swallowed. Words abandoned him.

"Okay," The sheriff plopped a heavy fist onto the table, silencing both of them, then he darted his eyes from Thomas, to Ronnie, and back to Thomas. "Here's what we're gonna do… we need to find out where in the hell Benjamin went. It doesn't matter what either of you did, if we don't find this sonofabitch, you may never see your daughter again."

"Don't matter," Ronnie said, "If he wanted her, she's gone."

"That's enough of that!" The sheriff spoke through clenched teeth. He took a calming breath and asked Thomas, "Your daughter or wife have iPhones?"

Thomas nodded and said, "I tried calling them right before you got here. No one answered."

"Try again. You sharing location with them?"

Thomas remembered Abby setting something like that up on their phones, but wasn't for sure. "We might be" he said, "but I don't know."

He grabbed his phone off the counter and dialed Linda's number again. It went straight to voicemail. He dialed Abby's. Hers rang, but no answer. It rolled to voicemail and Thomas said, "Abby, I need you to call me right away." He tapped the red phone to hang up and tried to think through his haze of confusion. How does he find someone's location?

"Ya have to go to a text message from Abby and click that little *i* thing," the sheriff said.

Thomas's fingers trembled as he tapped his way through. As he did, Ronnie said, "Chances of finding her now are next to nothing."

"Goddamn it, Ronnie," the sheriff shook his head.

"We needed to get here *before* he took her." Ronnie ran a hand through his hair. "Ain't likely to find her now."

Thomas clicked the *i* icon next to Abby's name and it brought up a map with a blue dot floating in the middle. "That's it!" he yelled. Hope surged. "I think I found it!" How did he not know that this function existed?

"Lemme see," the sheriff took the phone from him and stared at it. Then said, "That's only a few blocks from here."

Ronnie stretched over and looked at the phone. "Donna Johnson's place," he said.

A troubled look crossed the sheriff's face. "I hope he didn't throw her phone out the window or something." He handed the phone back to Thomas. "Let's head over there."

Thomas pictured Abby's phone lying in a ditch with his picture splashing the screen as he tried to call. God, he hoped she had it with her. *Please have it with you, baby.* In the past three years, he'd never seen her without it. She slept with the damned thing, for God's sake! Something he'd never been sure he should be letting her do.

They all three exchanged a glance then Thomas led the way to the door. They shuffled out and down the sidewalk. The sheriff said, "We'll take my cruiser."

Thomas was fine with that.

Part IV
Absolution

Chapter 28

Remember, this all happened last Spring. Hopefully, you'll understand why I'm upset that the Loggins are packing up to leave. Our little stroll through Black Rock is nearly over and we've arrived at their house. Looks like they're still packing up the car. The back hatch stands open and I can see someone loading a large duffel bag. The dim glow of the dome light illuminates the inside and casts an eerie glow across whomever is standing there. We're still too far away to tell who it is, but it won't be long now. They leave the hatch open and go back inside. We'll step a little closer and wait for them to come back out.

It's close to 10 PM, and that's late for the little town of Black Rock. Folks are winding down, most preparing for bed. Jean Tallman and her group of Bingo friends are probably still down at the Lion's Club, gossiping. I doubt they'll play much longer. Old women around here don't like to stay up late.

Jesse England likely arrived at his empty apartment a few minutes ago, as he does every night. He'll sit and stare at a blank television. He'll mumble to himself and talk about absolution. God knows what's wrong with him.

Ah, look, someone is coming back out of the Loggins' house, hauling another box. We need to move closer. I can't imagine what must be going through their head. That box looks heavy too.

I just hope they're not leaving town for good, though I suspect they are. We could use them around here. Of course, I wouldn't blame them if they left, though, and neither would anyone else for that matter. Ever since it came out about Pastor Loggins's incident with the girl back in college, a lot of people turned their back on the pastor and his family. Bad deal no matter how you look at it. The Indiana State Police even questioned that woman, Emily, and apparently, she admitted that she couldn't remember what happened that night almost a quarter of a century ago. She even stated she'd had a little crush on Thomas back in college. Emily lives in Indianapolis now, married with children, doing fine.

As Bill Hoskins, the bartender down there at Ada's Bar would tell you, and often does, *you never know what a guy is capable of. That pastor seemed like a hell of a nice guy and ain't none of us know what kind of situation he was in. He never did nothin' but good around here.* And so the debate rages on.

All I know is that I felt damn sorry for the guy. I don't think he deserved what happened to him.

The silhouette of a person slides that heavy box into the back hatch and now just stands there, hands on hips, staring into the back of the Jeep as if taking a mental inventory of all the stuff they've loaded, making sure they haven't forgotten something. As they turn their head and glare toward the street, as if staring straight at us, it's hard not to feel uncomfortable. Things are not the same here, that's for sure. I can remember when the Loggins first arrived here; you could always count on a smile from any one of them. Even the teenage daughter, Abby.

Not now though. The Loggins are barely seen nowadays. Recluses. And judging by the amount of stuff they're loading into that vehicle; they may be leaving for good.

I'd guess they're leaving to escape the bad memories that haunt them here, because there are so many in a town like this. Small towns come bundled with their own culture and history. Stories are passed down from generation to generation. Some of them are even true. In my experience, most aren't. For instance, many people around here believe that Al Capone had a hide out here in Black Rock, and some even believe there was a shoot-out at the site of the present-day library. But God help you if you even insinuate that Al Capone never set foot in Black Rock; those who believe he did will let you know how wrong you are. But I can assure you, Al Capone never spent time in Black Rock. Not to my knowledge, anyway.

Stigmas. That's what a small town brings with it. And it sticks to you like the stench of something rotten.

Before we step into the Loggins's driveway and speak with whomever is loading that car, let me finish telling you what happened that night.

The night the pastor made his choice.

Chapter 29

Abby's eyes fluttered open and the world swam into focus. Flickering candlelight danced in dark shadows. A picture hung on the far wall; a wall covered with ancient, faded-green wall paper – a painting of a woman walking next to a barn. Abby's fuzziness drained away. *Where am I?* The leather boot on pavement. Someone grabbed her and tossed her into a car. Her head collided with the door. *Someone hit me!* Her mother crying in the backseat...

Oh my God!

She sucked in a harsh breath and sat up, staring at a sheer covered window with an orange cat sitting on the ledge watching her. It yawned, flicked its tail, and turned its attention back to the outside. She scanned the room and took in the unfamiliar setting; an old dresser with two burning candles perched on top, a matted and worn maroon chair in the corner, a closet full of nightgowns. The quilted bedspread looked old, like someone might have hand-stitched it a hundred years ago.

Think Abby. What happened?

Michael was supposed to come by and dimly, she wondered if he'd ever shown up, perhaps wondering if she'd stood him up. The text, *pulling up now*, and then the car appeared. But it was an old man, not Michael.

My phone! She padded her pockets and darted her eyes across the bed, the floor, and the dresser with the candles on it. Nothing. Her chest tightened and she planted a trembling hand on her mouth to stifle a cry.

Abby swung her legs off the bed, sat up, and stopped instantly as a sharp pain in her stomach seized her. She doubled over and gasped shallow breaths. She clamped a hand over her mouth to stifle her whimpers. It was as if someone placed a hot piece of iron inside her.

I'm going to puke.

But she didn't. Slowly, the nausea passed, but left a dull throb in her belly that she worried may be there forever. She took a cautious breath, braced for another wallop, but the pain didn't come. She exhaled and glanced back over at the cat. It blinked and turned its head, as if saying, *oh, it's you again.*

Abby fought off the urge to scream for help. *Don't do anything stupid, Abby.* Gotta get out of here. Did anyone know she'd even been taken? Besides her mom, of course. Her dad had no idea she'd even gone outside. How could she have been so stupid?

Tears welled and she felt a cold trickle down her cheek. Where was the man who took her? *Am I locked in here?* Did *he* lock her in here? She listened and heard nothing.

Does Michael know that old man?

She eased herself off the bed, still treating that threatening pain in her belly with respect, knowing that if another cramp hit her while she was on her feet, she'd probably end up on the floor. She moved in shuffling steps. Darkness pressed against the window and the cat minded her with only subtle curiosity. She had to get out of here. That was the first thing. She had to get out and find her mom. And figure out where the hell they were.

Why is this happening? Another burst of tears trailed down her face, but she kept quiet.

She grasped the doorknob and then heard steps echo, like someone climbing stairs. *Oh my God!* She froze, then glanced around the room. *Under the bed!* She could dive under the bed or wedge herself between that dresser and the wall and remain hidden in the shadow.

Open this door and run! She'd seen movies. Read stories. They *always* find you.

She twisted the knob from side to side, careful not to make noise. Locked, solid and immovable.

"Please," she whispered and gave way to a subtle cry. "Please open."

The heavy footsteps continued the slow trek up the stairs, echoing against old wood, growing more ominous. she had to get out of this room

169

and hide. But all she could do was stand here and twist this stupid knob back and forth.

Do something!

Those horrible footsteps crested the top of the stairs and clomped toward her. She let go of the doorknob and stepped back, dreading what might happen next. A wretched sob burst from her mouth and she nearly crumpled to the floor in a defeated mess. Her cries seeped into the worn, wooden floor as the footsteps stopped outside the bedroom door.

"Abby?" that voice, *Michael's* voice.

The cat's ears laid back and it hissed.

"Michael?" Her heart knew the truth, but her brain wouldn't accept it. He was here to save her. He'd seen everything happen and followed her here and now he was saving her!

"Yeah, it's me." His sweet voice! "Sounds like you're awake in there."

"Help me!" She yelled. Her hair, sweaty and matted, hung in her face and she swiped it behind her ears. She shot forward and grabbed the doorknob. "Open the door!"

"I can't," his muffled voice dug into her chest. "It's not your fault, though. Just know that, okay?"

Damn him! "What? What are you talking about? Open the door!" She cried and clamped a dirty hand to her mouth. How in God's name had this happened to *her*?

"I gave him a choice," Michael said. "Times up. It'll all be over soon. They'll follow your phone here and soon it'll all be over."

The cat meowed and stared at her, as if to say, *how about trying the window, dumby*. How had she not thought of that? She turned toward it, shuffling quietly, with a hand clamped to her mouth to stifle the cries bubbling up within her.

"We'll have to leave soon, Abby."

She moved faster, not focusing on his words, and kept her gaze locked on the window. The *window*! Please be unlocked.

"Your dad," his voice darkened, growing deeper and gruff, "he'll be here soon. He and the people with him don't think I know, but I know. I know everything. I doubt it'll change anything, though. I doubt he's here to do the *right* thing. More likely he's here to try to stop me to save himself."

Dad?

She stopped. *Dad!*

This is a crazy man. *What if he's lying to me?* But what if he's not?

Keep moving! She reached the window and gripped the ledge with her fingers.

"They'll try to stop me. But they can't."

The window didn't budge at first, but then suddenly gave way with a noisy screech. *Shit!*

"Abby, what are you doing in there? Don't do this Abby. This isn't about you."

"I want my father. Let me out of here, Michael."

"I told you, I can't do that. Don't worry. I'm not going to hurt you and this will all be over soon." He paused. "One way or the other. Truth be told, I'm hoping we can be together after this is done."

"You're a psycho! I'm not going anywhere with you."

The window opened! *Oh, thank god!* She hoisted herself onto the edge and peered out into the darkness. The roof awaited several feet below. Too far to jump. It was too dark to see what was out there, but she could see trees with skeletal branches stretching up into the starlit sky. The cat hopped down from its perch and walked arrogantly over to the bed, rubbing against the maroon chair with its tail in the air.

The metallic scrape of a key slithering into a lock flooded the room. Panic seized her. The door swung open with a whine. She spun and fell onto her butt, sliding down the wall and smashing herself into the corner as if the walls might absorb her and hide her. She moaned and gazed into his horrid face looming in the doorway. Those eyes like pits and the mouth wide and full of teeth, opening and closing in wretched succession.

"You can't escape me," he said and he no longer sounded anything like the Michael who'd deceived her. The Michael she'd adored.

He took two booming steps across the room and she lifted her hands up in front of her face. This was it. Fifteen-years-old. *I'm sorry to everyone.*

She braced for his rough hands to clamp onto her arms, to yank her up and do what he must with her. The anticipation of pain filled her with dread so deep and so profound, her sanity teetered. Her screams echoed loud and awful and it wasn't until a moment had passed that she realized, he hadn't touched her yet. She opened her eyes to find him looming over her, but his head was cocked to the side, as if listening to something.

"I'll be back," he said.

Michael stormed out of the room and left her sitting, alone, gasping. She sucked in a deep breath, and that's when the stomach pain slammed into her again, locking her lungs. How bad had he hurt her earlier when he tossed her into the car and she'd banged her head? When he punched her in the stomach? She fell to her side, then rolled clumsily to her hands and knees. Her mouth opened and closed in silent, painful motions with only a weak strain escaping her throat.

Hot vomit rushed up her throat and spilled from her lips in disgusting, hitching gulps. The smell of the slippery liquid caused her to retch again. Her stomach tightened and she nearly blacked out from the strain. Abby clenched her trembling fist, fighting against the urge to faint. *If I pass out, my face will go in my puke!*

Tears flooded her eyes and she rocked back and forth.

Mom, where are you?

Then Michael's voice thundered from downstairs, "You meddled in the wrong place boy!"

. . . . .

Scott Kee pushed down the kickstand on his bike and parked it behind Mrs. Johnson's car. He expected a light to be on somewhere. He'd never actually been inside her house, but he'd peered in the door as Mrs. Johnson held it open many times in the past when he'd approached her for school fundraisers. He'd even asked her once if he could mow her yard for $10 and she'd abruptly told him, *no, maybe some other time.*

He stepped toward the darkened front porch.

She'd never been mean, though. Always nice in that grandmotherly way old women had.

Scott's dad told him once, *she's an odd old lady and she doesn't like people.* Which deepened the mystery as to why Abby would be here to start with. Maybe she's not. Maybe Abby hadn't gotten into Mrs. Johnson's car at all.

"But I heard something," Scott whispered to himself. Darn right he did. And Mrs. Johnson had parked in front of Abby's house and Abby hadn't been there when Mrs. Johnson pulled away.

Leave, Scott. The Spidey sense again. He'd never tell Abby about the Spidey sense because she'd likely think the Spidey sense was silly. *Leave now. Everything is wrong here.*

He stopped at the foot of the steps. He considered yelling for Mrs. Johnson, but that seemed stupid. A fifteen-year-old standing in the driveway yelling. But he didn't like this at all. He wished Abby would just respond to his text.

Something huffed behind him. Then a growl.

He froze, then whirled.

A dog. A *large* dog. He spotted two others slinking toward him. Close.

His eyes darted to his bike. Could he make it? His heart walloped and his breath grew shallow, raspy. He yelled, "Mrs. Johnson?" *Oh, please be home.*

His hand crept down to his jeans pocket and felt his phone.

The largest dog charged.

Scott moaned, unable to draw breath, then spun and shot up the steps to the front door. He grasped the handle and yanked. It swung open and he scrambled inside and tried to slam it shut behind him, but the dog crashed into before it could latch. He cried out and stumbled away as the dog wiggled its way into the house. Its nails clicked on the linoleum as it paced toward him. It was so dark in here. Nothing but shadows.

He dug for his phone and caught the silhouette of someone standing at the foot of the stairs. His breath locked. *Thank God.*

"You meddled in the wrong place, boy!" The person roared. That sound, that voice, zapped his hope. His Spidey sense screamed that he was trapped. He'd lost control of the world.

The other dogs entered from outside, butting their way through the swinging, unlatched door.

"Help me," Scott said weakly.

The dogs attacked.

. . . . .

A crash echoed from downstairs, shattering glass, dogs growling, barking, howling, and then a scream. Something familiar resonated in that scream, something she knew.

Abby cried.

Then another crash, this time like wood breaking. That scream again, pain-filled. Dogs growled and barked, that sound they make deep in their throat when pulling on a toy.

"Stop it," she said and cried harder. She clamped her hands against her ears. "Stop it!"

Scott Kee. He was so stupid! Why didn't he call the cops or something? Reality slammed into her like a slap in the face and she blinked against pain blossoming inside her. The reality of what was happening downstairs settled in behind a childish hope that Scott might save her.

The screaming stopped, replaced by a dark moan, and Michael's voice, muffled and subdued, "You shouldn't have come, boy. I'm rarely surprised, but you have truly surprised me."

A dog growled.

Scott screamed again, his voice weak and defeated, and then, like flipping off the television, his voice cut off. Silence. A silence that thrummed up the stairs, livid and terrible, death echoed its ghostly promise. *Oh god… Oh my god…*

Get out now, Abby. Your only chance.

She stumbled to her feet. The window. Any moment those heavy footsteps would come stomping up the stairs again, and he was angry now and the thought of what he'd do to her while angry made her head swirl. She flipped her hair out of her eyes and climbed out onto the window ledge.

One chance, Abby. You've got one chance and now's the time.

Too far to jump down. But pain or no pain, if she didn't get out right now, that'd be it.

She prayed that the dull throb below her ribs would not flare into the agony she knew could ensue at any moment. *Just let me get out of this house… please…* and then what? She pictured herself actually making it down from the roof (though she had no idea how she'd actually do that yet) and there would stand Michael, patiently waiting for her.

If she could only find her mom. Mom would know what to do.

Do it now, Abby.

She swung her legs out the window and leaned forward. A jagged piece of metal protruding from the window frame sliced the side of her arm and pain shot through her bicep like an electric shock. She cried out. Blood dripped like a faucet and she didn't glance at the cut, afraid of what she might see. God, nothing more now. At least let me get out the window.

Get out now, Abby... jump.

Chapter 30

Jack eased the car to a halt on the edge of the road, avoiding streetlights, and gazed through the side window. "See anything?"

Ronnie squinted and stared into the darkness of Donna Johnson's long driveway. It twisted through bushes and trees for at least a hundred feet, or more. He'd never been up to her house; only ridden past it on his bike twenty years earlier. Not a single light was on, but he thought he could see the reflection of a car parked next to the house. "Dark as shit," he said, "but it looks like a car's parked up there. I'd guess hers." Ronnie squinted, seeking a better view. "Seems weird, but there's also a bicycle up there, I think."

Thomas spoke from the back seat. "Doesn't look like anyone's home."

Ronnie rubbed his hand through his hair. This wasn't right. No one understood what they were dealing with here. Jack and the preacher may *think* they do, but they'd never felt the house shake or seen the wings expand. Michael would not take that preacher's daughter then run to a house two blocks away to hide. Something far more sinister lurked at the bottom of all this.

"Phone location still saying they're here?" Jack asked.

"Yeah," Thomas answered.

Jack reached over and keyed the mic hanging on the dash. "Patti?"

A hiss of static, then, "Yeah, sheriff?"

"I need you to send a unit to my location in Black Rock. Donna Johnson's place." Jack released the mic's button, then keyed it again and said, "Also, get ahold of the state police and let them know we've got an abduction in Black Rock and need them out here."

"You got it, sheriff."

He clicked the mic back onto the dash mount then rubbed his chin. Ronnie bit the inside of his lip and dug his fingers through his hair. "We gonna wait on them to get here?" he asked.

"We should. There's just three of us, and I'm the only law here," Jack said.

Thomas said, "But this isn't a matter of the law. We all know that, right?"

Ronnie agreed with Thomas; if they waited, Michael would be long gone. Especially if Michael knew they were parked out here, spying on him. "If we wait, we'll lose our opportunity. They'll be gone."

Thomas locked eyes on him, "What are you saying?"

Ronnie recalled how he'd searched for weeks after Sherri's abduction. Wandering through woods, through old barns, through houses. Nothing. "I looked everywhere after he took Sherri. Never found Michael or any trace of Sherri. It was like he just vanished with her."

Thomas gawked at him for a long second, then opened his door and climbed out. The dome light bathed them in dull light and Jack squinted. "Hold on, Pastor," he said, but then Thomas's door shut and darkness shrouded them.

Jack's window hummed down. "Pastor!" he hissed.

Ronnie watched the pastor stop at the edge of the driveway, then he shuffled back to Jack's open window. "We need to find out if anyone's up there," Thomas spoke above a whisper, but Ronnie sensed the panic roiling beneath the surface.

Jack said, "I get it, but you runnin' off on your own doesn't help us. Get back in here."

The pastor seemed to consider this, but then said, "I'm gonna go up and check it out. See if there's any movement inside. You think Donna is still up?"

Jack shrugged. "Hell if I know."

Ronnie leaned over. "I doubt it. She's old. But if you could peek inside a window or something, we'd know if anyone else is here. Might be a false alarm."

"Yeah," the pastor rubbed his forehead. "Let me run up there real quick. I gotta know if Abby's around here. I'll let you know."

Before Ronnie or Jack could respond, the pastor slipped around to the front of car.

Jack shot a glance at Ronnie. "Way to go. We already know those phones are here somewhere. I don't like him wandering up there by himself."

Ronnie shrugged. "Didn't you say the phones could've been tossed out a window, or something like that?" He'd hadn't owned a cell phone since high school and wasn't sure how a phone could tell you where a person was. "I was just sayin', if Michael leaves, then we may never find him again."

Jack tapped his thumb against the steering wheel and Ronnie grew more anxious. Were they just going to sit here and let that preacher go up there alone? Surely not. Ronnie wanted to go up there. He needed to see Michael again. "We should go with him?"

Ronnie and Jack gazed toward the house and watched Thomas step timidly to the edge of the driveway. The preacher shot a glance back at the car and then faced the house again and disappeared into the shadows.

"We won't be able to see him once he's all the way up there," Ronnie said. "Too damn many bushes and shit everywhere."

"Yeah," Jack spoke low.

A few seconds later, a dog's bark drifted through the open window. Close. Then another. Ronnie said, "You hear that?"

Jack nodded.

Ronnie said, "Sounds like it's coming from up there."

Jack said, "I found that dead goat about a mile from here, then Haddenfield's boy gets killed about a mile from that. Then Tillwood out at the County Home." Ronnie listened as Jack spoke more to himself than to anyone else. "County Home's only about a quarter mile from here. If it's Donna Johnson's dogs, then they're doing a big circle and might've returned here. Likely why we ain't found 'em yet."

"Distraction," Ronnie said and Jack shot him a troubled glare. Ronnie's heart kicked into high gear and his palms tingled. "Maybe Michael called them back here. Maybe he knew we'd come here."

"What the hell is he?" Jack's voice dipped low.

Ronnie shook his head. "I honest to God don't know."

"Demon." Jack chuckled, but there was nothing funny in that sound.

"Or angel." Ronnie had always wondered that himself.

"One shitty angel, if that's what he is," Jack rubbed his chin again while they both stared into the darkness of Donna Johnson's darkened yard.

Then something else popped into Ronnie's head, a simple yet unsettling thought. "If those are Widow Johnson's dogs, and if Michael's there, what the hell is *Widow Johnson* doing?"

Ronnie and Jack exchanged worried glances, no words needing to pass on the subject. They both knew they'd be finding out soon enough.

Jack shifted into gear, kept his lights off, and pulled up the driveway.

Chapter 31

Jack spotted the pastor shuffling back toward them and stopped the car halfway up the driveway. "Now what the hell's he doing?" Jack grumbled and shifted into park.

Ronnie shrugged but said nothing.

The pastor reached the car, his eyes wide and desperate, his breath puffed in small clouds. "I heard something," he gasped.

"Heard what?" Jack asked.

The pastor craned his neck toward the house and spoke in a breathless hiss, "I don't know, like thuds or something. They're here. I know it."

Jack said, "Look, the only thing we know for sure is that their phones are around here, somewhere." But was there any doubt at this point? *The preacher's right, they're here.* Jack shook his head. The state police would most likely be coming from a town called Gainesville, they'd be at least 10-15 minutes. That's if they hauled ass. "Meet me back by the trunk. Both of you." Jack shut the car off, pulled the keys from the ignition, and then reached up and flicked the dome light off. "Be quick and don't slam your door," he said to Ronnie and then opened his door, Ronnie did the same, and they both climbed out.

The pastor hesitated, shot a quick look at the house, then joined them at the trunk. "We need to hurry," Pastor Loggins said, his voice quivered.

Jack nodded and opened the trunk. He glanced at the house and froze. Three dogs clamored out the side door, running fast toward the back like someone had called them back there. Jack whispered, "Don't move." The last of the three dogs stopped just before it rounded the corner of the house, as if sensing Jack there, and turned toward him. *Oh shit.*

Jack's hand crept to his gun. The animal hunkered, glared at them, then its attention snapped toward the back yard and it shot around the corner of the house.

"Jesus," Ronnie huffed.

"Yeah," Jack spoke low and wondered where in the hell his other unit was? His deputy, Howard, should've been within minutes. He'd call Patti back and check on it in a sec.

He pictured Amy clasping his arm at a time like this and saying, *there's no way I'm going up to that house.* The wrongness oozed from the walls like blood from a wound.

"Donna still live here?" Ronnie asked.

"Far as I know," Jack said and reached into the trunk. "But I'm guessing she ain't here now." He grasped a flashlight and slipped it into his utility belt. He'd for damned sure need that thing. He leaned against the trunk lid, growing frustrated that Howard hadn't shown up yet.

"What are we waiting on?" The preacher asked.

"My deputy," Jack said.

"When's he getting here?" The preacher's voice rose and he kept stealing furtive glances at the house.

"I was hopin' he'd be here by now. Depends on where he's comin' from. Taylor County is a big damn county." Jack lowered the trunk lid, slowly easing it shut until it clicked.

The preacher shook his head. "We can't just stand here and wait. I need to get up there. I *heard* something."

"Agreed," Jack said. He looked at Ronnie. "Michael got any weaknesses you know of?"

Ronnie shrugged. "I honestly have no idea."

That didn't help a whole hell of a lot. "Alright," Jack said, "We'll circle around the house, see if we can spot anything. Ronnie, check the backyard. See if you can tell where them dogs were runnin' to. I'll check the front, and Mr. Loggins, you go around the other side." He glanced at Ronnie, who nodded back, and then at the preacher, whose wide eyes would've been comical in any other circumstance. "Let's stay where we can see each other."

"I need a light," Ronnie whispered.

Jack slid his flashlight out of his belt. "Only turn it on if you need it." He handed it to Ronnie, who took it, grimaced, then stepped away toward the back corner of the house.

Jack turned and glared at the street. "Damn it." He'd hoped to see headlights coming.

"What?" Pastor Loggins asked.

"Thought he'd of been here by now." Jack stepped around to the driver's side door, reached through the open window, and snatched the radio off the dash. "Patti?"

A short burst of static, and then Patti's voice burst on the line, "Sheriff?"

"Where the hell's Howard?" Jack wondered if he hadn't screwed this up. Should've waited down on the street.

She came back, "He was clear out by Grant, Sheriff. That's at least twenty-five miles from you. Everyone's heading your way, but you're looking at another 10 minutes, at least."

He squeezed the button to talk and caught the preacher scrambling away out of the corner of his eye. Jack stood straight and hissed over the top of the car, "Wait!" but it was too late; the preacher's silhouette disappeared around the corner of the house, the opposite way Ronnie had gone. *I heard something,* the preacher had said.

"Goddamn it." *You're losing control, Jack.*

He squeezed the radio button and said, "Tell Howard to hurry."

"Roger that," Patti said.

The radio fell quiet.

Jack tossed the mic onto the front seat. Feeling awkward and stiff, he drew his weapon and hurried past the front of his car. He spotted Ronnie's dark shape stepping cautiously through the backyard. Several yards beyond Ronnie, a large barn loomed in the darkness, blotting out the back portion of the property.

Jack slowed as he neared the side door where the dogs had run out. His heart thumped and blood throbbed in his neck. He passed by a car, then a bicycle standing lonely on its kickstand. The porch steps led to the side door which waited, dark and foreboding, as if telling him *stay away,*

Jack, you don't want to come in here. He listened. He breathed. He gripped his weapon and lifted it.

That's when Ronnie yelled, "Jack! Jack!"

A scream tore the darkness. A woman. Not a girl. A woman, screamed "In here!" or something like that. Jack scrambled away from the side door and lumbered toward the back yard. Toward that scream. A dismal feeling swept through him as he charged into blackness. Heart banging, he swept around the side of the house.

Sweat soaked his skin as he charged toward the shadow of that dark barn. His grip slippery. Jack yelled as he ran, "Ronnie?" *Watch for those dogs, Jack. They're out here.* "Ronnie!"

"Jack!" Ronnie yelled again. That yell came from *inside* the barn.

Jack's eyes darted toward every shadowed crevice as he ran. His feet ka-thudded on the cold ground, rattling his teeth.

From behind him, the preacher's voice echoed faint and muffled, "Abby!"

Christ on his throne! Jack couldn't stop, *wouldn't* stop. He'd get back there in a second. What the hell choice did he have? Everything's happening at once.

He halted hastily at the mouth of the barn. The light from a distant streetlamp casted dim and distorted shadows. Jack's breath came in gasps and he hissed, "Ronnie! You in here?"

A whimper drifted out of the darkness, a woman. *Goddamn it, I'd shit a razor blade for that flashlight right now.*

"Jack!" Ronnie's voice from inside the barn. "We're okay, I'm up on a rafter, but I dropped the damn flashlight. Watch out! They're everywhere!"

"What's everywhere?" Jack squinted, seeing nothing but black. Blackness thick enough to touch.

Then another sound drifted horridly out of that dark, straight in front of him. And then another behind him. Growls. Jack wondered if Wayne Tillwood had heard this same thing just before they killed him.

The dogs.

Chapter 32

Thomas brushed his fingers against the cool siding as he shuffled alongside of the house. Abby's voice, though distressed, danced in the cool breeze, somewhere out here. He'd heard it while the sheriff was on his radio. Abby sounded hurt. *Please, God… Please.* He braved ahead, following her voice.

"Abby?" he hissed. His eyes scanned the dark ground, the shadowed trees, the edge of the house.

Answer me, sweetie.

"Daddy?"

Thomas stopped. His breath caught. He'd heard *that*.

"Baby, where are you?" he asked. He stepped forward and placed his hand on the house.

"Up here," she said weakly.

He looked up and saw the edge of the roof looming above him. But he couldn't see her and his mind raced. Climb up? Have her slide down? Just do something. *There's evil in the air.*

"Can you slide down?" he asked. "I'll catch you."

"Where is Michael?" she asked.

He recalled the conversation with the sheriff and Ronnie. Michael and Benjamin were the *same* thing. Thomas glanced around, then backup. "I don't know."

"He's here, somewhere." The pain buried in her voice bore into him and his heart broke for her.

Make your choice.

"Baby, can you slide down?" he asked. He needed her to get down.

"I'm hurt, daddy." She coughed, followed by a short whimper. "I don't think I can do it."

"Okay. I'll come up there. Hold on."

A twig snapped behind him. Thomas whirled and sucked in a breath.

Benjamin stood before him. Looming. Taller somehow, and wider. Way wider. He was *spreading*, growing, blotting out all other shadows and consuming the night. *Oh my God...*

Wings. *Those are wings.* They unfurled like massive curtains.

What in God's name am I looking at?

"Pastor," Benjamin's gravelly voice bored into him. "I'm glad you came."

Chapter 33

Ronnie gripped the edge of a small beam and balanced about six-foot off the barn's dirt floor.

"What's everywhere?" Jack asked from the barn's open front. Growls seeped from the shadows.

"Dogs!" Ronnie called back. "They chased me in here. I barely got up out of the way." He'd dropped the flashlight while running and cursed himself for it.

"Who's with you?" Jack yelled.

Ronnie cast his gaze down at the woman pressed into a small, shadowed corner where the dogs couldn't reach her. In the dark, he could only make out the edge of her hair and the glistening sweat on her arm. "What's your name?" He asked her

Her weak voice drifted up to him, "Linda Loggins." She coughed, then said, "Can you help me, please."

That preacher's wife.

Ronnie yelled out to Jack, "Her name's Linda." He focused his attention back to her. "Can you climb up here?"

She shifted, as if she was about to try, then she said, "No, I don't think so. My leg is hurt."

Goddamn it, he'd have to get down there to her. Of all the things he didn't want to do. "Wait there."

He lowered himself down and quickly wedged into the tight, closed-in space, safe from the dogs, and he slipped his hands under her arms, then hoisted her to her feet. A deep growl drifted though the dark. The woman nearly slipped away, but he held her in place, feeling awkward and exposed. Her shredded leg hung uselessly and dripped blood like a leaky sink.

Now what the hell were they gonna do? She can't climb.

He held the woman, listening to her sluggish breathing and watched in dazed excitement as Jack Snider stood in the shed doorway, his gun drawn. *Do something quick, Jack, or me and this woman are about to become dog food.*

Jack's voice boomed. "Can ya get to me, Ronnie?"

"Oh god," the woman retched and swallowed something back, then gagged. "I'm gonna be sick."

Ronnie yelled, "Not sure," then turned his head, but kept his arms tight around her waist. The muscles in her body tightened and contracted with each punishing gag. "Just hang on," he said to her. "We gotta move."

But to where? Jack stood a mile away. They'd have to cross a swath of darkness to reach him. Climbing wasn't an option for this woman and there was no other door that he was aware of.

Two dogs lurked to the right, their heavy feet padded the ground as they paced and planned. Their breathing echoed, hoarse and raspy.

The woman gripped his hand tight and said, "I'm gonna be...", and then fluid spewed from her mouth and hit the ground in wet splats. Ronnie just kept his head turned, not focusing on it. The woman tried to breath, but another wave of puking gripped her body and more vomit splashed down her front. Ronnie's own stomach turned as the warm liquid splashed his arm. The sour stench engulfed them and he swallowed hard. He was not unfamiliar with puke, but having someone else's puke on you changed the game a little.

"Hang onto this," he whispered, "Don't let go." He shuffled back against a wooden beam. Panic slithered closer.

Her hand raised and she snaked her arm around the beam. She maintained her hold and nodded. Ronnie shifted his grip, *oh blessed relief,* and wrapped his arm around her shoulders.

He saw Jack at the Barn's opening.

Ronnie watched Jack's silhouette drop to one knee. *Now what the hell is he doing?*

Chapter 34

I should go check the car for the other flashlight, Jack thought as he dropped to one knee. This might be a stupid move.

He pictured the damn flashlight lying in the trunk; long, black, and cylindrical, nestled safely next to those propane tanks he'd been hauling around for the fireman's Spring chili cookoff.

But those dogs would attack him before he made ten paces. And God only knew what was happening in that barn; he could barely see anything. The preacher's wife was in there. So no going back, whatever had to be done, had to be done right here, right now.

He heard clambering inside and thought he saw Ronnie climb down from the rafters. Holy Christ. Jack drew his Glock 9MM. Scuffling. Then voices. Then… puking?

Help me, Amy, don't leave me now. And she would help him, he was sure of that.

He dug quickly in his pocket for his iPhone, finding it easily enough, and pulled it out. The harsh, growl-filled breaths of the dogs floated in the darkness, only a few feet away. He occasionally caught the reflections of their eyes, like catching the twinkle of a distant firefly, but not enough to take aim and be sure. He needed light for that.

And the iPhone came with a flashlight built in!

His swiped up on the iPhone screen with his thumb and levitated his thumb over the flashlight icon. His hands trembled worse than he thought. *Make sure the flashlight's on before you slide the phone out there, dumb ass.* He needed both hands free. What if he clicked on the flashlight, tossed it out there, and the damn phone landed upside down? If this didn't work, his only option was to fire blindly, and probably die just as Wayne Tillwood had died in a hail of useless gunfire.

He felt he could lob the lit iPhone out ahead of him if he were down on one knee, closer to the ground. "Get out of the way, Ronnie!" Jack yelled. He wouldn't wait long.

More scuffling. Ronnie's voice from inside the barn, "Grab it." *What in the hell's going on in there?*

Then came the yell, "Now, Jack, now!"

Jack tapped the flashlight icon and the world illuminated in a soft, gloomy glow. He tossed the phone out in front of him and watched the shapes of the dogs materialize like hellish shadows. No time to think. He chambered a bullet.

Jack fired, catching the closest dog square in the snout. It dropped with a painful yelp. The other dogs charged.

He squeezed the trigger and watched fur explode from the chest of an enormous German Shepherd. The body slid to a stop at Jack's feet.

Two others attacked from his left. Jack grimaced and hissed, "C'mon you bastards." He hit another dog in the hip. It fell hard and squirmed on the ground in a hail of yelps. Jack whipped around just as another animal reached him. The dog's jaws clamped onto the bare skin of Jack's exposed wrist, just as he squeezed the trigger. The bullet exploded from the top of the dog's head, but the animal's momentum knocked him backward onto the cold ground. *Whatever you do, don't lose the gun!*

Another set of teeth clamped onto Jack's arm. As the dog yanked and growled, Jack felt *his* skin ripping away. He cried out more from shock than pain.

Jack jammed the pistol into the dog's belly and fired. Once. Twice. The dog yelped and leapt away, collapsing onto its side.

That's six shots. Eleven left.

Jack rolled back up to his knees and held his mangled arm close to his side. He gulped for air, struggling to maintain control. Three snarling faces glared at him through the glow from the cell phone. He raised the gun.

He fired, hitting the dog on the left. It yelped and fell away in a snapping fit, but the other two didn't budge. A big black one bared its teeth.

Is that thing smiling at me?

Saliva dripped from its mouth. Its head hunkered low and it moved to the left. Jack aimed.

And then the iPhone's light went out.

Chapter 35

Thomas slipped and held out his hand to break the fall.

Benjamin loomed over him. The wings spread from his sides as he grew wider still, and then to Thomas's shock, and horror, Benjamin rose into the air. Whooshing wind gusts blasted thick clouds of dirt into his face. Thomas covered his eyes with his arm.

Christ Almighty! Do something!

He fought awkwardly to his feet and scrambled along the edge of the house. The whipping wind pelted Thomas with tiny stones. Benjamin levitated higher. The massive wings flapped and cut the air in sharp whistles as Benjamin hovered.

Thomas's legs felt like lead as he tried desperately to get around the side of the house and break this wind. He also had to get up to that roof. But how?

Can't even breathe!

Please God. Please.

Several gunshots rang out into the night. *What the hell was that? No time, have to get Abby.*

He had to find a door. A way inside.

I'm hurt, daddy.

Thomas turned away from Benjamin, squinting and searching along the house for a way in. He trudged along, slipped, then spotted a door. And for one horrifying second, he knew he'd never make it. Benjamin's hands would descend upon him at any moment. He broke into a lumbering run. *Please God.*

"You can't get away, Pastor." Benjamin's voice.

Thomas took the front steps in a single leap. He crashed into the door and fumbled it open. He fell inside and slid across the carpet. The room was dark with only ambient light seeping in through the windows. Thomas tried to make sense of the eerie shapes and shadows when suddenly Benjamin's silhouette filled the door frame. Thomas kicked at the door to close it.

Like it would do any good.

He scrambled to his feet. *Gotta get upstairs.* He lumbered and gasped. "Abby!"

He fought desperately to catch his breath. There had to be a way upstairs here somewhere. He glanced around. His vision adjusting to the weak light.

A dark substance, almost black, covered the walls and floor. *Oh God, that's blood.*

He screamed, "*Abby!*"

Blood smeared everywhere.

"*Abigail!*" A sob lurched from his throat.

A broken coffee table lay in what might have been a living room. Thomas covered his mouth and nose against an awful stench, something raw; a wet stink that clung to his nostrils and to the roof of his mouth. It got worse the deeper into the house he went.

His breath locked as his eyes settled on something lying against the far wall. His mind knew what it was but his heart refused to accept it. A body. Thomas gagged against thick bile bubbling into his throat. The legs sprawled awkwardly apart with flesh ripped away. The torso torn open and something soft, wet, and slippery protruded like a bulging balloon. Worst of all was the face; young and dead.

Don't look at it. He tore his eyes away and gagged.

Then Abby's voice. "Daddy!"

The stairway loomed ahead of him.

He stumbled forward with the image of that mutilated body forever seared into his memory. "I'm coming, baby."

He broke into a run, taking the steps two at a time, his mind on autopilot. But something wasn't right here. *Where is Benjamin?*

At the top, he noticed only one room with dull, orange candle light. He scrambled through the doorway, searching frantically. An open window. Except there was blood smeared all around it.

"Abby!" he yelled at the dark mouth of the window. *He'd just heard her!*

Nothing in return.

Chapter 36

For a hopeful second, Ronnie thought Jack might kill *all* of the damn dogs.

Then the light went out.

Right before the darkness engulfed them, Ronnie spotted tools hanging on the far wall. Shovels, picks, an axe, and shit like that. Stuff handy to swing at dogs. From where he stood holding onto the woman, he could see Jack at the mouth of the barn door and the dogs had him in their grasp.

"Fuck," he hissed. Then said, "We've gotta get out there. I gotta help him."

The woman said, "I can't run. You go."

Ronnie touched her shoulder and said, "Stay here. I'll be back."

The woman nodded and Ronnie slipped out of the small passageway. He sprinted toward the barn door and slid to a stop. Jack fought with both dogs, kicking and swinging.

"Goddamn it!" Ronnie said. *Those tools!* He darted to his right, through the dark, and fumbled along where he remembered seeing the hanging tools.

"Hang on Jack! I'm coming!"

Finally, his fingers clasped onto something heavy and metal. Ronnie wrenched the axe loose from the holder. He gripped it firm, relishing the weight.

He ran to where the dogs had Jack curled up on the ground. Jack's face twisted into a painful grimace.

"Hey!" Ronnie yelled at the dogs. "Hey you sons of bitches!"

The dogs ignored him. He'd need to swing the axe baseball style; connect with the dog broadside. *Smile, you bitch.* He swung the ax in a wide arc and buried the blade into the dog's side with an aching crunch. The wooden handle shuddered in his hands and he let go as the dog yelped and slumped to the ground.

The last dog, the black Labrador, turned from Jack and faced Ronnie; teeth bared. Ronnie reached down and grabbed the ax handle, yanking it loose. The dog snapped at him.

Ronnie backed up a step as the black dog hunkered its head low and advanced.

The roar of a gunshot blasted through the darkness and the dog's snout disintegrated. A grotesque shard of bone protruded from its head and its lower jaw flexed wildly. The Labrador's eyes bulged and it ran, slammed into the side of the barn, then fell to its side. Its claws scratched feebly at the barn wall.

Ronnie released a tightened breath. Jack sat up on his knees with the gun outstretched in one shaking hand.

"That all of them?" Jack asked, his voice cracked and hoarse.

"I think so," Ronnie huffed.

Jack climbed to his feet and winced. Ronnie took a step to help him when a familiar and ugly voice drifted out of the darkness.

"Well done," the voice said. Michael's voice.

Ronnie locked his eyes on Michael's shadowed face. *No.* Ronnie's chest fluttered and his hands began to tremble. Sherri's screams echoed horridly in his mind and he fought a sudden urge to run and hide. He glanced at Jack who stumbled, swayed, and then stood firm.

Michael emerged from the darkened shadow of the house. An old man dressed in a black suit with gray hair swept back. His eyes were blackened pits, as they'd been that day so long ago, and Ronnie cringed.

Michael stopped, glanced at both Ronnie and Jack, then settled his eyes on the dead dogs. "You killed them all." Michael lifted his hands. "Bravo!"

Ronnie's breath hitched.

Jack raised his gun and aimed at Michael. "That's enough," Jack said. "You're through here."

Ronnie said, "Jack, no. Don't."

Michael's face remained stoic. He looked at Jack and said, "I can assure you, sheriff. You won't need that. I'm not here for you. The ones I need are inside that house." Michael pointed his thumb behind him. "But I *did* want to say to hello to my old friend, Ronnie."

Ronnie's arms broke out in goosebumps. A chill raced through him.

"I mean it," Jack stepped closer. "Get your hands where I can see 'em."

"Jack…" Ronnie held up his hand.

Jack yelled, "I told you, get your -"

Michael shot forward with impossible speed, slamming his hands into Jack's chest. The force of the blow blasted Jack backward through the air. Ronnie blinked in disbelief as Jack crashed onto his back. The impact of the earth sent his gun another ten feet away.

Michael locked eyes with Ronnie. "Mr. Castle, what a pleasant surprise. I didn't expect to see you again."

Ronnie licked his lips and fought for words. Her screams were branded into his memory forever. Sherri's screams. He asked the question he'd always wanted to know. "Did you kill her?"

"Oh, Ronnie. That's none of your concern. You gave up that right," Michael said. "You made your choice."

Ronnie's face contorted and he was unable to stop the sob from lurching from his throat. Dimly, he saw Jack roll to his side and crawl. Nothing mattered now. Her screams would never leave him. It was the only thing he still carried of her. Had she known he could have saved her?

"Did she know?" he asked.

"What, that you chose yourself over her?" Michael shook his head. "Of course, she did. I made sure she knew that."

Ronnie felt faint and wobbled on his feet. He doubled over and braced his hands against his knees to keep from falling to the ground. He hated Michael. No doubt. But he hated himself more. Fifteen years of self-loathing had come to a head, right in this moment. Instantly, Ronnie realized what he wanted most. Not revenge. He wanted atonement.

A different choice.

Ronnie wanted to do what he'd replayed thousands of times in his head. To stand up from behind that counter and yell, *leave her alone! Take me!*

Michael said, "Run along, Mr. Castle. Our business is done." Michael pointed toward the house. "Pastor Loggins is a different story. I really must get back to him."

"Why are you doing this?" Jack's voice.

Ronnie glanced to his right. Somehow Jack had gotten to his feet again and stood hunched over. One hand pressed to his side, the other held a gun.

"Ah," Michael said, "I'm here to do what I do. Absolution. To bring things back into balance."

"The preacher?" Asked Ronnie.

"The preacher." Michael nodded.

"Why now?"

"Because he wasn't *here* before," Michael spoke as if everyone should know this. "Black Rock was my town before anyone ever knew it was mine. I discovered it, I claimed it, and I keep it clean." Michael shrugged and said, "The preacher brought his filth into my home. I demand absolution."

Ronnie looked up at him. "But you punish the innocent. How is that absolution?"

Michael stared at him, as if confused, then said, "Oh, come on Ronnie. You can't be this stupid. You think you're innocent? Look at yourself. I've been punishing you since the day you made your choice."

Ronnie dropped to his knees, unable to stand. His strength seeped away and he finally understood.

Michael gazed at the sky and said, "We're done here. I must get back to the pastor. He'll start to think I've left. You made your choice, Mr. Castle. Live with it. Or not."

Michael turned and Ronnie yelled, "Wait!"

Michael breathed a sigh. "What is it now, Mr. Castle?"

Silence dangled between them. A void filled only with the darkness of this infernal night, and then Ronnie said, almost too quietly to hear, "Take me."

Michael stared at him again, as if debating on what that meant, and then said, "It's too late for that, Mr. Castle. I can't take two for the same sin."

Ronnie's chest fluttered and a hollowness spread inside him. "For the preacher. Take me instead. The preacher's a good man. I'm not. Take me."

Michael appeared to be struck silent. Perhaps a scenario he'd never encountered.

Ronnie caught Jack's shadow lumbering away. The sheriff's feet scraped the ground as he shuffled toward the car. Getting away.

Good for him.

Chapter 37

Thomas crossed the dimly lit room in two loping strides and leaned out the window. "Abby!"

"Daddy!"

He spotted her crouched below the window sill, a good five-feet below him. Thomas's chest loosened, like a band suddenly snapped, and a sob swelled and burst out of him.

"I couldn't get back in," she cried. A small, dark stream of blood flowed from her arm. She lifted her hand toward him, stretching.

"I'm here, baby!" He reached down and gripped her cold hand.

He pulled her up, shocked at how heavy she was. *Don't drop her!* Abby hooked her leg over the window's ledge and Thomas pulled her inside. Into his arms. Her tenderness pressed on him and he placed a hand on her head, holding her close. He cried and said, "Are you okay?"

She nodded against his chest. "I cut my arm."

"Can you walk?"

She nodded again.

"We need to get out of here." Thomas held her out to see her face, her reddened eyes, and said, "It'll be okay, we just need to go."

Holding her close to him, they both made their way out the bedroom and down the stairs. As they neared the bottom, Thomas pressed his hand over her eyes to hide the bloody mess on the floor. "Don't look here," he said. She didn't argue. Her heart thudded against him and he hurt for her. *Is this my fault?*

All of this?

. . . . .

Jack fumbled with the trunk lid, wrenched it open and grasped the two propane tanks he'd been hauling around for over a week. He grabbed two road flares. His legs ached and his body bled. Blood trickled down his back from somewhere, but he didn't dare reach up and touch it, not yet.

Whatever had hit him and knocked his gun away, whatever the hell *that* was, Jack had never felt anything like it. As if an invisible hand shoved him, but yet, not invisible. Something that *looked* like an old man. A very strange old man. A very dangerous old man.

Jack heard the cavalry echoing from the darkness. Sirens wailed, but still so far away. A few miles from here. Minutes. Five at the most. But too much time to just sit down and wait. Ronnie may be dead by then, Michael would be long gone, and who knows where the preacher had gone.

He hoisted the tanks out of the car and plopped them on the ground. The road flares were rubber-banded together. He stuffed them into his back pocket and grasped the tank handles, one in each hand, and broke into a lumbering run back to where he'd left Ronnie.

And Michael / Benjamin.

Chapter 38

Jack rounded the corner carrying the two propane tanks.

Michael stood staring down at Ronnie, who was sitting on his knees, gazing up as if he were praying. How in the hell would he do this without killing both of them?

"Ronnie!" Jack yelled and lumbered closer.

Ronnie's eyes shifted from Michael to Jack. Jack dropped one of the propane tanks and waved his hand, signaling Ronnie to get the hell out of the way. But the dumbass didn't move and only sat there. Then, shockingly, Ronnie shook his head, as if he knew Jack's plan and didn't want him to do it.

Too late, slick. No way he was risking Michael escaping. Not this time.

Jack twisted open the tank valve, heard the hiss of escaping gas, and hurled the tank as far as he could toward Michael. This would be so much easier if he could find his gun! The tank fell well short of Michael and rolled to a stop in the grass. Too far away.

Sirens blasted. So close. Minutes? Maybe seconds? This had to be done and done now.

Jack grasped the other tank and found a better grip with more leverage. He opened the valve, heard the hiss, then twisted his body and slung it. He lost his balance and plopped onto the ground, but watched the tank sail past the first one and land within a few feet of Michael's legs.

Michael looked down, flashed a glance at Jack, then turned back to Ronnie.

Jack grabbed the road flares from his pocket, pealed one out, and lit it. He yelled, "Get down, Ronnie!" and tossed the flare toward the tank closest to Michael. Perfect shot! It landed on the grass just inches from the tank and burned deep red.

Michael stepped back just as the gas ignited. Jack closed his eyes, but could do little else before the flames rushed him. The explosion tossed him backward and he knew he was on fire, but was helpless to stop anything.

He landed hard and his head flopped back and collided with the ground in a teeth-shattering whack. Flames covered his shirt and he smelled hair burning. Weightlessness.

Nothing.

. . . . .

`Thomas shoved the side-door open and hurried down the rickety steps back outside. The sheriff's car should be in the driveway, around the house. Sirens echoed in the darkness. Such a blessed sound.

But Benjamin was out here. Somewhere.

And Benjamin would never forget. *This has to end.* Even if he and Abby did get away this time (which he highly doubted they would), Benjamin would find them. And Linda. He had to find Linda. Get them out of this nightmare.

I've made my choice.

Take me.

Thomas turned Abby so she faced him. "Listen to me," he said, cradling her face in his hands. "The driveway is around the house. I want you to go down it, get to the road." He swallowed, as even in the dark, her eyes swelled open. "It'll be okay. It's me he wants." Her eyebrows furrowed as Thomas watched the questioning look cloud her face. "Do you - "

A brilliant flash lanced the world white and for an instant, Thomas saw every detail lit up around him. Abby's face brightened and he saw her looking at him, and she blinked. Then the air ignited and hurled fire into the sky, stretching like fingers to touch the stars.

My God! Was is that?

He pushed Abby to the ground, threw his body over hers, and screamed.

Chapter 39

"Jesus Christ," Jack muttered.

The world swam into focus. He blinked away the blurry shadows moving around him. People. People moving. Close to him. The taste of soot stuck to his mouth and he swallowed and it was as if the inside of his throat had changed to sandpaper.

He gritted and clenched his teeth. Christ, everything hurt. Moving seemed impossible.

Who were all these people? *Where was Ronnie?* Jack sucked in a breath to yell but a sharp pain shot through his chest and stole the words.

One of the people wandering around hustled over to him and shined a flashlight in Jack's eyes. "Over here," they yelled, "Jack's awake."

Jack forced himself up onto his elbows and blinked heavily. The skin of his eyelids hurt!

"You shouldn't move, sheriff." A lady. He tried to see who it was, but his eyes wouldn't focus.

"Was I out?" Jack asked, his voice scratchy.

"Out cold," the woman said.

"A body," Jack croaked. "Did you find a body?"

"Two," the lady said. "One inside and one out here."

"Who?" Jack sat up. His strength slowly seeping back in. The woman protested, saying he should wait for the doctor, but she didn't stop him.

"We think one was Donna Johnson," the woman said, then added, "We're waiting on the coroner to identify the one inside, but it appears to be a young male."

He'd hoped to hear that they'd found Michael, fried to a crisp, but wasn't shocked that they didn't. Somehow, he knew they wouldn't. He needed to know everything this woman knew.

Jack looked at her. "Donna Johnson? The woman who lived here. Where?"

The woman glanced toward the barn and pointed, "Behind there. It appeared she may have passed some time ago, but the clothing strewn about the dog pen matched what were likely hers. Probably why the dogs went nuts; they starved without her to feed them."

"Jesus," Jack pressed a hand to his side. Something may be broken inside there. The woman squatting next to him wore a blue State Patrol uniform. If it weren't so damned dark, and if he could see better, he'd likely know who it was. "Who are you?"

"Jen," she said. "It's Jen."

Jack nodded. He'd only met her a couple of times, but always liked her. Good cop. "What else did you find?"

"We found a man and his daughter, Thomas and Abby Loggins, around back. They're beat up, but okay. We also -"

"There's a woman in the barn." Jack blurted. "May be Mrs. Loggins."

The woman, Jen, nodded. "Yep," she said. "Found her too."

"A man named Michael or Benjamin? Older, likely..." Jack thought about it, debating on how to describe him, then just asked, "Anything?"

She looked at him. "No, nothing yet."

"Ronald Castle? Mid to late thirties, male. Find him?"

The woman's eyebrows furrowed. "No one matching that either."

Jack cringed and thought, *goddamn it.* "He should be around here, somewhere."

Jen clicked the radio strapped to her shoulder and spoke into the mic. "Be on the lookout for a middle-aged white male named, Ronald Castle. Also, an older white male, named Michael or Benjamin."

Jack nodded, holding his wounded arm close to his chest. "Yeah," he said, "Yeah that's them."

The woman shook her head and said to Jack, "We'll keep looking. Were they both out here with you?"

Jack nodded.

The woman flagged down another officer and said, "Jack said that both of those guys, Ronald Castle and Michael or Benjamin, were out here with him." Then she turned back to Jack and said, "We'll find them."

Jack nodded, but he knew they wouldn't. He swiped a dirty hand across his face and thought again, *goddamn it.*

He knew.

Chapter 40

Distance. He had to get distance.

He tripped and fell, landing face-first in the muddy creek water. It splashed into his eye, or what had been his eye, and he stuffed his fist into his mouth to stifle a scream. *They might hear me.*

And they could kill him.

For the first time in Benjamin Clark's long life, he struggled. He couldn't fly. He'd never been hurt like this. Never. That shit-bag sheriff couldn't leave well-enough alone.

Benjamin pushed himself back to his feet and continued his awkward gait across the shallow creek and into the dark woods, dragging Ronnie Castle's body. *What if they chase me?*

It wasn't supposed to turn out this way. It never had before.

But nor had Benjamin ever changed his mind before either. *Maybe that was it. I changed my mind and didn't hold the preacher accountable.* I didn't make him *choose.*

Because of Ronnie Castle. Even now, amongst the pain and the fear, Benjamin couldn't help but admire the purity of Ronnie's choice. True atonement. True Absolution. So rare. So beautiful.

Tree branches swept passed his face, scratching and snagging.

He broke through the tree line and found a gravel road. He decided to walk along it for a while. If he saw headlights, he'd hide. He needed to heal.

He needed to be ready. For the next time. And there was always a next time.

Chapter 41

Damn, it's good to be done telling that story. I hate recalling that awful mess, especially in such detail. I'm not like Jean Tallman down there playing Bingo, who likes to gossip to whomever wants to listen. Hell, no. Nor will you hear Daisy Howard running around, spouting off about what happened with Archie out at the County Home. In fact, a lot of people worry about her and think she should retire. I sure as hell wouldn't blame her.

But none of that matters right now. We've reached Pastor Loggins's house.

There stands Abby Loggins, leaning heavily against the back of that Jeep, probably wondering if we're planning to talk to her. Well, me at least. She can't see you. She looks so frail standing there, so lonely. It pains me to see it after everything she's been through.

Abby probably got the worst of it. Her and her dad. We rushed the whole family to Indy on one of those life-line choppers. They took Abby into emergency surgery and had to remove a ruptured spleen and repair a kidney that, from what I heard, will probably never work right. She had to have twenty-six stitches in her arm and she lost nearly three pints of blood. And if all of that wasn't enough, her nose was broken! I haven't talked to her since that night.

Up until now, that is.

Her mom had a lot of surface damage, but aside from losing blood, she came out okay. She had to have a lot of stitches in her leg, but it sounds like the scars are healing and she should regain full use of her leg. Oddly enough, she doesn't remember much about what happened. She recalls looking for Abby and walking down the street just after dark, but doesn't remember a thing about Benjamin kidnapping her, the ride out to Donna Johnson's house, or being tossed to the dogs. If you ask her about a guy named Ronnie Castle, she has no clue who he is or what he did.

But Abby worries me. She's hell-bent on finding Benjamin (or Michael, as she calls him). I'm concerned that it's more than a *want*. I think she's obsessed with finding him. In the few times I've seen that girl since Ronnie disappeared, I can't help but notice the rage pent up inside her. The fake smiles that never touch her eyes.

That's why I'm here. I want to make sure she's not thinking of doing something crazy. Something dangerous.

Abby or her dad.

And what was Benjamin, you might ask? I honest to God don't know what he was. I wish I did. Perhaps as Ronnie said, a demon of some sort, but if that's the case, he was an odd demon. He believed he was serving justice in some twisted way. Maybe he was an angel.

But that also seems a bit of a stretch.

I've even considered that Benjamin is nothing more than fate manifested. The whole, *what-goes-around-comes-around* thing. Who knows. We'll likely never find out.

Ah, Abby is staring right at us.

"You coming over here, or what?" She asks. She places her hands on her hips.

I'd best get over there. I feel responsible for her; though I'm not exactly sure why. I never actually met her before all the shit happened.

"Got a sec?" I ask as I make my way up the driveway. I'm sure she doesn't like me much.

"What do you want?"

"Just checkin' on ya. Heard you folks were leavin'."

She nods and says, "What do you want, sheriff?"

Christ, she doesn't even talk like a teenager anymore. "Just curious where you're goin'," I say.

She glances away and I notice her scars are barely visible in the dark. I guess it has been three months, enough time for flesh wounds to heal. Then she blurts out, "We read about a strange man spotted down by Little Rock. He's all scarred up, like he's been burned. And he's old."

When she says *read about*, she's referring to these internet groups where people claim to have had a similar experience as us with Benjamin; and they've got their own little online community. I joined a few of them myself, if I'm being honest.

"And you think it's him?" I ask.

She shrugs and says, "I dunno. But it could be."

I nod. "Why?" I let the question hang in the air, then I ask, "Why not just leave well enough alone."

She shrugs. "I hate him," she growls. "He nearly killed all of us. He killed Scott. I want him dead."

I consider saying, *the dogs killed Scott*, but I keep quiet. No sense stirring shit if it stops stinkin'. But damn it, that hate is gonna burn that poor girl up.

Just then, Pastor Loggins comes out the front door and steps down the driveway. He stops next to his daughter and wraps an arm around her shoulders. His hair is longer. He's unshaven. He wears a flannel shirt, unbuttoned, perhaps unwashed. I heard he quit his pastor role shortly after the run-in with Benjamin, but I never came by and asked him about it.

He looks at me and says, "Sheriff," and sticks out his hand.

We shake.

I ask him, "Abby right about you goin' down and checking on a possible sighting of Benjamin?"

He glances at Abby and I'm not sure if he's aggravated that she told me or if he's proud of her resolve. "We may," he says.

"Not that it'll do any good, but I wish you wouldn't," I say. I've never told Abby about Ronnie Castle. Not sure if her dad has. About *the choice* and the circumstances that lead to the pastor *and* his daughter being spared. Surely the pastor told her. "You need to let it go." But do I *really* mean that? Did I walk all the way across town tonight and tell you that story so we could let Benjamin go?

The pastor nods and says, "Yeah." But he doesn't elaborate and I don't ask any more about it. "Linda isn't going with us." The pastor speaks quietly and stares up at the young stars. That look on his face tells me there's trouble here.

A pause settles between us and then Abby turns and closes the back of the jeep. "We gotta go," she says to her dad. The pastor makes his way to the driver's door and pulls keys out of his pocket. He stops and looks over at me and I shoot him back a quick nod.

The pastor climbs into the car and starts it, then he glances at me through the open window. "You wanna to go with us, Jack?"

My heart flutters. *Be honest with yourself, Jack.* If my Amy were here right now, she'd tell you; it's the real reason I walked down here tonight. The reason I told you the story. The reason I waited until now to drop in on the pastor and his family.

The reason I no longer sleep at night.

I take one last glance at the town behind me, at Black Rock. My town for so long and now in the hands of someone else just as I now belong to someone else.

A man named Benjamin Clark.

About the Author

David Odle is the author of the novels *Markus* and *Kate's Lake*. David spent seven years in the military and after earning his Bachelors Degree in Business Administration, worked for over twenty years in the IT industry. David lives in Indiana with his wife and children.

Note from the Author

Word-of-mouth is crucial for any author to succeed. If you enjoyed *Black Rock*, please leave a review online—anywhere you are able. Even if it's just a sentence or two. It would make all the difference and would be very much appreciated.

Thanks!
David Odle

We hope you enjoyed reading this title from:

BLACK ROSE
writing™

www.blackrosewriting.com

Subscribe to our mailing list – *The Rosevine* – and receive **FREE** books, daily deals, and stay current with news about upcoming releases and our hottest authors.
Scan the QR code below to sign up.

Already a subscriber? Please accept a sincere thank you for being a fan of Black Rose Writing authors.

View other Black Rose Writing titles at www.blackrosewriting.com/books and use promo code **PRINT** to receive a **20% discount** when purchasing.

www.ingramcontent.com/pod-product-compliance
Lightning Source LLC
Chambersburg PA
CBHW010734100726
47899CB00009B/3052